THE
SITUATIONSHIP

Taylor-Dior Rumble is a writer and actor, born and raised in South-East London. Writing is the only thing she's ever really loved since she was a child, expressing her passion as a fashion blogger during her schooldays.

Taylor-Dior started her journalism career at BBC News, producing and writing stories ranging from the politics of Black hair to colourism in Hollywood and the Oscars, until she realised she didn't just want to write about other people doing cool and creative things – she wanted to do something cool and creative as well.

THE
SITUATIONSHIP

TAYLOR-DIOR
RUMBLE

PENGUIN BOOKS

UK | USA | Canada | Ireland | Australia

India | New Zealand | South Africa

Penguin Books is part of the Penguin Random House group of companies
whose addresses can be found at global.penguinrandomhouse.com

Published in Penguin Books, 2023

004

Typeset by 12.5/15.25pt Garamond MT Std by Jouve (UK), Milton Keynes
Printed and bound in Great Britain by Clays Ltd, Elcograf S.p.A.

The authorised representative in the EEA is Penguin Random House Ireland,
Morrison Chambers, 32 Nassau Street, Dublin D02 YH68

A CIP catalogue record for this book is available from the British Library

ISBN: 9781529198652

www.greenpenguin.co.uk

Penguin Random House is committed to a sustainable future
for our business, our readers and our planet. This book is made
from Forest Stewardship Council® certified paper.

For my dad, Martin Antonio Rumble.
My most favourite storyteller in the world.
I love you and miss you always.

I

Tia had been to the toilet three-and-a-half times since she'd rushed home from work. The first time was as soon as she walked through the door and begged her sister to hurry up and get out of the bathroom. The second time was after she had got out the shower, the third was while her concealer was drying, and the half was when she thought she had to go, in the middle of drying her hair. She spritzed her round face with a finishing spray and swiped layers of brown gloss onto her plump lips, and Tia was finally ready for the night ahead. She took a deep breath while smoothing down the sides of her knitted dress that held on to her hips, disguising her bumps and hugging her curves in all the right places, admiring her reflection and the slit that drew attention to her left thigh. She gave herself an approving nod while fluffing out her curls once more – she had to look flawless. Her primping was disturbed by a text from her best friend Hannah, asking for the reservation time again despite Tia having sent it to the group chat that morning. She rolled her eyes and replied, reminding the squad not to be even a second late: everything had to be perfect tonight.

After months of texting, countless voice notes, and many hours spent overanalysing everything he posted on his Instagram Stories, Tia couldn't wait to welcome Aaron back home with wide-open arms, and wide-open legs if he wasn't too tired from his flight. But even if he was, anything remotely close to the kiss they'd shared the night before he left would be all that Tia could possibly want after eight months of being apart. It had been the longest the two had ever gone without seeing each other, but since he was now back at his parents' house, just a couple of roads away from Tia's, they could slip right back into their old routine. In fact, she had already planned to try and synchronise their journeys home after work, maybe grabbing a drink at her favourite bar or showing him the best places to eat near his new office. She couldn't wait, she thought to herself while adding the final touch: a pair of gold hoop earrings.

The restaurant she'd chosen sat on the corner of a bustling high street by Deptford Market, humble and unassuming in its location, but chic and cosy on the inside. Bare walls, dark wooden floors, and dim string lights that hung above candlelit marble tables. Tia gazed around the space with a grin, pleased that it looked just as romantic as it did online – she'd spent days searching for the perfect location. She was even happier to spot her best friend Luca, already sat at their table with a half-empty drink, still in his suit from another day at the law firm that worked him too hard. He looked around the restaurant and slicked his dark gel-covered hair back, until he saw Tia being escorted to their table and looked her up and down.

'Oh my God.'

Tia body-rolled and giggled before leaning over to hug him. 'You like?'

'I love,' he said, giving a little round of applause. 'Now, here's the drinks menu.'

'I love the way you think.'

'Figured you'd need one before your boyfriend gets here,' sighed Luca, returning to his phone.

'He's not my boyfriend!'

'The slit on that dress says otherwise,' he said, tickling her thigh. 'Hannah's gonna be so proud to see you in something other than a Tupac shirt.'

'Fuck you!' she laughed. 'Speaking of, where she at?'

'Probably running late cos of Sean.'

'Sean? But the table's only booked for four.'

Before Tia could complain, she saw Hannah at the door and her disinterested-looking boyfriend walking in behind her.

'Guess she couldn't leave the ball-and-chain at home,' whispered Tia.

'More like he couldn't stand the fact she has a life

outside their relationship,' said Luca through gritted teeth.

Hannah looked every bit the effortlessly cool fashion intern. Her long legs were encased in a pair of flared jeans, and she wore a fitted white T-shirt she had no doubt cut and cropped herself, accessorised with a pair of ankle boots, chunky hoop earrings, and Ruby Woo, which drew even more attention to her full lips. Her bum-length braids swayed as she sashayed between the tables.

'You look insane!' she said, planting air kisses to the sides of Tia's cheeks.

'Just tryna be like you, sis.'

'Oh, please! I would've made more of an effort if someone wasn't rushing me.'

'Tia would've had our heads for dinner if we got here late!' Sean said while shaking Luca's limp hand.

'Not gonna lie, he's right, still,' Tia said, forcing out a laugh while glaring at Hannah for bringing a plus-one the group could've done without.

After ordering a round of drinks and browsing the menu, Tia adjusted the extra chair that had been brought over to their table, then drained her Mai Tai as soon as it arrived. Every time the sounds from the high street got louder, she turned around to see if it was Aaron walking through the door. She checked her phone and held it up in the air several times just to check whether she had bad signal – he'd usually text if

4

he was running late. Hannah rested her hand on Tia's shaking leg under the table before leaning into her ear, covering their faces with the menu.

'Will you relax? You look amazing and happy hour doesn't end for another hour – he's gonna be haps.'

'Haps about me? Or the two-for-one cocktails?'

'Both.'

'No, but seriously, it's just Aaron,' said Luca, reaching over the table and grabbing the menu. 'You're acting like you haven't known him for a million years.'

'I know but I can't help it! I've missed him so much.'

'Bitch, please, you missed those lips!' Luca hissed before taking a sip of his drink. 'A sesh ending with that many love bites has gotta be unforgettable.'

Tia shook her head into her hands. 'Oh my days, allow me, please!' she begged.

'Nope, you're never living that down!' cackled Hannah. 'Legit thought we were back in colly the way you searched for hickey cover-up tutorials.'

'Not my finest moment.'

'But I'm sure there'll be plenty more after tonight,' huffed Luca, before waving his hand at a waiter to order another round.

Tia could feel the second Mai Tai take the edge off her nerves. She looked at her friends around the table, grateful that their bickering was putting her at ease. The only thing that was missing was Aaron, she thought. She smiled at the blissful thought of him sitting beside her, their arms interlinked, laughing at Hannah and Luca arguing over something dumb like they had always done for so many years. She couldn't wait to get back on track.

As she took another sip of her drink, she caught a glimpse of a dazzling smile nestled in a dark, thick beard. She put down her glass and strained her neck to look past the group of people in front of this person, and gasped when she realised it was Aaron. His deep brown skin glowed beneath the string lights, and she could just about make out his razor-sharp shape-up, smiling at the trouble he must've gone to trying to get a haircut as soon as he landed in London. He was already laughing with the maître d' who was escorting him through the crowd, which was just so typical of Aaron, Tia thought to herself. Just like his classically handsome looks, his boyish charm was irresistible. Her heartbeat accelerated as he walked closer, revealing the rest of his outfit, which Tia mentally approved of. His broad shoulders were draped in a camel coat, and beneath it he wore a grey sweatshirt and blue denim jeans. She smiled at his Jordans, which he had no doubt bought for a ridiculous amount from a reseller.

Before anyone else on the table noticed what she was looking at, Tia leaped up from her seat and launched herself into Aaron's chest, wrapping her arms around his neck and taking in the scent of his spicy bergamot cologne.

'You're here!' she squealed into his ear as he began to laugh.

She felt a single arm around her waist and held on to him even tighter, rocking his stiff body side to side. Tia overheard gasps coming from her table, no doubt over how much hotter Aaron had got, and broke away from him so she could get a better look for herself, her hands resting on his shoulders. Tia's toothy smile faltered when she saw his pursed lips, and she stood back a little, now realising his other hand was holding someone else's. Her eyes travelled up the arm and were met by a wrinkled nose and a cutesy grin. Tia immediately whipped her arms back from Aaron's shoulders and held her own hands behind her back, squeezing her fingers in an effort to centre herself and not collapse.

'Tia, right?' the woman asked. 'Aaron's told me so much about you!'

She reached out for a hug, enveloping Tia in the patchouli musk of her perfume.

'Oh, you're a hugger!'

'I am I'm afraid!' she laughed before letting go. 'It's so great to finally meet the famous Tia!'

Her voice was chirpy and bright in a way that drew even more attention to her American accent. Her sleek, dark hair was parted in the middle and slicked down into the kind of bun Kendall Jenner would wear. The girl was wrapped in an expensive-looking floor-length cardigan, which elevated the skinny jeans and T-shirt she wore underneath. Her thick black glasses and minimal jewellery made her look even more polished and put together.

'Don't know about famous,' Tia laughed. 'I'm sorry but I didn't get your n—'

'This is Olivia,' announced Aaron. He looked at her with a warm smile before turning to everyone else. 'My girlfriend.'

2

Girlfriend?!

The word echoed over and over again in Tia's mind until she registered the fact that Aaron really was referring to someone that wasn't her, that this was actually happening.

She froze for what felt like an hour, until she realised she was blocking the couple's way and moved to one side so that everyone could greet them properly. Tia wrapped her arms around her stomach, feeling as if the words had left Aaron's mouth and punched her straight in the gut. She could feel the concerned stares of her best friends burning a hole into her head and looked at the floor, feeling every gland in her eyelids swell, knowing she'd most definitely burst into tears if she made any eye contact with them. She gripped the backrest of one of the chairs until her nails left marks in the leather, as Aaron continued making his way around the table before realising there weren't enough seats for everyone. Her stomach lurched at the thought

9

of giving up her own chair up for this random girl so she waved down a nearby waiter, asking if it was possible to get another. He sighed and gave Tia a look that screamed 'Fuck off', before going over to the maître d', who also looked visibly annoyed but did a better job at disguising it.

'I'm so sorry but we're at full capacity,' he said gesturing to the packed restaurant. 'But you could always have your guests wait by the bar until another booking frees up a seat?'

Just as Olivia looked as though she was going to volunteer as tribute, Tia took her arm and insisted she sit. *There's no way you get to be a fucking saint tonight,* she thought to herself, grabbing her clutch bag and her coat, which was hanging from the backrest. Olivia, Aaron and the rest of the table began to protest until Tia waved her hand in the air.

'Guys, it's fine! Honestly. Aaron, sit down!' she said. 'You guys must be so knackered from the journey.'

'But what about you though?' he asked. He looked around the restaurant as if a chair would magically appear. 'Let's just go somewhere el—'

'Oh my days, don't be silly!' She cleared her throat and chugged the rest of the watery Mai Tai. 'Look! I need another drink anyway. Don't worry.'

She reassured everyone with a smile and scurried off to the bar as fast as her legs could take her, plopping herself onto the spindly stool, inhaling and exhaling until she was ready to string together an actual sentence that didn't consist of 'What the fuck?!' She desperately waved her arm at the bartender who had already ignored her twice.

'Erm, hi, can I get, uh—'

'Two Mai Tais and two tequila shots, please.'

Luca slapped his debit card on the bar and slid it towards the bartender. He put his arm around Tia's sunken shoulders.

'What are you doing? Go sit down, I'll be there soon,' she said in a shaky voice. She struggled to lift her gaze from the napkins and straws in front of her.

'And fifth-wheel Sean and that fake-ass Huda? I'm good.'

In any normal case, Tia would've probably laughed at Luca's shade but she was too busy trying to remember how to breathe. She held her hands together and exhaled, debating if it was too extreme to ask God to strike her down and put her out of her misery.

'No, but what the actual fuck? Like, is this actually happening?'

'Breathe. Your eyelashes look way too good to ruin right now.'

Tia looked up at the ceiling, hoping her teary eyes wouldn't loosen the glue she'd painstakingly applied to her strip lashes with the help of a TikTok tutorial she'd barely understood.

'He never mentioned her once,' she sniffed.

'Yeah, fuckboys tend to leave out important details like that,' said Luca, glaring at Aaron across the restaurant.

'He's not a fuckboy though. He's Aaron.'

'Stringing someone along for months just to come back with a girlfriend is Fuckboy 101, babes, history or not.'

'So that kiss the night before he left . . . it meant nothing to him?' Tia could feel her throat closing up and exhaled again. 'Like, nothing at all?'

Several Spanish swear words left Luca's mouth as he peered down the bar to see what was taking their drinks order so long.

'All those FaceTime movie nights, the daily "good morning" texts, the random selfies throughout the day . . . What, was I just practice until he found someone else?'

Before Luca could swear again, the barman placed their drinks in front of them. Tia's voice began to crack.

'I feel so stupid. After all those years of back and forth, I thought we'd finally got to something real. I can't believe this is happening.'

'No, no! Come on!' Luca grabbed hold of Tia's hands before forcing a tequila shot into one of them. 'Crying over wastemen is not our brand: drink.'

She looked at the serious expression on his face and nodded, before clinking her glass to his and swallowing every drop of the shot. Tia shuddered as the alcohol hit her empty stomach.

'There,' said Luca, popping a lime wedge into Tia's mouth. 'Now doesn't that feel better?'

Tia shook her head then felt someone's arms wrap round her shoulders from behind.

'Hey, sis,' said Hannah. 'They've brought another chair now, you ready to come over?'

Tia shook her head again, spat out the lime (much to the bartender's disgust), and reached for the Mai Tai melting in front of her, while Luca reached for her phone. He unlocked it and began to furiously tap away until she finally looked up from her half-empty glass and glanced over at him.

'Wait, what are you doing?' she asked tentatively.

'The cure to getting over someone,' he said, showing the girls the screen, 'is getting under someone else.'

Hannah laughed while Tia sank into her arms even more, groaning at the dating app profile Luca was currently filling out.

'You can't be serious,' she said.

'I'm deadly serious.'

'Shouldn't she process this first?' asked Hannah, rubbing Tia's back. 'It's too soon to get thrown into the jungle. She's never even used Hinge before!'

'Hannah!' Luca slapped her shoulder. 'How long have we been trying to get this nun to join the rest of this generation? There has never been a better time than now!'

Tia kissed her teeth. 'Nun, you know.'

'And you ain't had *none* since you've been waiting for that prick like a fucking military wife or some shit,' he hissed, pointing his sharp chin towards the table. 'He's taking the piss.'

Hannah shrieked into the air while Tia tried her best to hold back her laugh but cracked a smile anyway. The alcohol was finally hitting.

'I don't know, man, I don't think I'm built for apps,' Tia whimpered. 'I like it the old-fashioned way, y'know? Locking eyes with a mysterious stranger across the bar or bumping into a peng ting at a party, exchanging some witty banter . . .'

The three immediately peered over their shoulders, scanning their surroundings for even a speck of potential, but alas, the nearest thing was a couple of hipsters raving about the bottle of natural wine that had just arrived at their table.

Luca rolled his eyes. 'That's nowhere near efficient enough, babe.'

'You make dating sound like a job!' laughed Hannah.

'It is when you're trying to build a brand! Can't just have any random near you.'

'But you know what, babe, this could be the start of something new!' Hannah held Tia in her arms and looked back at the table. 'Me and Sean met on Tinder!'

Luca cleared his throat as Tia giggled into her glass. Hannah's point didn't fill her with much confidence but she appreciated her efforts either way. A waiter then walked past with a slab of something smoky and sizzling, suddenly reminding Tia that she was in fact starving and should probably eat something if she was going to carry on drinking. There was no way she'd get through this evening sober.

'There she is,' said Aaron from across the table, as Tia pulled out a chair and sat down.

'Here she is,' she said faintly, waving her hands in the air.

The alcohol had most definitely hit her. She smiled immediately after seeing his smile, but it soon vanished when she noticed Olivia's hand wrapped around his on the table. Throughout dinner, dessert, and the constant stream of Mai Tais Luca was plying her with, Tia seethed with rage, unable to decipher whether she wanted to scream or cry. She sat and quietly observed for most of the evening, trying to work out what made this girl so much more special, disappointing the feminist within her. Was it the way her poreless olive skin radiated like a Glossier model's? Was it how she sat up straight with princess-like posture and took the tiniest bites of her grilled vegetables? – because she's plant-based, of fucking course. Or was it the way you couldn't pin down where she was *from* from?

Aaron and Olivia began to explain how they met, practically finishing each other's stupid sentences, making Tia want to barf.

'I was pretty low when I got to Cali,' Aaron said.

'Like, Google was obviously amazing, and the guys on my scheme were cool, but it was a little overwhelming. And I guess I got homesick and just wasn't being as social as I probably should've been.'

'Yeah!' Olivia said, grabbing his shoulder. 'This guy would literally code all day, all night and never come out for drinks! And I was like, "He's way too cute to be living like this!"'

'I mean, I only had a couple of months out there so I wanted to do a good job, innit!'

'No, no! You're so right, I'm kidding!' she beamed as Tia mentally begged her to shut the fuck up. 'But anyways, I asked him if he wanted to hang with me and some of the other developers and he flat out said, "Nah, I'm good!"'

Oh fuck, she's actually smart too, Tia thought, sinking even further into her seat.

'So we all went anyway and then he showed up,' Olivia went on.

'Yeah, I figured it'd be dumb to reject an invite from someone this gorgeous.'

Olivia covered her mouth to giggle. 'So we talked and drank some more—'

'Then she offered to be my *tour guide* at, like, one in the morning?' he gave the table a devilish grin before she urged him to stop talking. 'And we, uh . . . spent the whole night together . . .'

'Oh my God, don't say it like that!' she squealed. 'We

mostly talked, and then I took him out to this amazing spot where you can see the Golden Gate Bridge – *classic move.*'

'She failed to mention this *amazing spot* was damn near an hour away from campus.'

'You're never letting that go, huh?' she laughed. 'It was worth it, though. Right?'

The more they went on, bantering and nudging one another, the tighter Tia's throat felt, as she tried her best to feign interest in their vomit-inducing story, struggling to tear her eyes away from their intertwined hands on the table. Their love story took a turn when they were forced to work together on a business idea that would win them an actual job back in London and, as luck would have it, their app proposal won. It was called SaintHood, the wannabe power couple explained with glee to Tia's disdain, and it was designed to match businesses and start-ups with local charitable organisations. Aaron's charisma and creativity partnered with Olivia's technical abilities made them unstoppable in the office, while the lunch meetings and late nights proved their attraction to be undeniable.

'I was certain we weren't gonna get it. It was so competitive!'

'She's being modest,' added Aaron. 'She was one of the best developers on our scheme, plus our idea was fire! We won by a landslide.'

Everyone politely laughed as Tia loudly sipped the remnants of her drink.

'But when we did win,' said Olivia, looking at Aaron, 'it just felt like fate, you know?'

'Moving across the world for a boy?' said Tia, finally breaking her silence and playing with the crushed ice in her glass. 'That is pretty ballsy, Livvy.'

Hannah's eyes shifted to Tia's as she glared at the happy couple over the rim of her drink. Luca slipped his hand under the table and gave her thigh a tap, telling her to calm down.

'I mean, it was more so for the job and the benefits but I think he's also worth it, too,' Olivia said, wrinkling her nose at Aaron in that cutesy way Tia already hated. She huffed into her glass, wondering why the waiters were trying to avoid making eye contact with her.

'And what about you, Tia?' asked Olivia. 'Aaron tells me you're way too busy being a total boss at London Central News to even bother dating!'

'More like busy being a workaholic – LCN is her life!' he laughed. 'She was even late to my goodbye party cos she was busy writing suttin!'

They exchanged looks as if there was an inside joke Tia wasn't part of which instantly got her back up, but before she could say anything, Luca put his hand on her thigh.

'Actually, I was just saying to Tia how much I've missed her!' he began. 'Because when she's not working, she always out on a date or two, or three!'

Tia's jaw dropped before turning it into a wide smile, clocking his game plan.

'Yeah, she's always being wined and dined!' Hannah added.

Luca nodded approvingly at her cooperation and continued, 'And maybe even sixty-nined, eh, babes?'

Everyone laughed as Tia squeezed Luca's hand under the table. His cackling was especially loud from trying to mask the pain of his right hand being crushed. This wasn't her style in the slightest, but she appreciated her friends' support, as messy as it was.

'Oh, rah! Is that what you're on, T?' Aaron raised his eyebrows. 'You failed to mention that during our catch-ups.'

'Yeah, well, you failed to mention a lot too,' said Tia without thinking. He squinted his eyes at her from across the table and she shakily rose to her feet.

'Luca, Hannah? Cigarette?'

Before Hannah could refuse, Luca grabbed her arm and ushered the girls outside.

'What the fuck, guys?!' hissed Tia.

She fumbled in her pockets for her lighter and dropped it. The sudden blast of fresh air had made her feel even woozier than before, and she was getting sloppy. Hannah tutted and picked it up for her, lighting the cigarette hanging from Tia's rum-tinged mouth.

'Oh, don't be like that, T! Miss Tour Guide was

doing my head in,' Luca argued. 'Is she the bloody FBI or something? So fucking nosy.'

'Maybe she was just being polite, tryna make conversation and that?' Hannah suggested.

'No, she was trying to take Tia for a dickhead! Like she's a hag with no life outside the office.'

'I mean, *you* were the one who called me a nun,' said Tia, crouching down on the concrete. She wasn't sober enough to stand and felt less prone to falling over if she was closer to the ground.

'It actually seemed like Aaron was tryna say that,' added Hannah. 'Dunno why he's acting like such a prick.'

'See! Even more reason to jump on Hinge, Tia!' Luca took out her phone from his pocket and triumphantly held it out. 'Look, you've only been on here for an hour and already have twelve matches!'

'Fuck off!' squealed Hannah. 'Tia, this is such a good sign! Any one of these could be the perfect distraction.'

Tia looked up at her friends through hazy eyes and cigarette smoke, smiling at their attempt to secure her some dick. It's not like she didn't date or had sworn off men completely (though she'd read somewhere that that would probably extend her life by a few years); her and her friends had just always thought she and Aaron were endgame. Like Chuck and Blair or Issa and Lawrence — they were that annoying, on-again-off-again pair within the friendship group, driving Luca and Hannah insane because there never seemed to be a right moment for them to be together. When they'd first started hanging out in sixth form and word had got out that they were doing more than studying, their unlikely union had sent shockwaves through the school's ecosystem. Tia was a bit of a nobody and Aaron was the popular boy who everyone either wanted to be or be with, but the weight of all the gossip and rumours quickly became too much, and they'd decided to call it quits and remain friends. Despite everything, they'd remained each other's first phone calls whenever something good or something bad happened; they always left parties early to go smoke in Aaron's car; they knew each other inside out, and they were proud of it too. They'd both dated other people throughout their friendship, but had never really approved of each other's choices, especially since Tia had always secretly held a candle for Aaron – though she'd never have admitted it out of fear of losing what they had. So, when Aaron had seemingly risked it all, kissing her the night before he was leaving to live abroad for eight months, she couldn't have been happier. It had finally felt like they were in this together.

But none of that mattered now, Tia thought as she stood up to look inside the restaurant. His arm was around the back of Olivia's chair, the happy couple laughing and beaming in each other's faces.

Far too drunk to make the journey back to their

table, Luca and Hannah told Tia to wait on a bench while they went inside to pay. Tia shoved her card into Luca's hand, who flat-out refused to accept it and forced her to sit down, insisting she'd been through enough tonight. She leaned her head back against the brick wall and took deep breaths, shivering when she felt a chill go up her uncovered thigh. Tia kissed her teeth at the slit of her dress, as if it had failed its job in securing her man.

She waited for everyone to come out of the restaurant, the couples coming two by two, Hannah linking her arm through Sean's as he complained about the shitty weather, and Aaron holding Olivia's petite manicured hand. Tia shivered as another cool breeze went past and Aaron put his arms around Olivia in a cute attempt to warm her up. Tia felt a lump at the back of her throat and looked at the ground.

When Luca joined her on the bench, he returned Tia's phone but was too occupied typing away at his own. She glanced over at his screen as he texted his ETA: the name at the top of the message chain read 6'7" + DIMPLES'.

'Now I know that ain't the name on his birth certificate.'

'Who cares what his name is?' Luca scoffed. 'He'll only be saying mine in about an hour.'

The two giggled together until Luca could sense her side-eye. He continued to type and switch between apps on his phone until she sighed, and he couldn't ignore her any longer.

'Go on. Say it.'

'What?'

'I can tell you wanna say something.'

'I don't know what you mean.'

'Tia!'

'You don't think it's a bit soon?' she winced, as Luca rolled his eyes.

It had been three weeks since he and his ex-boyfriend, Hassan, had broken up. Luca had said it'd been a long time coming, sharing details of their explosive fight – there were the numerous little digs about how Hassan couldn't stand Luca's lawyer mates, and the green-eyed situations on nights out, all of which had culminated in a full-on shouting war between the two when Hassan had decided at the last minute that he didn't want to accompany Luca to a colleague's house-warming. They had both said things they couldn't take back, and in a fit of rage Luca had suggested they should break up. Hassan had been taken aback, but according to Luca, hadn't had the balls to push through and fight for their relationship, so that was the end of it.

The first post-break-up weekend was spent binging Netflix's finest, tackiest rom-coms in Hannah's room. Tia had ordered copious amounts of Chinese food to line the gang's stomachs for the bottles of rosé they went on to down, while cursing Hassan between Toni

Braxton's greatest hits. The second weekend, Luca had gotten a new PT at his gym to prepare for his return to the streets, and by the third weekend he had reacquainted himself with all the dating apps he had deleted not long after meeting Hassan. He had handled the whole thing in the way he handled his work: sequential and methodical with very little room for emotion, much to Tia and Hannah's concern.

'No. I'm done being depressed! I'm not wasting another second mourning that idiot,' Luca argued. 'If he wants someone boring like him he can fuck off and find them.'

'You don't mean that.'

'I do. I'm not gonna waste time on someone who can't appreciate what's right in front of them. I changed so much for that prick and I'm not doing it anymore.'

Tia sighed and nodded. 'This is the kinda energy I need to be on.'

'Best way to get over someone is to bend someone else over. No, wait, that came out wrong . . .'

'Nah, you meant every bit of that shit!'

The two cackled into each other and Tia slapped Luca's knee, almost forgetting the night from hell she'd had, and Hannah skipped over to see what all the fuss was about. Her boyfriend followed closely behind, reminding her about the train times and how far they were from the station. She sighed and air-kissed the two, and yelled goodbye to the other couple before catching up with Sean who had already started to walk off. Luca began to cuss him in Tia's ear until Aaron walked over, his fingers interlaced with Olivia's.

'Yo, T, did you want a lift home?' he asked.

Olivia nodded, her face full of concern. 'Yeah, you don't look so good.'

Did this bitch just call me ugly? Tia asked herself, tilting her head at the smug picture-perfect couple in front of her. She wanted to tell Olivia that she didn't look so good because the guy she was currently hanging on to for dear life had had his tongue down her throat the last time they had seen each other.

'She's fine,' barked Luca. 'Don't worry, I've got her.'

'You sure?' asked Aaron.

Tia gave a resounding nod. 'I'm great. Don't worry about me.'

'Well, it was so awesome meeting you guys!' added Olivia.

'Uh-huh. Likewise, sweetie!' said Luca with an American twang, which she laughed at.

He was so immature sometimes but Tia lived for the pettiness, especially as her blood began to boil, seeing the two walk towards Aaron's car. The car she'd helped him pick, the car she'd ridden shotgun in after every motive and hang-out, the car they'd kissed in the night before he left.

After Luca had ordered Tia an Uber, she snatched her phone out of his hands and opened the new dating app. They all looked the same to her and she began to swipe right as fast as her thumb would let her, barely reading the profiles let alone taking a proper look at their pictures. Luca jigged in his seat as Tia was finally practising what he'd been preaching for so long. She'd had enough of being the eternally single friend without so much as a sneaky link to keep her warm, and besides, she could do with the distraction – anything to take her mind off Aaron.

3

'Tia.'

'Tee-ah?'

'Tia!'

Gbemi elbowed her into paying attention, making her jolt in her seat, spilling tea on her trousers. Tia put her cup down and kissed her teeth without thinking, then quickly looked up at her colleagues around the Collaboration Zone (a stupid name Camilla had come up with for the large table where their meetings were held), and gave their glares an apologetic smile. The faint grin she'd struggled to produce quickly vanished when she saw the unimpressed look on her manager's crepey powdered face.

'Do you have anything new to share? Any new ideas?' asked Camilla, raising the intonation of her voice.

Being put on the spot like this caused Tia's already fragile stomach to do a somersault.

'I . . . um . . .' Tia cleared her throat and held the side

of her throbbing head. 'I'm actually waiting to hear back on something I pitched last week?'

'Oh? Remind me what it was again.'

'It was, erm, the Windrush grocers in Brixton? They're being forced to close due to a private members club buying the building.' Tia flicked through the pages of her worn-out notebook as she spoke, trying to find her pitch with all the newsy buzzwords. She could feel her throat closing itself and cleared it again. 'The couple have been there for decades, helping low-income families eat healthier, but I thought we could open it up and look at the wider gentrifica—'

'Ah yes, I remember!' said Camilla. 'Sounds fab, but I think the whole gentrification thing is a bit . . . well, done to death. What do you think?'

Her manager had this habit of presenting her opinion like it was fact then asking everyone for their thoughts in an attempt to appear as though she invited collaboration, which Tia couldn't stand. Camilla looked around the table for additional comments and an inkling of agreement when her unofficial protégé Petra decided to weigh in, of course.

'Yeah, I see what you mean, Camilla. I think we need to flip the conversation on its head,' she began, explaining with her hands. 'It's a bit of a downer, isn't it? What about looking at gentrification through a more uplifting lens?'

Tia sighed as more people began to enthusiastically

nod and chip in with comments of their own: Harry
mentioned how much fun Peckham was now that there
were so many 'bangin'' places to hang out, and Arjun
couldn't stop going on about his brother's new flat in
Hackney and how much safer the neighbourhood was
now compared to when he was at school. Before Tia
knew it, her idea had been shelved and Camilla was
advising her and Petra to put their heads together and
come back with something more solid next week, much
to Tia's dismay: she knew the grocers would be long
gone before she managed to pitch the story again. She
was just about to tune out of the rest of the meeting
when in sauntered Marc; he took a seat beside Camilla
without even looking up from his iPhone, transforming the entire energy of the group. Tia rolled her eyes
at the sight of her colleagues suddenly adjusting their
posture and adopting looks of faux interest and enthusiasm, a few even laughing and nodding ferociously at
the ideas being presented, clearly all desperately vying
for Marc's attention.

Marc was something of an enigma to Tia. His wild,
wiry hair and penchant for Doc Martens could fool you
into thinking he was a member of some bygone rock
band from the eighties rather than an editor at LCN,
though he probably wished he were the former. In the
three years that Tia had known Marc, not a month had
gone by without him telling stories from his glory days
as a music reporter for the *NME*, *Q* and whatever else

old white liberal men read. Some of that anarchist spirit was still in him though, as he was probably the most radical editor at LCN; his more strait-laced counterparts were forever scratching their heads at how Marc got away with so much. His every other word was either 'fuck' or 'bollocks', and he almost always did the opposite of whatever the higher-ups said. He also frequently butted heads with Camilla, which was largely the reason why Tia was such a big fan of his. He cleared his throat, indicating he couldn't stay for long, and Camilla gave him the floor to speak.

'Right, everyone, sorry for the intrusion but I've got some good news,' he began, crossing one leg over the other and folding his arms. 'Due to the increased traffic our recent content's been bringing to LCN's website, our department's being given some extra funding, which means we'll be creating several new permanent roles.'

Tia raised her head like a meerkat in a David Attenborough documentary. Though Marc couldn't sound any less enthusiastic, a permanent role at LCN was rarer than a unicorn. She knew this could be the ticket to get her out of her three-year stint as a researcher.

'I'll be sending a more detailed email by Monday so do look out for that,' he said before abruptly getting up to leave.

'So start working extra hard on all those pitches!' Camilla added.

The thought of having to think of an idea her infamously difficult manager would actually want to commission was enough to give Tia chest pains. When the meeting finally adjourned, her and Gbemi beelined to their usual sofa around the corner from the communal kitchen. Not only was it their favourite spot to gossip and avoid doing real work, but it also served as a sacred space for the two to check in with each other between mundane meetings and microaggressions. It was part of their routine. Whether it was figuring out what to message someone back, bitching about an annoying colleague (or three), or refining some ideas before a big meeting, it all happened on the crimson sofa.

'No, but what kind of dickhead schedules a meeting for Friday afternoon?'

Tia crossed her legs and rubbed her pounding head, asking God why the Ibuprofen she'd taken earlier hadn't kicked in yet.

'I think it's cos she has that running club with some of the editors?' Gbemi explained. 'She emailed this TED Talk the other week about how exercise increases productivity or some shit.'

'Everyone in the world knows Friday afternoons are basically write-offs. No one does any real work.'

'Not in the world according to Camilla Hastings.'

'Innit.'

'No, but did you see everyone's faces when Marc

mentioned them jobs? Everyone's gonna be moving mad.'

'I know!' groaned Tia, resting her forehead against Gbemi's shoulder. 'How does it feel not having to worry about a job anymore, O great one?'

Gbemi laughed, trying to downplay her recent promotion. She'd just been made an assistant to their department's social media team after implementing a very successful TikTok campaign that had made Marc smile for the first time since his second divorce. And while Tia couldn't have been prouder and was her work wife's biggest cheerleader, she couldn't help but feel pangs of inadequacy looking at her own lack of progress, especially since she and Gbemi had started together as interns.

'Just apply! If I have to read another one of Petra's longreads defending appropriation I'm actually going to rush her.'

'Oh my days, it was the audacity for me!' said Tia, as Gbemi pulled up the article on her laptop, shaking her head at its booming stats and engagement. 'Like, we get it, you went to Carnival once.'

The girls cackled over each other's laps before reluctantly deciding it was probably time to get back to their real jobs before anyone noticed they were gone. As Tia peeled herself off the sofa, she reached into her pocket to check the time on her phone and was met with a blank, dead screen. She sighed at the distinct memory of blasting Adele through her phone's speaker while crying herself to sleep the night before, and asked Gbemi if she could borrow her charger. The phone was still lifeless after plugging it into the outlet. Her stomach began to rumble. Remembering that the last proper meal she'd had was the one she'd shared with Aaron and his perfect plant-based girlfriend, Tia marched to the Five Guys round the corner and scoffed down a bacon cheeseburger, as if she was somehow getting back at Olivia, though the grease and saltiness did ease her hangover ever so slightly.

When she got back to the fourth floor, she could see that her colleagues who sat near to her desk looked more annoyed than usual. Before she could even remove her coat, Camilla walked over, sending pains into Tia's chest, and she immediately began to explain that she'd already WeTransferred the research she had requested earlier.

'I've got it. I just wanted to remind you to keep your phone on silent.' Camilla folded her arms. 'It's been pinging for ages and is quite disruptive, m'kay? Let's be considerate.'

After Camilla had disappeared into another meeting, Tia slumped into her chair and snatched the phone from her desk, mentally telling it off for getting her into trouble. After flicking the button on its side, she froze when she saw the crowded but unfamiliar notifications on the screen:

I've been told my face makes a great seat ;)
Do u have snap?
Ur a feisty one still! I like dat u knw
How do you feel about animal costumes? Xx

Tia could feel the bacon cheeseburger climb its way up her throat and slapped her hand over her mouth as she continued to scroll, her widened eyes blinking in disbelief at what she was seeing. She scrolled through several chats filled with aubergines, peaches and laughing faces, then clicked on her own profile and gasped, slamming her phone down on her desk.

Tia remembered swiping right quite a bit during the journey home, but not on every fucking man in London.

4

Luca was screaming from under the pillow covering his face, his gangly legs wriggling in the air. In desperation he began to thump the mattress beneath him.

'Tia, please. He could pass out!'

Tia struggled to keep her elbows on top of Luca as he tried to sit up. Hannah scooped spilled Sensations off her bed and back into the bowl, mostly unfazed by the murder attempt happening in front of her.

'He deserves it after the shit he pulled on my Hinge profile!'

When Luca finally stopped resisting, she released her grip on the pillow and threw herself down on the carpet, realising that killing her best friend wouldn't change what had already happened.

'I was only trying to help!' Luca said, gasping for air.

Hannah jumped on top of him and picked up Tia's phone from beside him. '"Swipe right if you want to stop imagining me naked. I suck at chit-chat but can suck on something else . . ." Are you on crack, Luca?!'

'You can't say it didn't get her results!'

'Yeah, if those results were a future STD,' Hannah shouted. 'Do you want her to get over Aaron or get gonorrhoea?'

'Well—'

'Shut up!'

'I knew this was a bad idea,' said Tia, finally lifting her head. She leaned back against the bed her besties were lying on and looked up at the ceiling. 'I told you guys I'm not built for apps!'

'No, no, no. You can do this!' Hannah grabbed on to Tia's shoulder and gave her a shake. 'You just need to stop listening to Luca and you'll be fine.'

'Erm, fuck you!' he said, pouring himself another glass of wine. 'Finally getting her on Hinge was down to my hard work, thank you very much.'

'Whatever,' Hannah shrugged. 'You're just attracting creeps because your profile is way too horny.'

'She *is* way too horny.'

Tia kissed her teeth as Hannah began to scroll through the photos Luca had selected, full of ample cleavage, pouts with tequila shots in hand, and the thirst traps she'd taken on their Bank Holiday week-ender to Croatia last year.

'It needs balance: you need pics that cover all the bases. Your profile is basically an advert for you.'

'What do you mean?' asked Tia.

'You need a gym pic to show that you're healthy.'

'But I can't even do half a Chloe Ting video without crying.'

'A pic with your friends to show you're not a loser; a travel pic to show that you're cultured, and maybe one with a puppy to show that you're wholesome.'

'But I don't have a pupp— Sorry! Why is this so complicated, please?' asked Tia as Luca cackled in the background.

'It's just not giving wifey material right now, sis,' said Hannah, shaking her head.

'Who cares about being wifey material, please?' shouted Luca. 'We're children.'

'Thirty isn't even that far away you know,' sighed Tia.

'Exactly!' Hannah clapped her hands. 'What else is the point of dating? You can't seriously expect to survive off hook-ups for the rest of your lives – that's so depressing.'

'No, what's depressing is being trapped with the same boring penis for the rest of your life.'

'It's not boring when you're in love with it, Lucaaa!'

Hannah bellowed the lyrics of a long-forgotten Trey Songz ballad as if the three were back in Year 10 again. She wrapped her legs around Luca, humping the side of his body and re-enacting all the things she and Sean had got up to the night before, as Tia rolled her eyes from the floor, laughing at their shrieks.

'How is Sean, anyway?' Luca asked after finally pushing Hannah away. 'He seemed bare aggy yesterday.'

'He's just getting sick of Foot Locker and is dying for a new job. We couldn't even finish properly because he had to be up early to open the store.' She rolled onto her back and sighed. 'Plus he kept getting shook about his mum busting in.'

'Oh, now that would be mad,' laughed Luca. 'Could you imagine?'

'Don't! There's been so many close calls lately, we're seriously thinking about getting a place together.'

'Wow, already?' said Tia. Her eyes darted to Luca who looked equally concerned.

'I dunno, I think it'll be really good for us.'

'Has it even been a year though?'

'This week is our fourteen-month anniversary actually.'

'Babe, that's not a th— Y'know what, never mind.' Luca held his hands in the air, already deeming Hannah a lost, loved-up cause.

'Why wait any longer? We love each other. This is the next step.'

Though Tia wasn't in any rush to shack up with someone or race down the aisle, a part of her envied how comfortable Hannah seemed with Sean. She had someone to leave with and natter to after a night out; she had someone who'd listen to all the pointless nothings that had happened throughout her day at work, and she had someone to plan her tomorrows with. Perhaps that was why the idea of moving in together didn't scare Hannah so much, Tia thought. You're less scared of life's unpredictability when you know you won't be facing it alone – or rather, you'll be facing it with someone who's just as clueless as you are but nevertheless still by your side. And here Tia was, depressed over a guy she'd known for ten years who was moving forward with someone he'd known for months.

Tia snatched the bowl from between her bickering friends and shoved a handful of crisps into her mouth before refocusing her attention on her abysmal dating profile. She started by deleting Luca's choices and replacing them with a more wholesome selection: her current favourite selfie (which she'd already plastered all over her Twitter and Instagram); a full body shot of her at an exhibition by her favourite photographer; another selfie in which her curly head of hair took up most of the space; an incredibly orchestrated candid Hannah had once taken of her at an overhyped restaurant, and of course, she reinstated one of the thirst traps from Croatia, for balance.

By the following week, she was almost certain she'd sprained her thumb from swiping left so much. Dwayne from Romford had a weird head shape; Josiah from Hackney only had group pictures; Robert who was based between London and Oxford screamed jungle fever, and though Tosin looked tall and only lived a few kilometres away from Tia, he was wearing stained T-shirts in three of his photos. She managed to hold a conversation with an estate agent from Beckenham until she could no longer hack the way he spelled 'you' with a single letter. The only other guy that she was speaking to was pleasant enough, but Tia would have been lying if she didn't admit that his photos on a fancy-looking boat were the only thing keeping her interested. But no matter what or who she tried, she couldn't find someone better looking or more interesting to talk to than Aaron. She hated that she still thought about him when he wasn't even hers to think about anymore.

Han:

Maybe cast the net a little wider?

Don't be so picky x

Tia:

Picky? I'm not picky!

LuLu:

@Han we prefer the term SELECTIVE

Tia:

THANK YOU!

Han:

Okay Clueless 🙄

But even if they're not 100% your type
on paper, just give it a chance innit.

Tia:

Can I least fancy them? Or am
I too single for that now?

LuLu:

Don't listen to her babes.

Never settle, never chase. YOU'RE THE PRIZE.

She knew messaging her friends for advice would only confuse her more. But when she returned from her shower to zero notifications bar a text from Pizza GoGo, she sighed at her reflection and sat down in front of her bedroom mirror. She roughly parted her dripping-wet hair into untidy sections and scooped out a massive blob of her fragrant hair cream, raking it through her strands and carefully squishing the ends until her curls began to form again.

Am I being too picky? Tia asked herself. She jiggled her thick thighs and stared into the mirror, tugging at the dark circles under her eyes, then pinching her chubby cheeks, pushing the fat back to see what she'd look like with an actual jawline. Sure, she wasn't exactly Beyoncé reincarnate, or anywhere near as flawless as the girls she followed on Instagram, but she still thought she deserved to be with someone she was actually attracted to. Surely she wasn't so hopelessly single that she had to compromise on something as basic as liking the other person's face.

Tia proceeded to scroll through everyone else's much-cooler lives before getting stuck into a K-drama, simultaneously living vicariously through Luca's blurry story updates from the sticky dancefloor of Heaven and Hannah's video of Sean tucking into a dessert they had just ordered. Her phone screen suddenly flipped to a boomerang of someone's glossy hair blowing in the wind in front of London Bridge. It wasn't until Tia noticed it was posted by Aaron that she sat up to get a better look. She lost count of how many times she rewatched the flash of Olivia's grin. *Such a fucking tourist,* Tia thought, flopping onto her back, nitpicking at any detail to tear apart in her mind. She attempted to screenshot the post to send it to the group chat, but the phone slipped between her clammy fingers and plummeted right onto Tia's nose. After howling at the pain, her heart began to thump so hard she felt as though it was about to tear itself out of her chest.

'NOOOOO!' she yelled, looking at the screen. 'NO. NO. NO. NO.'

She'd reacted to Aaron's story. With a fucking laughing emoji of all things.

Deleting her entire online presence and moving to her grandma's house in Jamaica felt a bit dramatic but Tia was tempted. She was still coming to terms with the fact that Aaron was actually with someone who wasn't her, and she definitely couldn't handle a conversation revolving around Olivia. She raced to their DMs, wildly hoping it was an aberration or a mirage, but no such luck. He'd already seen it and had started typing. Tia was about one more embarrassing event away from a nervous breakdown and quickly locked her phone before she could see his reply, rubbing her tender nose bridge.

'T, you alright?' her mum asked from the other side of her bedroom door.

'I'm fine!' she groaned, throwing her duvet over herself. 'Just dropped something.'

When a notification sound pinged, she cried out to God, begging for it to be another text from Pizza GoGo and not something weird from Aaron. She stuck her arm out from under the covers and felt around for her phone, pulling it back under the cocoon she had made for herself. She sighed when she saw the Hinge notification.

'Great. What now?'

Tia raised her eyebrows at the message. This was a positive sign and a first since Luca had downloaded this godforsaken app for her. The stranger was referring to her line about swiping right if they needed a concert buddy.

Nate:
I'd go and see literally anything with you

It would've been corny if he weren't so gorgeous, Tia thought while trawling through his profile. He had reddish-brown skin, looked a bit on the thin side, but quite tall, and thankfully didn't use his height as a prompt. His short, fluffy beard straddled the fine line between fashion-forward and unkempt, but judging by his dress sense the scruffy aesthetic definitely seemed like a deliberate choice: a flannel shirt and a pair of Dickies in one pic; a navy overcoat, what looked like grey suit trousers, and JW Anderson Converse in the other – his look appeared carefree but was very much curated. He looked every bit the artsy fuckboy you'd bump into a dozen times at Boxpark. He wore some kind of hat in every photo, leading Tia to suddenly panic about whether he had a receding hairline, but beggars couldn't be choosers, and even if he was bald, his handsome face more than made up for it, she thought to herself, scrolling further down to read the rest of his profile.

It felt too good to be true, and she was reassured to see the icon linking to his Instagram account. The display picture still looked similar to the ones on his Hinge profile. Though it was private, his post-to-follower-to-following ratio looked real and human, dispelling worries of him being a catfish or some kind of bot. A few of Tia's mutuals already followed him too, but before she could examine further, her phone pinged again.

Nate:
And I love The Internet too! Did you catch their last show in Brixton?

Oh my days, he actually read my profile? Up until a couple of days ago, something as minuscule as reading a few sentences would never have stirred Tia's hopes like this, but after more than a week on Hinge, she knew enough to realise that these crumbs of decency and non-wayward behaviour were few and far between.

Tia quickly typed out a reply before talking herself out of it and dropped the phone from her hands, smiling to herself at this sudden glimmer of hope.

5

With less than fifteen minutes until she had to run for the train, Tia quickly scooped small handfuls of Eco Styler onto her damp hair and brushed it down into a low bun, her least favourite hairstyle but the one that was least likely to become topic of the day at the office. She sighed at her reflection as she tried to slick her edges down into a swirl that she liked, frustrated at the effort she had to make, all so she could avoid her colleagues' questions and remarks. She slathered her face with cream and brushed her overgrown eyebrows into place with a spoolie and a mixture of soap and water, before swiping her lips with a tinted balm Hannah had talked her into buying. She sighed at her dark circles and bare face until she quickly threw on a pair of hoop earrings, the only thing that could make Tia feel more done.

South-East London railway was crap on a good day, but on a bad day, and one on which Tia had woken up late, it felt like a personal attack against her life. She was so out of breath from running across Catford Bridge station that she wasn't even able to kiss her teeth when the doors of her train slid open to reveal a sea of grey suits and ugly but very practical-looking backpacks. She squeezed herself into a tight corner by the carriage's overflowing bin and rested her head against a dingy poster about withholding money from beggars. With little to no room to break out her headphones and drown out the sounds of people coughing and turning the pages of their *Metro*s, Tia fished out her phone from her pocket to open Instagram, begging for a morsel of Shade Borough nonsense to ease the pain of such a shitty morning. She scrolled past glossy photos of younger, far more accomplished celebs, annoyingly productive morning routines, and elaborate one-pot recipes.

By the time Tia arrived at work, Camilla was already four pitches into their morning meeting. She darted her beady eyes towards the corner Tia had tried to slip into undetected before fixing them back onto a writer pitching an idea about a local artist working with schools to destigmatise periods through sculptures made from sanitary-towel wrappers. It was the writer's third period-themed pitch, and Tia respected the tenacity, though she thought it was very Goop-esque and could tell the novelty was wearing off for Camilla, who rejected it of course. She said something about how LCN's mostly older readers hadn't been too keen on the last period story they'd run, about a singer's viral ode to menstruating, and swiftly moved on. Harrison, a staff writer who'd been tapping his fountain pen on his knee until it was his turn to speak, gave a smug grin, as if he already knew Camilla would love his idea. And he was right, because as soon as the words 'war veteran', 'reunited' and 'lost dog' were mentioned, the table erupted with glee, knowing it would secure over a million page views in a single weekend. Tia and Gbemi had a running joke about how much easier it was to get an animal story commissioned as opposed to something focusing on women, black people or, more controversially, both – though the joke got less funny the longer they worked there.

'Tia?' Camilla seemed have picked up on her lack of enthusiasm. 'Would you be able to assist Harrison in getting some archive images and whatnot?'

Tia nodded and forced a cheesy grin at Harrison, who gave her a wave and mouthed how they should have a quick chat afterwards.

'Since you haven't got too much going on and all,' Camilla added, scribbling something into her leather journal. 'Oh, wait – do you have an update on your and Petra's idea?'

Before Tia could open her mouth to say something, Petra spluttered in with a barrage of breathy laughs, explaining how they were just waiting to hear back from some potential interviewees.

After an unnecessarily long conversation with

Harrison, followed by Tia evading his questions on how she managed to slick all of 'that hair' down into a bun, she returned to her desk with a cup of tea that may as well have been warm dishwater and absolutely no desire to rifle LCN's archives for Second World War photos. She slid her headphones over her ears and plugged them into her MacBook, placing a notebook and pen she had swiped from the office stationery cupboard beside it, giving the illusion she was going to be productive and far too busy to talk to anyone sat around her. She wanted to procrastinate a little more before skimming through her inbox though, and dug out her phone, pleased to discover several new messages on Hinge.

One from the estate agent she'd matched with last night; another douchey joke from the Tory who had a boat, and two from her current favourite, Nate. Since she'd reclaimed her profile, the slew of matches and messages were considerably less thirsty than before, but were still overwhelming for a first-time user. It had now been nearly two weeks since she'd started using Hinge, and though these sorts of apps were always branded as quick and convenient solutions for finding love, Tia was already exhausted by how taxing the whole thing was. For one, she usually found herself swiping left, because almost every other profile looked like someone she'd bump into in the office. Tall, thin and white with names like Matt and Ollie, all dressed in some kind of button-down, hands clasped around a pint of beer and their hair slicked back. Their profiles always mentioned something about *The Office* and how they were looking for someone to go rock climbing with; she could just about catch her breath after walking up a flight of stairs so that was a hard pass. If she did manage to match with someone, they were either not interested enough to reply within a day, or the conversation got too creepy too quickly, like with that electrician she'd matched with who was more interested in requesting feet pics than learning her favourite cuisine. But Nate was different.

She smiled at the four letters of his name and saved his messages for last, as if it they were an indulgent sugary treat. He wished her a good morning and apologised for falling asleep during their debate on how Joe Goldberg from *You* was still attractive despite being a bloodthirsty psycho. Most of their conversations were silly little arguments over stuff that didn't really matter, like pizza toppings, unpopular film opinions, and which post-2016 Kanye album was the worst. He paid attention to the parts of her personality she'd attempted to inject into her profile, like suggesting his favourite dim sum restaurant for their hypothetical date because he noticed how much she loved Asian food. Nate even took note of things she hadn't even realised, like how she wore black in almost all of her profile photos. He teased her hard about the fact that she hadn't watched a single one of the year's biggest TV shows, and though she felt a little embarrassed about how boring she must be coming across, she was delighted that his solution was to spend a future weekend together binge-watching everything she had missed out on. Whether he meant it or not, she loved how eager he seemed to spend time with her that didn't involve a bedroom or anything remotely sexual, which she'd quickly learned was a rarity on dating apps.

A few days after they'd matched, they'd crossed the all-important voice note threshold. Nate had started it off by apologising, explaining how what he wanted to say was too long to type, which thrilled Tia. To her, this was an indication of his level of investment into not only their conversations but getting to know her beyond a few handpicked photos on her Hinge profile. Luca, the realist of the group, didn't think it was that deep, though Hannah, the hopeless romantic out of the three, revelled in Tia's excitement.

She replayed this morning's voice note over and over, smiling to herself over Nate's perfect laugh. It was a little deep and raspy but didn't feel unnatural, or like he was trying to flex his masculinity by forcing some macho tone. *Even his voice is peng,* she thought to herself while smugly scrolling through his photos, as if she hadn't already done so a dozen times.

'I've just clocked, all you do is argue with me till the morning. Is this healthy for us?' he said with a laugh sprinkled in at the end. 'I pressed "snooze" on my alarm twice this morning because I was so tired from you defending a literal serial killer.'

She slightly panicked over what to say back, suddenly forgetting how to speak in a cool, calm, collected way and took a swig of her tea before speed-walking to an empty meeting pod by her desk, pretending she was chatting to a very important contributor. Though voice notes were essentially just diluted phone calls, she found something so intimate about sharing fragments of one's breathy musings to someone who actually cared about what you had to say back. Though she mainly used the function to spill some untypable tea to Hannah and Luca, it felt different with someone she'd never met, like a newer, more intimate level of communication. After practising her reply in her head a few times, she finally spoke into her phone and then released the "record" button, already anticipating Nate's clapback.

Tia reluctantly returned to her desk, figuring she should probably do some work and look busy, and plopped herself into her chair and swivelled her body back towards her MacBook, stroking her fingertips over the trackpad. The screen lit up and she sighed a little louder than intended, scanning her full inbox. She skipped emails about collections for colleagues who barely looked in her direction, drinks being organised for someone's leaving do in the same dreary pub her team always holed up in after work, and, of course, more research pointers from Harrison, just in case Tia had suddenly forgotten how to do her job. She hit the backspace button over and over until she reached the latest email from LCN's very own press office.

LCN LAUNCHES LCN LEAD: 'A BOLD STEP INTO A MORE INCLUSIVE FUTURE,' SAYS DIRECTOR SIMON BODEN

Tia rolled her eyes at the headline in its sleek Bodoni font. *Yes, there's nothing bolder then yet another diversity scheme,* she thought to herself as she read on. LCN Lead was a fancy new leadership initiative designed to reinvigorate the organisation's editorial output, prioritising things like diversifying the newsroom and making an effort to target under-served audiences. Her scepticism increased the more she listened to the clip of Simon's speech from the launch breakfast that had happened the previous day, talking about how LCN was committed to appealing to all of its readers, while standing alongside other directors and executives who all looked like a variation of him (salmon-coloured, half-bald, with rolled-up sleeves in an attempt to look approachable) and had all probably gone to the same university as him. She scrolled further down to the photos of the lucky few and smiled to see her mentor, Yvonne Anderson, one of the only black women in attendance, in her signature bob-and-blouse combination.

Yvonne had shot to fame in the early nineties after she'd been photographed for the cover art of her then-boyfriend's single. He was a toff by day and a house DJ by night, had a bit of a coke problem, and was a total prick (probably due to the coke, Yvonne had suspected). She had been a beautiful but bored university student and they had bonded over her love of free VIP entries to all the best clubs in London – while he earned major Brownie points by having a drop-dead-gorgeous woman on his arm, so theirs was a mutually beneficial relationship. The track itself was pretty forgettable, and today you would only ever hear it as part of a question on *The Chase*, but at the time it was huge and played in all the biggest dance venues across Europe. Yvonne's deep copper-brown skin, gap-tooth grin and signature Bantu knots were everywhere and practically made her the face of the UK rave scene, which then catapulted her to a brief but very busy modelling career. Hers was one of the few Black British faces, besides Naomi Campbell's, that had graced the covers of *i-D*, *Dazed & Confused* and British *Vogue*, to name a few, and she'd been a permanent fixture on the catwalks for Yves Saint Laurent, Jean Paul Gaultier and Vivienne Westwood (who, to this day, still credited Yvonne as a muse).

After years of living the high life in New York, both literally and metaphorically, Yvonne had grown tired of having to work twice as hard as her paler counterparts and had decided to settle back in London and put her English Language degree to use. Yvonne had penned an exclusive op-ed for the *Guardian* detailing the harsh realities of working as a model and the exploitative nature of the industry. It was the first time an insider had been so open and honest about the fashion world, and she'd blown everyone away with her refreshing candour and wit, proving that she wasn't just a pretty face. But because she was also a very pretty face, opportunities to appear on television and to write even more about her experiences had grown, which had eventually led her to pivot to journalism. LCN had taken her on as one of its first Arts and Culture correspondents in the early 2000s, and she'd spent the next two decades reporting from the red carpet, producing award-winning documentaries about fast fashion, and had spearheaded a focus on emerging designers and creatives from the capital. Everything Yvonne touched turned into gold – or rather, everything she touched turned into BAFTA gold, as quoted from Simon Boden himself.

Tia could hardly believe that such a legend had even had the time to take her under her wing, but Yvonne had been gracious and regal as ever during their first coffee together two years ago. Since then she would occasionally ask Tia along to gallery openings and press events she was invited to, and had introduced her to the coolest theatre-makers and artists around the city. They'd have talks about the highs and lows of LCN over drinks, and Yvonne would always have a crazy tale or two from her heyday, dotted with pearls of wisdom that Tia would try and apply to her own path.

After sending Yvonne a congratulatory email, Tia took another look at her inbox in case Harrison had decided to nag her even further, then jolted up from her seat when she saw Marc's unread email in bold lettering. It was the all-important message about the new jobs. Tia's eyes skimmed through all the generic stuff he'd already mentioned in the meeting and scrolled all the way to the bottom to see just how many spots her department would be fighting over: three senior journalist roles, two video journalist ones and only one writer's position.

'One?!' she whispered to her screen.

The Hunger Games would be easier than this, Tia thought to herself. She ignored the line about further contract extensions, since she'd had more than enough of those as a researcher. This time was going to be different, Tia assured herself while downloading the lengthy edit test and application forms. She didn't know how she was going to beat all her other colleagues who were quite literally born to work at a place like LCN, but she wouldn't give up without a fight.

Throughout the day, Tia's attention kept being stolen by the buzz of her phone, Nate's messages being the only hits of endorphin between Harrison's incessant need for discussing every single detail of his pitch and the ever-growing bits of research he absolutely needed.

Listen. I blame you for having me up till 4! Just not quite in the way I'd like ;) Nate wrote, making Tia grin and look away from the screen like an idiot. How about we grab a nightcap tonight? Maybe it'll help us get to bed earlier lol, he said, sounding all laidback and sexy.

She quickly consulted the group chat with Hannah and Luca, who begged her to stop overthinking everything and to put her vagina first for once in her life. Under Luca's command, she waited another five minutes so as to appear busy at work, then replied with a very lowkey Sounds good to me x.

The girls sprawled on their red sofa, savouring the last ten minutes of lunch, when Tia giggled at something on her phone.

'That TikTok was jokes, innit?'

She looked over her phone's screen at Gbemi with a puzzled look on her face.

'The aunty praying for her dog?'

'Oh no, sorry. I'll watch it now.'

'I swear the only times you've smiled today have been when you're replying to your new bae.'

'Not true. That Oloni thread you sent finished me.'

'Asking his date to go halves on the petrol, y'know. Men are actually scary.' Gbemi shuddered.

'The scariest.'

'Except the one hitting you up though, right?'

'He's cute or whatever. I'm actually seeing him tonight.'

Gbemi rejoiced, looking up towards the ceiling to thank God before slapping Tia's thigh.

'Finally! You lots have been doing up penpal way too long, man.'

'Is two weeks really that long?'

'In the world of Hinge and Tinder? Yes, babes,' she laughed. 'D'you know what you're gonna wear?'

'Fuck, I don't even know. Jeans and a nice top?'

Tia tapped on her camera and reversed it to inspect her face, annoyed with the lack of effort she'd put into her appearance that morning, dragging a dark circle down with the tip of her finger, while Gbemi begged her to at least show some breast.

'Okay, I will. But only for you,' laughed Tia as Gbemi dragged her up and off the sofa.

The pair linked their arms and cackled over towards the communal kitchen to make a cup of tea, dragging out every step of the brewing and stirring process just so they could spend even more time chirping about Tia's first date in forever. As the best dressed in the office, Gbemi schooled her on the dos and don'ts of what to wear, threatening to drag Tia to the shitty pub after work the following day if she dared showed up to her date in anything wide-legged, despite Tia's defensive plea.

'Actually you better send me a pic so I can approve the fit,' ordered Gbemi. She wagged her manicured finger in Tia's face and began poking her sides until Tia agreed between her giggles.

After breezing through her work for the rest of the day, Tia sprinted out of the office to Oxford Circus station, just as the huddle of equally exhausted workers was slowly starting to form outside of NikeTown. She darted down the escalators, bumping into shiny yellow Selfridges bags and clunky backpacks, and slipped through the sliding doors of the tube. The anticipation of finally getting to meet Nate was enough to distract Tia from the musty bodies that fused to her as she squeezed herself onto the train back to Catford. She ran to the bathroom the moment she opened the front door of the flat, shouting to her mum over the gushing sounds of the showerhead blasting tepid water into the tub that she and Luca were going out tonight. The church kid within her didn't see any point in possibly worrying her mum, or raising her matrimonial hopes up over what could be a one-off, so the white lie was the simplest way to go, Tia thought, as she ripped her clothes off and leaped into the shower, eager to scrub and rinse away the mind-numbingly boring day.

'And don't suggest to split the bill like you always do, yeah?' said Hannah over speakerphone 'We gerrit, Miss Independent! But sometimes let the man be a man, d'you get?'

Tia rolled her eyes while carving out her non-existent cheekbones. 'It's not that deep.'

'Yes, it is. And if he uses a voucher, run for the fuckin' hills.'

'Oh my days, how jokes was that Oloni thread though?'

'Listen! The streets are rough, I don't ever want to return,' Hannah cackled. 'And who knows, you may even leave them if tonight goes well.'

'I was never in the streets!' shouted Tia, trying to hold in her laugh while carefully applying brown lipliner.

'I'm just saying, you never know what fate may bring!' Hannah said in a spooky voice. 'Just be open, innit.'

'Uh-huh.'

'That applies to both your heart and your legs.'

'Oh, fuck off!' Tia giggled.

'Where's he taking you anyway? An *art gallery*? Or an *independent cinema* perhaps?'

'I don't even know. My phone died before I could read his reply,' Tia laughed, knowing she should've never shown Hannah and Luca the hipster photos on Nate's profile. 'And I feel like imma probably be late. Hold on, lemme check.'

After spraying her face with far too many spritzes of Fix+, Tia pulled on the charging cable trailing up to her bed and dragged her phone down into her hands. She tapped on the Hinge app.

'Erm, what the fuck?'

'What?'

'What the fuck!'

'What the fuck's happened, T?'

'FUCK.'

'Tia, what the fuck, bruv!'

'He's gone!'

'Who's go—'

'Nate!' Tia blurted. 'Our chat, my profile, it's all gone! "Your account has been removed,"' she read out loud, baffled at the sentences before her eyes. '"You have been banned from using Hinge for violating our Terms of Service."'

'Woah,' said Hannah. 'What the fuck did you do?'

'How should I know?' Tia shrieked. 'This doesn't make any sense!'

She paced up and down her room until she became dizzy and threw herself onto her bed, frustrated with herself to the point where she could feel her face burning up, and stared at the ceiling, imagining Nate waiting at some bar for hours on end. The image of him sipping on a watered-down Negroni, looking at the door for her every time it opened made Tia physically cringe and curl up into the foetal position. She whimpered when she noticed she was ruining her make-up, then realised it didn't even matter. No matter how many times she tried to rationalise the disaster of the situation, a sharp pang of guilt and disappointment repeatedly hit Tia's chest. *He's never gonna chat to me again,* she thought, wiping off her lip gloss with the back of her hand.

6

'I've been thinking.'

'Uh-oh. Go on.'

'And it was either the Tory I told to go fuck himself.' Tia paused. 'Or the electrician who sent me the dick pic . . . who I told to go fuck himself if he could wrap his hand around something so small.'

Gbemi cackled into her mug of coffee while Tia continued to retrace where everything went wrong. It had been over a week since she had been banned from Hinge. A week since she inadvertently stood Nate up on what would've been their first date, and a week since she had given up on dating, despite her friends begging her to download a different app.

'I mean, they both sound petty and gross,' said Gbemi. 'And definitely the kind of guys who'd be into that revenge-reporting shit.'

Up until her unjust ban, neither of the girls had ever heard of this apparent phenomenon, until Tia had done an FBI-worthy internet search for any kind of answer as to how she could get her profile and her chat with Nate back. All she'd found, however, were Reddit threads and screenshots of the same thing happening to other women, and stories of them appealing to Hinge without receiving so much as an automated reply. Her stomach lurched when she stumbled into Incel Twitter and came across tweets from men advising one another to report an account anytime a girl was being 'bitchy'. The journalist in Tia was almost tempted to turn this whole ordeal into a pitch for LCN, until Gbemi begged her to stop thinking about work for once. Plus, Tia heaved at the thought of having to disclose her dating life to the likes of Camilla and Petra around the Collaboration Zone table.

'Ugh. Fuck this,' Tia wailed. She threw her head back and folded her arms, like a spoilt toddler throwing a fit in the middle of a supermarket. 'Can we talk about something else? Like how your date went?'

Gbemi sighed and kissed her teeth; the sharp sound tore through the air like thunder.

'Stoppp. Was it that bad?'

'Deaddd. It was dead.' Gbemi slumped her body further into the red sofa. 'He just kept forcing the deadest jokes. Like, you know the ones who try to make everything sexual? Gave me instant ick.'

'So jarring.'

'Like, how you gon utter the word BBW before our main course reaches the table? Are you alright?'

Tia's jaw dropped. 'Fuck off. Where did you meet this creep?'

'Nowhere, bruv! My mum set me up with her church friend's son.'

'Stop it.' Tia covered her mouth with her hand then shook her head.

'Church boys are proper weirdos though, innit. Always mad horny. That's why they get married after like two months of dating.'

'I am dead!' Tia giggled. 'How did your mum even convince you to go?'

'She happened to have a migraine the day she showed me his photo and said she hopes she doesn't die before seeing her future grandchildren.'

'Wowww,' said Tia before bursting out laughing.

'Yeah, Viola Davis ain't got nuttin on Nigerian mums.' Gbemi rolled her eyes, completely unamused. 'What you got planned for the rest of the day?'

'Not much,' Tia sighed, as they began walking back to their desks. 'Gonna try and think of some ideas to pitch though. If I can't secure a babes I should at least try and secure this role.'

'You know you can do both, right?'

'Nope. I'm done. I'm tired.'

The girls laughed as they went off in opposite directions to their respective teams, promising to grab lunch together from somewhere that wasn't the nearest Pret or Leon for once.

When Tia logged back into her MacBook, her Twitter feed automatically refreshed and she began to scroll down the timeline to see what she had missed: discourse on having kids at weddings, pretty photos of SZA, the new Timotheé Chalamet trailer, and a clip of a schoolgirl over and over again. It had been retweeted by a bunch of her mutuals, from old classmates to Twitter heavyweights with tens of thousands of followers. She saw cryptic but angry tweets around it but still didn't understand what was going on and so plugged in her headphones.

In the clip a few schoolkids jokingly chanted 'Black hair matters!' before bursting into laughter and being shushed by a teacher. Some then began throwing peace signs and middle fingers at the camera until it moved away from them, panning the crowded classroom and zooming in on a girl probably no older than twelve or thirteen. Her face was plump and glazed, as if her mum had lovingly slathered a thick layer of cocoa butter all over it just before she'd left for school, and her cloud-like hair was teased out into an afro with a red bow clipped to one side to match her familiar-looking tie. Her arms cradled a sparkly purple diary over her round belly, and her matching backpack looked as if the whole of WHSmith was packed in there. The camera zoomed in on her watery eyes and Tia could tell the girl was trying to hold back her tears while trying to plead with a teacher roughly escorting her out of the classroom, with another impatiently waiting by the door.

'I don't want to tie it up,' the tearful girl said as the teacher continued to steamroll her explanations. 'I washed it last night, I don't need to tie it up.'

Tia thought about her own twenty-four-year-old self getting ready for work, and how if her curls weren't perfectly sleek or were too frizzy then she'd brush and pull and police 'all that' hair into submission, just for a more peaceful day at work. She thought about the number of times she'd dodged wandering hands during her first few weeks at LCN as an intern, until a high-pitched voice from the video stole her focus.

'Miss Harrison always does this! Always gettin' onto us over the dumbest things, bruv.'

You couldn't see this other student's face but you could hear everyone else around her agreeing, chiming in with their 'Innit's and the occasional 'Wasteman!' It wasn't until the clip looped a second time that Tia got a better look at the badge on one of the student's blazers, the same blazer that was crumpled up and stuffed in the back of her own wardrobe at home. She shook her head the moment she realised that this was in fact happening in her old secondary school, and she readied her fingertips to type something. She stopped, though, her hands hovering over the keyboard. She couldn't tweet anything about it due to LCN's strict impartiality code, and Tia was already on thin ice since getting into an online spat with some Republicans a while back. She didn't regret it, but it had been her third warning regarding social media, and she didn't fancy having an unnecessary meeting with Camilla; her days had more than enough of those already.

The next day, the school released a public statement in response to the viral video, stating that the size of the child's hair had breached their uniform policy, which instructed students to keep their hair neat and/or tied back for health and safety reasons. And if that weren't enough, screenshots from the girl's classmates had been posted on The Shade Borough: Snapchat stories that had been re-shared over and over again, with students explaining how that specific teacher seemed to target particular girls over nail colours, earrings, and the music they'd play out loud during break. The comments on the post were somewhat divided, with some (mainly) men agreeing with the teacher, while many women chimed in on how they too felt unfairly scrutinised over similar issues. Even Tia could remember from her own school days the way that teachers would demonise specific kinds of students for how they carried themselves, cursing their futures with hypothetical prison sentences and unwanted pregnancies if they didn't wear their ties properly or tighten the belts around their sagging trousers. This wasn't a one-off incident, she thought to herself.

A part of her wanted to report on this but the other part couldn't see it as even being possible: this issue couldn't have been further from the kinds of fluff

Camilla loved to commission. Tia stared at the document she had already created, filled with links to tweets and articles by other news outlets who had already written about the video, until the text became blurry.

'Guh-bemí!'

Janine, a sub-editor from another team, walked into Tia's line of vision and stared into her face with one of those awkward grins white people do where their lips disappear. Tia blinked into the woman's face as she began asking about an edit Tia had zero knowledge of.

'Um, I'm not Gb—'

'Oh my goodness!' the woman's eggshell face began to turn bright red, and she tightly gripped the laptop cradled between her arms. 'I'm so sorry, I thought you were Guh-bemi.'

Tia clenched her jaw and stood up to put her coat on, taking a deep breath while pushing her arms through the sleeves as the woman continued to laugh about the honest mistake of confusing her with the only other Black woman in the office who looked and sounded nothing like her.

'It's fine,' Tia said through a forced grin. She pronounced Gbemi's name properly for the woman, instructing her as to where she could find her, before heading downstairs for a cigarette.

The hit of nicotine was just enough to take the edge off everything that had irritated Tia that morning, but not enough to erase the dread she felt about the afternoon she'd be spending chasing contributors for Petra's gentrification piece. She closed her eyes and threw her head back, exhaling the smoke, then looked around at all the red-brick buildings that surrounded LCN's steel fortress and the backstreets filled with Addison Lees dropping off and picking up journalists for their next big scoop, for stories they probably cared about. Tia was about to check her phone until she spotted the sharp padded shoulders of a Balenciaga coat slipping out of a glossy black cab. She smiled when she saw the perfectly tousled bob belonging to Yvonne, who clocked Tia immediately. Out of respect, Tia attempted to hide the cigarette before Yvonne sauntered over, but it was too late.

'You've been caught red-handed,' she laughed, air-kissing Tia beside one cheek.

'Sorry, Yvonne. It's been a crap morning.'

'Don't apologise, just give me a pull.'

'Haven't you quit?' Tia laughed but handed it to her anyway.

'I know but it's the smell! Just one – see?' Yvonne took two puffs and handed it back. 'No harm done.'

'How's it all been since the announcement?'

'A nightmare.' Yvonne opened the flap of her Celine tote, revealing wads of documents. 'Who knew restructuring the editorial guidelines of a century-old institution would mean so much paperwork.'

'Wow. I definitely don't envy you there.'

Tia's grin and chirpy laugh weren't enough to distract Yvonne from her downcast eyes. She studied them for a moment before shaking her wrist to reveal her Serpenti watch to check the time.

'I've got about twenty minutes until my next meeting. Coffee?'

7

Even within the safety and familiarity of LCN's cafe, Tia couldn't go anywhere with Yvonne without a gaggle of people wanting to say 'hi' or congratulate her for whatever award/honour/special mention she'd recently been given. But it never got old, the way people's entire demeanour changed when they met the perfect picture of grace and talent that was Yvonne Anderson. The baristas couldn't stop smiling while Yvonne was placing their order, and even brought their drinks to their table in cups and saucers instead of the flimsy takeaway cups.

'So,' Yvonne began. She ripped open a sachet of brown sugar and stirred it into her Americano. 'What are you working on? I want to know everything.'

Tia's chest always tightened whenever she was asked this. She never felt like *she* was enough, let alone that she was working on something worth telling to Yvonne. It almost made her feel guilty, having access to such a trailblazer when she could barely pitch something without her throat closing up. Her hands fidgeted under the table as she reeled off the list of research tasks she had been undertaking, blowing her duties way out of proportion in an attempt to appear productive. Yvonne smiled and nodded, but in that way she did whenever her contributors were waffling, which made Tia even more nervous.

'That sounds great, darling. But what are *you* working on? Your ideas, I mean?'

Yvonne took a sip of her coffee, smiling at Tia over the rim of her cup, watching her squirm from across the table.

'Actually . . .'

'Hmm?'

'I do have this one idea I'd like to pitch.'

'Brilliant.'

'But I don't know how it'll go down with my editor,' uttered Tia. 'It's trending everywhere right now, but she's not one for stories that rock the boat, or that focus on anyone other than people she can relate to.'

Yvonne grinned to herself: she didn't need Tia to explain any further. She knew exactly the kind of attitude Tia was referring to: she had been dealing with it for almost twenty years. She stayed quiet as Tia came alive, retelling the events of the viral video and the outraged aftermath that had followed it, nodding and asking her own questions about the school and its history of targeting Black students over trivial matters.

'Who else has covered it?' asked Yvonne, in editor mode.

'Sky News and *Metro*, but they literally just reshared the clip,' Tia explained. 'I'd want to open it up to a proper discussion about the politics around our hair, the adultification of school girls – it touches on so many thi—'

Tia paused when she saw the smirk on Yvonne's face.

'This, to me, sounds like a pitch worth commissioning.'

'That's because you have taste,' joked Tia. 'It's just so hard pitching this kind of stuff to people who don't even pretend to be interested in these perspectives.'

'It is hard, you're right. But that's our job. Fighting for these perspectives to be explored. Because if we don't, we'll never be heard.'

'Of course.'

'Furthermore, this is the exact kind of content LCN Lead wants to get behind.' said Yvonne, patting her handbag full of paper. 'So don't be afraid to drop that in. You've got my support.'

It filled Tia with confidence that an esteemed person such as Yvonne could see the potential in a story she had started to care about so much. Her sage wisdom lit a fire within Tia that she hadn't felt since her first few months at LCN, back when she was an intern. She returned to her desk with a burst of energy she couldn't waste on psyching herself out, and she began to fiercely type into her document.

The next day, Marc swanned into the pitch meeting and sat next to Camilla, his face buried in his iPad, completely unaware of how his rare presence sent a frisson through the other staff members, all of them giddy and eager to present their stories. A few uninspiring pitches later and it was slowly nearing Tia's turn to present her idea. Her chest began to tighten the more Camilla thrilled at the story that was currently being pitched to her.

'So let me get this straight,' she began, trying to hold back an actual laugh. 'A Maine Coon from Greenwich has more Instagram followers than David Beckham?'

Sophia nodded with glee as she passed her phone around to her other equally delighted colleagues. She was a staff writer on the team whose niche seemed to only be clickbaity crap with a sprinkling of animals here and there. Camilla laughed as she pulled up the cat's profile on her own phone and showed it to everyone sitting nearby. It was not possible for Marc to look any more disinterested.

'Brilliant. Absolutely brilliant! This is going to be a hit on Facebook, for sure.'

Fuck, Tia thought to herself. How the hell was she

going to compete with a mildly cute cat that had more followers than one of the most photographed men in the world? She sank in her seat ever so slightly as she heard the laughs and banter quietening down in anticipation for her to start speaking.

'Tia,' said Camilla. 'What have you got for us then?'

The smiles around the table vanished as everyone looked in Tia's direction. She could feel her throat starting to close up as she opened her MacBook and typed in the incorrect password, twice. She cleared her throat to recalibrate herself and slowly started explaining the video she had come across.

'I want to speak to other Black women about their experiences of being discriminated against because of their hair,' she said.

When she looked up from her screen, she could see an array of different expressions. Some stared blankly. One or two faces looked a little insulted, namely some of the older writers on the team, as if Snowflake Twitter had struck again. As Tia referenced similar incidents being reported in America and South Africa, the well-meaning older millennials offered kind smiles, but she could tell they just wanted her to wrap up quickly so they could show off their ideas while Marc was still present.

'I do empathise with the schoolgirl,' Petra weighed in. 'But surely all the tweets were a bit of an overreaction? We all had to obey silly school rules.'

Harrison laughed. 'Yeah! Like, I remember one time I got detention for wearing my muddy football boots.'

Another writer chuckled and chimed in with his own nostalgic anecdote, as others around the table nodded in agreement.

'I think shoes you can take off is a *little* different from the hair that grows from your scalp,' said Gbemi. Tia shot her a grateful glance.

'It definitely wasn't an overreaction,' said Tia. 'So many women of all ages have started sharing their experiences and the way it affected how they saw themselves. Even I could relate.'

A few people began to look as though they were starting to warm to the idea, giving that fake empathetic look. In a bid to silence everyone's scepticism, Tia rested her MacBook on the table and turned it towards everyone. An array of dark-skinned Black women, each wearing a unique hairstyle, from fluffed-out afros to elaborate braids and juicy twist-outs, filled her mood board. Most of the women were clothed in neutrals and varying browns and creams that complemented their deep skin tones, presenting a clear theme. Some of them gave toothy grins or moody stares into the camera. Others had their hands resting on their scalps or cradling their full faces. Tia had also added a few odd photos of a retro golden hot comb and the iconic jars and tins of Blue

Magic, DAX, and a gorgeous vintage bottle of Luster's Pink Oil.

'I don't want this to be an ordinary feature – I'd really love to photograph these women and make a visual scrapbook of sorts.'

Tia knew this would be a risky pitch given that LCN had never really committed this much effort into one-off ideas like this one, but she knew what she wanted. The more Tia had researched and redrafted her idea, the more her imagination had run wild with it. She didn't care about the byline or the predicted stats. She just wanted to see something beautiful and familiar on the homepage for once.

'Our hair, our appearance, being too loud, being too quiet – it's always picked apart, no matter what stage of life a woman's in.' She paused. 'No matter what stage of life a *Black* woman is in. The world is always telling us how we should look and behave, and a lot of people have had enough.'

Camilla pursed her lips but Tia carried on.

'Our pop culture, our history, our pain, our creativity are all things woven into our hair. There are so many visually beautiful things we could do to demonstrate this in addition to all their stories, and—'

'This sounds like it's going to be pretty expensive. Have you considered that?' asked Camilla.

While Tia had thought she was on a roll, the

all-important budget question threw her off her equilibrium.

'Oh, um. Not yet. I wasn't sure that was necessary at this sta—'

'And are you absolutely sure this couldn't be just a regular feature instead? We have some very talented illustrators who could knock something u—'

A small voice from the back of the crowd interrupted Camilla's suggestion.

'I think that would do this story a disservice.'

Tia looked round and saw a pale, slender arm raised in the air. It was Eloise, another researcher on the team. She was quiet, unassuming, and dressed like a school librarian from an eighties children's book in the best way possible: she was forever clad in knitted jumpers and chunky cardigans, clunking up and down the fourth floor in her trusty Church's loafers. Tia hadn't really crossed paths with Eloise before, and though she was eternally grateful to Gbemi, she was relieved to see someone other than the only other Black woman at the meeting sticking up for her idea, hoping it'd be enough to convince Camilla.

'I think seeing this kind of imagery will inform our readers far better,' she added, adjusting her circular-framed glasses. 'The whole story will be about hair so surely we'd need to see it too?'

Camilla held Eloise's gaze and fixed her mouth to say something.

'Also,' Tia cleared her throat as everyone turned their beady eyes back to her, 'a member of LCN Lead came across my pitch the other day by chance, and they really felt like this was something we should do more of.'

'And who might that be?' Camilla leaned in, with a smarmy grin.

'Yvo—'

'Yvonne Anderson?!' blurted Petra.

Oohs and aahs erupted around the table as Camilla sank back into her chair, until Marc loudly snapped shut his leather iPad case, silencing everyone, and rose from his seat.

'I like it.'

Everyone's eyes widened as their looks of doubt and scepticism started to trickle away in some half-baked attempt to get on Marc's good side. He took a sip from his Hydro Flask and started scrolling away at his phone.

'Just make sure your interviewees are good. We can talk about the money later,' he added, without even lifting his head.

Camilla couldn't even interject because by the time she'd picked her jaw off the floor, Marc had already trailed off to God-knows-where. Tia could barely suppress her Cheshire-Cat-like grin and looked at the floor to avoid all the gawping around the table. Getting a commission from Marc himself felt like receiving a handshake from the Pope.

When the meeting finally adjourned, Camilla asked

Tia to stay for a moment, before she could run back to the red sofa with Gbemi to squeal in celebration.

'I think Marc got a tad carried away with not worrying about the money,' she laughed. 'You know what he's like!'

Tia laughed along in a bid to speed the conversation up.

'You've never done something like this before, so I want Eloise to help you out, since she was so enthusiastic during your pitch.'

'Oh, I'm sure I'll be okay. I've worked on plenty of shoots before!' said Tia, in her chirpiest voice. It was vital to sound as cheerful as possible when disagreeing with an idea in the office.

'That's true, but she's had a bit more experience planning with budgets and whatnot, so she'll be a great help.'

The more Camilla spoke, the more resolute she sounded. Speaking to her often felt like a Wimbledon final, forever ensuring you prepared decent enough answers to backhand her incessant questioning. The constant back and forth always made what could have been a pleasant discussion into more of an interrogation. Tia's voice would often get higher and higher with each reply, ensuring she sounded as unaggressive as possible. If she refused accepting Eloise's help one more time, Camilla would probably schedule in yet another unnecessary meeting about 'teamwork' and 'collaborating effectively'. This wasn't Tia's battle. And besides, she had just received a commission from LCN's toughest editor, so she wasn't going to let some bullshit micro-management rain on her parade.

'Sounds great, Camilla. I'll be sure to catch up with Eloise later on today.'

8

Hannah had graduated from Central Saint Martins the previous year, and, like many other fashion graduates, was now more or less a slave to the back-breaking and underpaid (though mostly unpaid) internships across the city. Luckily for Hannah, though, her collection had caused so much of a buzz at her end-of-year showcase that she'd won a placement at FUNKI. FUNKI was a painfully cool Scandinavian brand that had just launched in the UK and it was throwing an uber-bougie party to celebrate its arrival. Tia and Luca had been so excited to finally see Hannah's designs come to life and take the fashion world by storm, but since starting the placement she'd been relegated to booking taxis, chasing invoices, and packing hundreds of goodie bags. Not quite the fantasy the three had had in mind, but it didn't stop them from taking full advantage of the open bar, especially Tia, who wanted to celebrate such a triumphant pitch in the face of her dickhead manager.

The narrow cobbled streets of Shoreditch were

crowded with wacky-looking creatives and PR babes with names like Holly and Charlotte, clad in ZARA's finest, texting the rest of their tribe to meet them at places like Tonight Josephine and Bounce. The balls of Tia's feet were already beginning to burn as she teetered along the pavement in her favourite pair of black ankle boots which made her feel like Zoë Kravitz, simultaneously relishing and regretting her choice of footwear. She really had had no choice; her friends would have rinsed her if she'd turned up in her trusty pair of Vans.

When she arrived at a building that had no clear signage (because what's an industry event without a 'secret location'?), she suddenly saw a group of trenchcoats emerge from a steel door. Each member of the platinum-blonde posse wore layered gold jewellery and odd earrings, Ganni's latest arrivals, and pastel Xou-Xous around their delicate necks, readying their skinny cigarettes and lighters. She was definitely at the right place, Tia thought, slipping into the building before the door slammed closed. She stepped into the antique elevator and pushed the 'PH' button. The sounds of a Tame Impala track got louder and louder the higher Tia went. When the doors creaked opened, she was met by two skinny white men weighed down by their unreasonably chunky Balenciagas. One had his hand fused to his headset while the other held a large clipboard with pride.

'LOVE the hair.'

'Oh my God, you look just like Ella Eyre,' said the other, in that deep, monotonous voice everyone who worked in fashion seemed to have. Tia thought that her bottle of NC45 would care to disagree.

'Literally twins,' said Mr Clipboard. 'Name?'

'Tia Martin?'

'Let me see . . . Yep. Got you, babe. Go right in,' he said, hanging her coat on the rail behind him.

Steve Lacy's 'Some' blared through the DJ's sound system as she made her way through the crowds of twiggy models and slick-looking professionals, hunting for a spot to stand and look cool, wishing she had worn something better than a nice top and jeans she could just about breathe in. When Tia settled on a random table, she fluffed out her hair in an effort to look like she had actually made an effort, then took out her phone so she could pretend to text and look important, when two glasses of something bubbly were placed in front of her.

'There she is!'

Tia laughed when she looked up to see Luca, filming a video of her for his Instagram Stories. She struck a pose before getting shy, waving him away.

'How sick is this?' he squealed, chugging half his drink.

Heavy-duty garment rails were scattered across the distressed wooden floors of the open loft space, each one filled with an array of colour-coordinated sweats and other expensive-looking basics. Campaign shots of fresh-faced models who ticked every box on the diversity checklist were blown up and displayed on temporary walls beneath dimmed spotlights, along with pithy typeface quotes like 'THE YOUTH ARE THE FUTURE'. The photos had been separated into different themes, such as 'Sustainability' and 'Female Empowerment'.

'Alright, don't look but that guy at the bar hasn't stopped staring at you,' Luca said into Tia's ear. 'Not yet . . . Now! No, wait! Alright, look now!'

She looked over her shoulder, trying to follow Luca's shitty directions and vague descriptors before turning back round to take a swig of her drink.

'I don't even know why I'm trying it.' Tia kissed her teeth. 'I'm done with dating.'

'Bitch, you've barely started!'

'Barely started what?' asked Hannah as she tickled Luca from behind. He informed her that Tia was done with dating after just a couple of weeks on Hinge. 'Bitch, please!' Hannah laughed.

'Are you still moping over the date that never happened?' asked Luca, to which Tia nodded. 'Look we're in East, plenty of artsy fuckboys in the sea. Literally, just take your pick.'

'Maybe getting banned was a sign, like I should just be alone now.'

'More like a sign to never voluntarily chat to a Tory ever again.'

'Can we talk about something else please?' Tia said with a wry smile. 'Like, what the hell you guys are talking about?' she asked Hannah, pointing at her headset.

'Ugh, I dunno why they got us to wear these. Everyone's just bitching about some ex-*Love Island*ers who just walked in.'

The three looked back at the entrance to see which C-list celebrity had just arrived, when their jaws dropped at the couple standing behind the Molly-Mae wannabe. Hannah slapped her hand over her mouth and began apologising profusely into Tia's widened eyes.

'Why are *they* here?' hissed Luca.

'I completely forgot Aaron had asked for a plus-one,' Hannah whimpered. 'I'm so sorry, T. I didn't think he'd bring her – he always brings his boys!'

Tia began to laugh hysterically before emptying her glass.

'Oh my days, don't apologise! Why shouldn't they be here?'

Olivia looked like a breath of fresh West Coast air in the sea of black and grey outfits, wearing a flowy cream blouse and a satin midi skirt Tia could only dream of squeezing one of her thighs into. Aaron was keeping it casual in jeans and a white T-shirt. Tia smiled fondly at the black jacket he was wearing on top, remembering the Black Friday sale she'd dragged him to three years back. She'd bribed him with Nando's and he'd complained the whole time, until he'd got gassed at how good he looked in the jacket Tia had begged him to try on – not that he'd ever give her credit.

Her smile soon vanished when she noticed his and Olivia's hands fused together as they waded through the crowd, looking around to spot a familiar face. Luca and Hannah kept asking if she was alright but the lump in Tia's throat made her unable to get a word out.

'I know I can't avoid him forever,' admitted Tia as she stood upright, primping and bracing herself.

'But we can until we find the bar,' said Luca, slipping his hand into hers. 'C'mon. I need a top-up anyway.'

'Go,' instructed Hannah as she popped her headset back on. 'I'll keep them distracted for a bit.'

Tia mouthed 'I love you' to Hannah as Luca pulled her through the crowd towards the bar. Upon arrival, he shoved a flute of something straight into Tia's hand without saying a word. She downed it in three gulps, then tipped her glass towards the bartender, who immediately refilled it without question.

'I won't force you to talk about it all right now,' said Luca, leaning against the bar. Their years of friendship gave him a sixth sense when it came to gauging her mood.

'Much appreciated.'

'But can we just deep where we are right now?'

He motioned towards the literal party happening around them.

'What's your point?'

'My point is we both look fire and we're in the middle of this pretentious-as-fuck party. We're basically Carrie and Samantha!'

Tia giggled as Luca made his case. He wrapped his arms around her waist and gave her a squeeze.

'Please don't be sad over some wasteman! You deserve so much better than . . .'

His voice trailed off in the direction of a model who was walking past. Tia laughed even more when she realised whom had caught Luca's eye.

'Go on. Go. I'll be fine. Go have fun.'

'Are you sure?'

'And be a cockblock?' she said, rolling her eyes. 'Go. I love you.'

Grateful for her blessing to hoe around, Luca kissed Tia's cheek then disappeared into the crowd. Left alone with her thoughts and her third glass of Prosecco, she decided to leave the bar in a bid to not repeat the drunken bitter vibes she had probably emanated the last time she'd seen Aaron and Olivia together. After pretending to check her inbox full of imaginary important emails on her phone, she looked around at the clothes and influencers around her and figured she should probably look at the reason this event was being thrown, and walked down the makeshift gallery. Between sips of her Prosecco, Tia read on the Helvetica-covered walls that FUNKI had collaborated with three of London's coolest rising photographers, each tasked with capturing their collection from their own artistic point of view. A portrait hung towards the back of the space, below a spotlight, caught her eye. The closer she got, the more details she noticed. It was black and white and grainy, as if it had been taken on a film camera. The girl in the picture was the spitting image of Brenda Sykes, with her big doe eyes and pixie-like features. Her mini afro was teased and fluffed out, and she wore a simple silk slip dress with a cropped cardigan that was slipping down her delicate shoulders. The structure in the background looked familiar but Tia couldn't put her finger on it, and the longer she stood in front of the photo trying to guess, the more annoyed she got.

The sound of a camera's shutter startled Tia. She turned and saw a tall, slender frame beneath a New Era cap, hiding his face behind a massive DSLR. Probably one of the event photographers trying to get a few shots of the party. He wore a crisp white T and a brown flannel shirt with the sleeves rolled up, revealing a pair of veiny arms and a tattoo on his forearm she couldn't quite make out. His khaki cargo trousers complemented the earthy colour palette of the rest of his outfit, and the hems stopped just above his ankles, as if they were tailored to his gangly legs, and his New

Balances looked old and worn out, as if he actually used them for running, unlike everyone else who had only copped a pair to look trendy.

She continued to stare into the portrait, crossing her arms to make it look like she was really concentrating. The photographer noticed her efforts and laughed from behind his viewfinder.

'Does this look pensive enough?' she asked, admiring the rest of the photos surrounding the portrait. 'The . . . um . . . brutalism is just sublime, right?'

'Sublime, you know. Okay, art critic,' he said. They both laughed as she mockingly raised a hand to her chin. 'Yeah, um. Their smiles really juxtapose with the harshness of Milford Towers,' he added, putting his camera down and standing behind her.

'Who's the art critic now?' Tia laughed, until she realised that the pictures really had been taken on the block in her neighbourhood. 'Oh shit, wait, you're right. I was wondering why it looked so famili—'

When she looked up she was met with piercing dark eyes beneath furrowed bushy brows and a warm grin nestled in a scruffy beard.

'And I've been wondering why you looked so familiar,' said Nate. 'Hey, ghost.'

Moments later, he tried disguising his laughs between sips of whatever was in his FUNKI-branded cup, as Tia apologised profusely about her disappearing act. She would've been dying of embarrassment if she weren't so tipsy, and started to laugh when she could tell he was trying to take the piss. Nate looked down at her through squinted eyes as if he still wasn't convinced, so she took her phone out of her pocket and showed him the screenshot of Hinge notifying her of her ban, taken around the same time their date was meant to happen. He moved closer to get a better look at her proof but barely glanced at the screen, and instead kept his gaze fixed on her until she looked back up at him, suddenly stumped for something to say. She still hadn't processed the fact that he was: a) Just as fine as he looked in his photos, finer even. b) Actually real. And c) Standing right in front of her, staring into her eyes.

'What?' she said

'I just can't believe you're here, that's all. I'm honoured that you graced me with your presence this time.'

'Ha-ha, very funny.' Tia rolled her eyes. 'I really am sorry though. I felt so bad about you being at some bar all alone.'

'Yeah, that was a first for me,' he laughed. 'But we're here now. Seems like the universe wanted us back together.'

'I'm sure that sounded way less corny in your head,' she said to the ground and he threw back his head to laugh.

'Wow! First you desert me, now I'm corny!' he said, and dramatically threw his hand over his chest. 'Didn't take you for a heartbreaker.'

'Oh, your heart was broken?' teased Tia as he nodded. 'So, what did you take me for?'

'I don't know. You're all sweet and pretty on the outside . . .' He looked at the curls surrounding her face and she began to blush the longer he stayed quiet. 'But then you like to argue with man till three in the morning, so!'

'You're so annoying!'

He laughed again and moved over to the bar to order another drink. He asked Tia if she wanted another but she refused, not wanting to get too drunk during their first encounter. She couldn't believe how well this was all going and how easy their conversation was flowing, as if her ban had never happened. It already felt like a distant memory, until Nate mentioned it once more.

'Maybe the ban was a blessing in disguise though, lowkey.'

'How so?'

'Because it got rid of the competition. I guess it's more of a blessing for me.'

Tia laughed. 'I take it you're pretty competitive then?'

'When I really want the prize, yeah.'

He subtly bit the bottom of his plump lip, staring down at the smile Tia so badly tried to hide, bashfully looking away from him so he wouldn't notice her flushed face. When she turned to face him properly, he handed her his phone.

'So I don't lose you again.'

95

Tia smiled. As she typed in her name and number, she could hear Nate being called by a group of guys standing near his photos; presumably his boys, judging by the way they teased him when they clocked what he was doing. He mouthed something in their direction. Tia gave him his phone back and he proudly smiled at his new contact. He looked as if he was about to say something else when another friend called him over. Tia laughed as he tried to wave them off and apologised on their behalf.

'It's fine,' she said, 'my friends are probably looking for me anyway.'

Tia's phone had in fact buzzed seven times since Nate had walked her to the bar earlier, the group chat all giddy at the sight of her talking to someone who wasn't the security guard or the venue's toilet attendant.

'Who'd you come here with?'

'My friends. One of them works for FUNKI.'

'So does my boy! He actually put them onto me,' said Nate. 'Come, meet them.'

He placed his arm over Tia's shoulder before she could say anything, gently ushering her towards the group, and she grinned at Nate as he introduced her to his friends, each one equally as fine as him. They smiled and stretched out a hand for a shake or an arm for a friendly hug, going round the circle with their names and occupations. Miles, the Kofi Siriboe lookalike, was a model (obviously), Sasha was a DJ and had the most flawless locs Tia had ever seen, and Reece, your generic light-skinned with green eyes, claimed to be both, which meant he sucked at the latter but his stunning face was enough to get him booked regardless.

'And how do you two know each other?' Miles asked with a glint in his eye.

'Oh, we don't,' Nate began. 'She ghosted me, innit, so I had to hot her up just now.'

'Woah, woah,' laughed Tia, startled by the accusation, as his friends began to commend her for her apparent decision. 'Ghosting is a bit of a stretch, no?'

'It's calm though, I got you now.'

He looked into her eyes with a confident but cool stare as Tia smiled back at him, her curved lips hiding behind the rim of her cup. Though this was their first real-life encounter, he was already the only thing she could focus on, almost forgetting about the party and crowd of people around them. She definitely wouldn't mind bumping into Aaron and Olivia now, Tia thought to herself, looking over shoulders in case she suddenly needed to laugh extra loud at whatever Nate was about to say next. Reece suddenly tapped his shoulder, motioning his head towards the balcony of the venue.

'You wanna hit this?' Nate turned back around to ask but Tia shook her head.

'Nah, I'm good but you go ahead. I should find my friends.'

'Alright, miss. I'll see you around then,' he said, walking backwards towards his friends.

Tia returned his smile as he slowly backed away. Nate fished his phone back out of his pocket, before tapping the screen and holding it to his ear. Tia didn't realise what he was doing until her own phone began to vibrate. She answered it.

'It's me again.'

Tia laughed while staring back at Nate, now a couple of feet away from her.

'Do you need something?'

'Hm. You to save this number. Just write "Leng Photographer" to jog your memory.'

'You're not serious.'

'As a heart attack,' he said. 'Just don't go disappearing on me again, alright, heartbreaker?'

'I won't.'

9

Several days after they'd reunited, Tia and Nate had already returned to the routine of their pre-ban conversations, bickering into the early hours of the morning, promising each other they'd go to bed earlier, and then doing it all over again. The recurring notification of his name was the only endorphin hit she ever seemed to get in the midst of trying to start on her feature under the micromanaging eye of Camilla, who'd been listening in on the interviews Tia had already started to conduct from her desk. Even seeking refuge in the other desks around the floor was futile because Camilla would tell Tia that sitting away from the group indicated a lack of team spirit or community cohesion or whatever the fuck she'd got from a *Forbes* article. Tia decided that if she was going to be able to do this project without every inch of it being tainted by Camilla's need for control, she needed to distance herself from LCN as much as possible. So when her third interviewee suggested Tia meet her elsewhere, she had never scrambled her things together so quickly.

It was a chilly but bright afternoon when Tia made her way down to the pub the interviewee had suggested. One of those rare clear blue-sky days, the kind that filled you with optimism and convinced you that London would be the best city on earth if the weather weren't so shit all the time. She didn't even care that the crisp air had frozen the tips of her nose and ears – just as long as she was far from Camilla. The heavy wooden doors drowned out the sounds of Peckham High Street's traffic jam as they shut behind Tia. There were one or two punters dotted around, and 'Sweet Love' by Wizkid quietly hummed in the background against the clinking of freshly washed glasses and the odd ruckus from the kitchen's pass-through window. She almost didn't recognise the sanctuary she had just sat down in, it looked so mellow and bare compared to the sweatbox it usually turned into on a Saturday night.

'Are you Tia Martin? From LCN?' asked a statuesque Black girl with a sweet smile. Her round face was bare and she brought with her a pungent yet sweet smell, as if she had dipped her entire body in a bottle of Razac.

'Yes! Leanne, right?' asked Tia. 'It's so nice to finally meet!'

Leanne was a PhD student whom Tia had found

commenting on the *Daily Mail*'s Facebook post about the suspended schoolgirl. She'd been battling Brexiteers and had made Tia physically laugh out loud with every witty comeback she'd posted. She knew she needed this kind of voice in her feature. Leanne sat down as Tia placed an order for the two of them at the bar.

'As much as I'd kill for a daiquiri right now,' she joked, from where she stood. 'I'm a bit worried I wouldn't get much work done.'

As soon as Tia brought over their pricey mocktails and sat down, she could already sense the small talk disarming Leanne as she started to wriggle into her seat further to get comfy. The niceties weren't always Tia's favourite part of interviewing people. In fact, it was mostly awkward at the best of times, but it always felt necessary in making the other person feel as comfortable as possible before getting into the nitty-gritty.

From exchanging woes about hot-comb burns and wrapping their hair at night, to Leanne's learned comparisons of Louisiana's Tignon Laws in the late 1700s to today's school suspensions, the conversation flowed as freely as Tia had hoped it would. She kept apologising to Leanne for her lack of eye contact, due to ferociously typing out all the gold nuggets her guest was dropping.

'It's just heartbreaking, you know?' said Leanne.

'Like, sometimes it feels like you almost have to fight the whole world just to get them to respect your natural state. Surely that's the bare minimum?'

Tia nodded. 'And if it isn't your aunties begging you to relax it—'

'Then it's some random idiot at work tryna touch your twist-out!' Leanne exclaimed. 'Black women are not your pets, for fuck's sake!'

The women shook their heads simultaneously and giggled together; bonding over the shared struggles was nothing new – laughing about those struggles, even less so.

'And then you have this literal child being chastised.' Leanne paused. 'For being herself! It's an absolute joke.'

By the time the girls were all talked out, the sleepy, hollow shell of a pub Tia had entered a few hours ago was slowly turning into the lively local dive she knew all too well. After thanking Leanne profusely, they stood to say their final goodbyes.

'I wasn't expecting this to be so . . . lovely.'

Tia laughed. 'I'll take that as a compliment.'

'No, it is! I'm just glad LCN has someone . . . like us.'

Working at a place like LCN either impressed people or completely disgusted them. When Tia had first started, she'd been overwhelmed with congratulatory messages from people at church and pats on the back from friends and family, for moving up in the big wide world and rubbing shoulders with some of the country's best journalists. But occasionally she'd get the odd rant from an uncle or two about Tory media scum and being a mouthpiece for the government. Both were valid concerns, though Tia didn't really care as long as she was getting paid to write. Leanne's comments weren't the first in this vein and they probably wouldn't be the last. Tia knew exactly what she meant and nothing more needed to be said.

'Thank you again. Look after yourself, okay?'

'And you better do the same, girl!' laughed Leanne.

After waving goodbye to her guest, Tia packed up her things and headed to an empty garden chair outside, patting down the pockets of her coat to feel for her cigarettes. She lit one, took a long drag, and lifted her face to the sky to exhale the smoke. Tia closed her eyes for a moment and quietly thanked God for such a smooth interview, hoping the rest of them would go the same way. Feeling like she never got much right at work, she was always grateful for the few moments when she felt like she did. Lately, it seemed as though she was always grasping for what she was meant to do at LCN, or why she was even there in the first place, because the Big Guy Upstairs never seemed to give her any clear answers.

When she opened her eyes to take another pull, she

spotted a familiar face saying goodbye to a group and walking towards her.

'Well, ain't this a nice surprise,' laughed Nate.

'Um, stalker much?'

'If only I had that much time,' he joked, then gestured to the laptop he was putting into his bag. 'Just wrapped up a meeting. You?'

'Same, actually.'

The warm lights from the pub's windows shone onto Nate's reddish-brown skin. He rubbed the back of his head, this time uncovered and revealing his curly high-top fade.

'At a pub?'

'To interview someone for work,' she said, throwing the remnants of her cigarette into a nearby bin. 'I was just about to leave to finish it off.'

He checked the time on his watch and asked, 'You always work this late?' to which Tia nodded.

'Now that can't be healthy,' Nate sighed. 'You should take a break. Let me buy you a drink.'

In the five seconds it took for her to decide, Tia estimated how long it would take her to catch up with transcribing the next day at work. Then she thought about how much Gbemi would cuss her if she mentioned turning down a drink from a peng ting in order to go home and transcribe. Nate had a cheeky but all too persuasive glint in his eye that Tia already seemed powerless to. There was something about his habit of getting straight to the point that made her feel all giddy on the inside. She mirrored his stance, placing her hands in her coat pockets.

'Alright. I'm in,' she said, as Nate smiled victoriously. He immediately took her arm and ushered her through the smokers' area and back inside. 'But just one!'

IO

Tia looked around at the empty tables and chairs dotted around the pub, letting Nate take the lead. He placed a hand on her back and guided her towards a chesterfield sofa in front of the fireplace. The embers glowed and crackled below the sounds of a Tems song quietly playing in the background. He sat Tia down in the warmth before asking what her choice of poison was. She replied with the name of the pub's infamous rum punch. He grinned and said, 'So you're a Wray girl?' and Tia smiled sheepishly before admitting that she'd lost count of all the messy nights she'd had because of that white spirit. As soon as Nate began chatting with the bartender, Tia dug out her signature lip tint from her bag and quickly dabbed it onto her pout in an effort to look more awake. She pushed a curl behind her ear then took it back out again and fluffed her hair out before checking her reflection in her phone's blank screen. She'd have made more of an effort today if she'd known she'd be on a date tonight. The spontaneity of it all was out of her comfort zone, but then again, so was everything else when it came to Nate.

Tia had always found first-date conversations so painfully slow and awkward, filled with lacklustre questions about how many siblings the other person had and whether they'd liked the *Game of Thrones* finale. And if they ever bothered to ask her about what she did for a living, they'd either say, 'That's sick, still!' and follow up with asking whether she could get their boy's song played on the radio, or, her personal favourite, 'You should write about me, you know.'

Nate was different though. Everything he asked was all about Tia: how she liked LCN, what other places she'd want to write for, who her dream interview would be. At times she felt as though she was rambling, but he listened intently to each and every word, giving her time and space to find the answers.

'Wait, so you didn't go to uni at all?'

'I hated school so uni was never on the cards for me,' said Tia with a scowl. 'Soon as I left sixth form, I interned my arse off at all kinds of places. PR agencies, a magazine here and there, that kinda stuff.'

'Okay, bad and boujee.'

'Barely!' she laughed. 'You know they don't pay interns. I was broke as fuck! So I worked at this football club on the weekends, pulling pints. It was the ghetto.'

Tia was surprised at how easy it was to talk to him, how their chat flowed so effortlessly without any space for an awkward silence or the dreaded 'So . . .' It made up for the time they'd lost to Tia's unjust ban, which Nate continued to tease her about and pepper into their conversation, all giddy and giggly, as if they were two naughty schoolkids reunited after a teacher had forced them to sit apart. She often found herself lost in Nate's expressions, soaking in all the details that couldn't have been shared though a voice note, like the way his forehead wrinkled when he laughed or how he spoke with his hands when he was making a passionate point. It still felt so surreal to her, opening up to him like this when just a few weeks ago they'd had no idea of each other's existence and weren't even in each other's orbit.

Nate laughed at her horror stories about match days against Millwall, but then sighed. Tia asked what he was thinking. He dismissed it at first, saying it was nothing, until he saw the look on her face, that she could tell that there was in fact something, and he laughed at her ability to already see through a little bit of him.

'It's just nice talking to someone who gets it,' he said. 'I feel like everyone around me comes from a totally different world sometimes.'

'So what world did you come from then?' asked Tia. 'How did you get into all of this? Or were you just lit from day one?'

Nate shook his head and laughed that that couldn't have been further from the truth. He told Tia that he got his first camera on the third Christmas he ever spent with his dad, when he was sixteen or seventeen years old. A little digital thing that wasn't very spectacular, but Nate said it was the best thing his dad had ever done for him on the occasions when he'd decided to act like a parent. His mum, on the other hand, hadn't been impressed, because it had nothing to do with getting a degree, though she was satisfied that her ex-husband had turned up with something more than a football shirt for a team Nate didn't even support. From then on, Nate had become infamous for carrying his camera around at house parties and drink-ups, uploading the best photos to his mildly popular Tumblr account, which had grown over the years. By the time he'd got to university, he'd wanted to take the photography more seriously and had started working all the jobs he could to save for a better camera and decent lenses.

'I worked in the library, the student bar, even the local takeaway. It was long.'

'How did you even balance all of that with your degree?'

'I didn't,' he laughed. 'I either slept during all my lectures or didn't bother getting out of bed at all.'

Nate argued that it had all been worth it though. With the upgraded equipment, he'd become more confident in his growing abilities and had created a portfolio, cold-emailing it to hundreds of ad agencies, magazines and photographers, until one had got back to him with an actual job offer.

'It was a glorified assistant role, but his name was French so I was gassed.'

'Some sound logic there.'

'Allow me, I was young and hungry, okay?' he laughed. 'So I dropped out.'

'What?! Like, just quit uni then and there?'

'Pretty much.'

'Your mum must've been pissed.'

'She slapped the shit out of me the day I came back home and my sister had to beg her not to kick me out then and there.'

'That's intense.'

'It was crazy, still. Education is everything to her.'

'When did she finally come round to the whole photography thing?'

'Not that long ago, you know,' said Nate, leaning back against the sofa. 'True say, now I got a couple of press features, two-two exhibitions under my belt and that, she's finally starting to get it.'

'Your risk really did pay off then.'

'Something like that.'

'That must feel really good.'

'Surely you know what that's like, Miss LCN?'

Tia leaned back on the sofa and the two sat

shoulder to shoulder. She looked at her empty glass on the table in front of her, avoiding his stare, and bit her bottom lip, trying to think of what to say, searching for some honest words that wouldn't scare him off. She found him so easy to talk to, but it was way too early to dissect her existential crisis – that was at least three dates away.

'I dunno. That place is just . . .' Tia sighed. 'Sometimes I wonder, what if this is as good as it's gonna get?' He nodded and remained quiet, allowing her to find her words. 'Like, it took so long for one of my ideas to finally get commissioned. Am I always gonna have to be proving myself this hard, all the time? Am I even good enough to be there?'

'Nah, don't do that.' Nate shook his head. 'You wouldn't still be there if you weren't good enough. And this hair thing sounds sick. You're the shit! Own it.'

She laughed. 'I just feel stuck there. I've been in the same position for years. I don't know how to break out of this rut. I feel like a fail—' She cut herself off when she saw the wide-eyed look on Nate's face and laughed again. 'Sorry, sorry! I'm rambling, my bad.'

'Nah, I hear you. I'm just thinking.' He looked at her a little longer. 'You ever thought about leaving?'

'Yeah, right.' Tia huffed. 'And go where? It's LCN. Doesn't get better than that.'

'And maybe do your own thing? Figure out the shit you actually like doing.'

'That just feels like I'd be going backwards.'

'A change in direction isn't going backwards. You're talented, you can go wherever you want.'

'You sound so sure of yourself.'

'Is that a bad thing?'

'No, no. I wish I was like that.' said Tia. 'Have you ever felt scared?'

'Of?'

'Fucking up. Failing.'

'Oh, one hundred per cent.'

'So what changed?' she asked.

'Realising that everything I want is always going to be on the other side of fear.' He paused, staring into the half-melted ice cubes in the dregs of his Old Fashioned and caught Tia's expression. 'Sorry, that's a bit deep for a first date, innit?'

'Nah, you're good. I like it deep.'

Their jaws dropped when they realised what she'd said, and they held their heads back in laughter. The cocktails had most definitely gone to both of their heads. Tia tried to recover but Nate wasn't giving her a chance anytime soon.

'But on a serious level,' he said. 'You have to feel the fear and do it anyway. Whether that's being honest with how you feel about something, or leaving an environment that doesn't let you grow, your happiness has to be the compass.'

Tia could never have imagined feeling this

enlightened on what was meant to be a first date, but that just made her all the more enamoured by Nate and how everything was so unexpected but shockingly easy with him. She gazed at him as he drained the last of his drink, not realising how much she'd been yearning for someone to talk to about all this stuff – that person was usually Aaron.

'C'mon, I wanna show you something.'

They shared a cigarette as they walked along Rye Lane under the dusky sky. The narrow pavements were still teeming with life. Aunties making their way home with blue scandal bags filled with tonight's dinner, schoolgirls waiting outside to be let into the hair shops, the shrill hum of electric nail files and laughter from the salons spilling out onto the road.

They turned left into an alleyway and Nate rummaged around in his pockets, revealing a set of keys. He unlocked a door and lead her up a dingy stairwell that reeked of fresh paint. Tia groaned with every step, offended that he would subject her to so much exercise after their drinking and smoking.

He laughed to himself but ignored her complaints and opened another door, before taking her hand to guide her into their final destination. Tia's footsteps on the wooden floorboards creaked and echoed the further she walked into the open space.

He removed his jacket and took her coat. 'Wait here a sec,' he said.

When Nate went off into the darkness, Tia explored the room a little more. Clothing rails were pushed together to one side of the room, bare but for a few hangers, and a couple of pairs of trainers were lined up on the floor. On the other side of the room a single bar stool rested on a vintage Persian rug; its faded pink colour complemented the room's terracotta-coloured raw plaster wall. Two softbox lights were switched on, and on a wooden table a laptop stood open, which Tia couldn't resist inspecting.

'Nosy much?' said Nate, returning with a camera weighing down his neck.

'What is this place?' Tia asked, looking up at the ceiling.

'An old mentor of mine needed someone to run this place. I had nothing important going on, so I thought, *Why not?*'

'Oh, shit. Okay, boss. So this place is yours?'

'Well, it's his studio. But he's letting me do whatever I want with it so long as the rent gets paid.'

'Still, that's so sick.'

She walked over to the mottled steel-framed windows, taking in the view of the train station across the road. After connecting his camera to his laptop, Nate patted the bar stool.

'Come, sit.'

Tia scoffed at his request.

'You don't want to be shot by London's hottest

photographer? Y'know . . . according to some random clothing brand that cut a nice cheque,' he laughed.

'Rah, where's your artistic integrity?'

'Yeah, turns out I can't always pay rent with integrity,' he said, fiddling on his laptop. 'C'mon, sit. I want to shoot London's hottest writer.'

'Oh my days, you're so corny.'

'If memory serves, you swipe right for corny.'

Tia cracked up. 'You are petty as fuck!' she said before rolling her eyes and dragging herself away from the window. She perched on the edge of the stool and adjusted her top before folding her arms to conceal any visible stomach roll, looking everywhere else but into the lens while Nate took a few shots.

'You look uncomfortable.'

She laughed and covered her face in some attempt to compose herself. Nate crouched down to Tia's eye level and started taking a few more shots. She alternated between crossing her arms and holding on to the seat out, not knowing what to do with her body.

'You camera-shy?' he asked.

'Perhaps.'

'Really? I couldn't tell from your profile.'

'You still remember it, yeah?'

'C'mon. Photographic memory and dat,' he joked.

'Oh, whatever, man,' she laughed, as he paused to examine the lighting. 'So, what have you got planned for this place?'

'To make this the go-to spot for anyone broke who needs to shoot something,' he declared. 'One of the hardest things for me back in the days was money. Shit, it still is now. So why not make things a little easier for others, you get it?'

She nodded as he flitted around the studio, talking about his hopes to start photography classes for local students, wishing there'd been something like that when he'd first started out with his flimsy digital camera. Tia couldn't help but smile as he explained away, sounding so determined and eager. She even hoped she'd be around to see it all come to fruition, though it was probably too soon to think that far ahead. The look on her face seemed to stop him in his tracks and he lowered his camera.

'What? I got somethin' on my face?'

Tia shook her head. 'You're just . . .'

'Just?'

'You're just really cool. The way you're doing your thing. It's cool.'

He looked at the floor and smiled, and for the first time looked a little shy, as if he wasn't used to hearing things like that. But Tia couldn't help but feel so inspired by how different he was, compared to how miserable she often felt at LCN. She was sort of jealous of Nate's passion, wishing she could bottle it up and take a swig of it before the weekly pitch meeting with Camilla.

'I don't know anyone who has it all figured out like this,' she added, looking up at the equipment around them.

'I don't think anyone ever truly has it all figured out.'

'I guess not. But still, going from a broke student to being able to help out other students? That's huge,' said Tia. 'Like, I know I don't know you like that, but, I dunno . . . I feel proud of you.'

Nate smiled again and walked over to his laptop and Tia winced a little.

'Sorry, that was weird. I made it weird, right?'

'Nah, not even,' he laughed and stared at his shoes for a moment before looking back up at Tia. 'I just haven't heard that in a while.'

'For real?'

'I get so caught up in thinking of my next move, wondering if it's gonna be good enough, I guess I never really deep how far I've come.'

He joined her on the set and looked around for anything he could adjust. Tia tugged at the hem of his shirt to get his attention and mimicked his motivational speech from earlier.

'You're the shit. Own it.'

'Ha-ha, very funny,' he scoffed. 'But thanks. It means a lot.'

'Anytime.'

Her eyes wandered along the veins of his muscly forearms while he messed around with the softboxes that stood in front of her and his T-shirt flashed a little bit of his stomach, which Tia couldn't help but stare at, trying to stop herself from wondering what he looked like underneath. It wasn't until the light was turned off that she realised he was actually putting it away completely, and he lowered the brightness of the other.

'Rah, was I that shit a model, yeah?' she laughed.

'Nah, I wanna try something different,' he said. 'Maybe you're stiff because of all this around.'

She rose to her feet and clutched her imaginary pearls, insulted at Nate's accurate observation.

'Stiff?' she asked. 'Stiff?! Stiff where, please?' she repeated while he laughed.

'I dunno, you just seem . . .' She saw him looking her up and down, trying to search for the word. 'Uptight?'

'Uptight? Uptight and stiff?'

He nodded and walked her over to the windows while she continued to cuss.

'I guess that's what years at LCN does to a person,' he joked. 'You've forgotten how to get loose.'

His last comment hit a nerve Tia didn't realise was even there. It's not like she was the company's spokeswoman, but hearing someone else finally say out loud how she'd been feeling, so unexpectedly, made her feel a type of way.

'I can be loose – I'm so loose!' she declared. 'I'm easily the loosest person in the office, I eve—'

'Oh, mad!'

Tia paused and shook her head when she realised what she had just said while Nate leaned over himself, cracking up. She tried to backtrack and kept restarting her sentence but quickly failed, too caught up in his ridiculous laugh to be bothered to clarify what she'd meant. Pushing her hair back, she started to fan herself from the heat of their dissipated laughter while looking out the window, as the high street below them was slowly quietening down. She turned around when she heard the camera shutter.

'Do that again.'

'What?'

'Look out the window,' he said. 'Now look back at me.'

His voice was low and his tone became more stern as he directed her. His soft gaze from earlier on had disappeared and turned into something more focused and steely. It made her nervous for some reason.

'Beautiful,' he said from behind the viewfinder.

He asked her to play with her hair a little more, which she was grateful for; it gave her something to do rather than emulate her best Blue Steel face. She was so far out of her comfort zone but somehow Nate made it feel so easy. When he had got enough shots, he walked back to his tethered laptop and started to look through the photos. She walked over and sat on the table beside the laptop, peering over it. 'Is that me, yeah?' she asked, jokingly.

The photos were actually pretty, much to Tia's

surprise. She hadn't doubted his abilities, but since she hated the way she always looked like a potato in group photos, she'd often designate herself as the squad photographer on nights out to avoid sinking further down her self-hate hole.

'God, I look so lost there,' she said, pointing at the earlier photos on the screen.

'Nah, you look fine.'

'Thankfully your directing helped,' she laughed and tried to mimic his deep voice. 'Never heard you sound so serious before.'

'What was that?' he asked as he burst out laughing.

'That low and slow sexy voice you put on when you were in the zone!' He grinned as Tia continued to take the piss out of his professionalism. 'Just don't expect me to listen to you anywhere else.'

'You sure about that?'

When she looked back up from the screen, the lines in his face that would appear when he laughed were gone. Instead, a palpable intensity spilled from his sleepy eyes. There was something about his gaze that made Tia want to stare right back, instead of cracking a joke like she'd usually do whenever she felt shy. She felt seen, but not in a needy way. She could see it in his eyes that he wanted her one way or another, and she liked it. Without breaking eye contact he closed the laptop beside Tia and stood in front of her.

'I said, "Are you sure about that?"'

She gulped without realising and glanced at his mouth and the facial hair that surrounded it, but before she could return to his eyes, he laced his fingers behind the nape of her neck and drew her face close to his. Tia's racing heartbeat matched the rhythmic clacking sounds of the train arriving at the nearby station, as the tips of their noses brushed against one another. Nate's lips hovered over hers for a moment before finally giving in to her silent pleas.

Tia's entire body tingled as the taste of his whiskey-tinged kisses unfurled all of her senses. The feeling of him pressing against her soft frame disarmed her natural urge to stop and think; all she could do was focus on how good this moment felt. Nate's firm grip around the back of her neck loosened as his hands made their way down to her waist, pulling her body even closer to his and wrapping her legs around him. He began to plant a trail of kisses down her neck, hungry and intense, taking in the scent of her sweet perfume as if it had been calling to him from the first night they'd encountered each other.

'You good?' he asked.

She poked the inside of her cheek with her tongue and grinned, baffled at how she could suddenly feel so shy.

'Hello?'

Her heavy eyes widened when she realised she had just spaced out. Nate chuckled and patted her curls.

'I said, "Are you good?"'

Tia nodded. 'I'm good.'

They laughed together and he kissed her again, his hands rubbing the sides of her thighs.

'Good,' he said, planting one last kiss on her forehead. 'Now let's get you home.'

11

By the time Tia had finished recounting her steamy make-out sesh with Nate, Gbemi was on the very edge of the red sofa, practically frothing at the mouth and hungry for even more details. *So this is what it feels like,* Tia thought to herself. The weekend recap that occurred between the girls over Monday's lunch break usually consisted of only Gbemi divulging details from a Hinge date gone wrong, or a sneaky link that felt so right but was still so wrong, while all Tia could ever contribute was a funny meme she had seen on Twitter or a mini review of a Korean sheet mask she'd panic-purchased online at 3 a.m. one time. Now she was the girl with the sexy, sordid tale. Seeing the excitement on her friend's face as she pried for more information made Tia feel like *that* bitch. Like she wasn't just some overgrown teen, twiddling her thumbs at home while all her friends were out living their best lives over the weekend; like she was finally participating in her twenties properly.

'I think it was the surprise of it all,' said Tia.

'Or the fact you could feel his dick between your legs.'

The girls squealed and collapsed against each other's shoulders, covering their mouths to conceal the cackling, ensuring there weren't any colleagues lurking around. Tia shook her head and fanned her now-blushing face.

'I knew I shouldn't have told you that.'

'Why not? You know you were thinking it too!' Tia's smirk all but confirmed Gbemi's remark as she continued: 'Besides, this is the first bit of action you've gotten in ages.'

'Thanks for the reminder,' said Tia as the pair peeled themselves off the sofa. It had been seventeen minutes since the official end of their lunch break, not that either one of them was rushing to get back to work.

A few hours of transcribing had gone by when at last Tia raised her stiffened neck up from her keyboard. When she walked over to the kitchen to stretch and refill her water bottle, she noticed Eloise sitting alone. Her petite frame was drowning in a chunky red cardigan, its sleeves covering her pale knuckles as she furiously typed away at her MacBook. The strawberry-blonde hair that typically covered her freckled face was instead scraped into a topknot. When she looked up from her screen and locked eyes with Tia, the pair exchanged kind smiles. Tia approached Eloise's makeshift workspace.

'I don't know how you get anything done out here. Isn't it loud?'

'It was either this or being stuck next to Harry and Arjun arguing about some football transfer.'

'Oh God,' grimaced Tia. 'Literally anything is better than sitting between that.'

'So you see my point?'

'Completely. I don't know how they get any work done.'

'I guess when most of your pitches involve animals and quirky old people you can afford to slack a bit,' said Eloise, folding her arms.

The girls laughed as they shook their heads in unison. Until recently, Tia had never exchanged much with Eloise other than the odd greeting if they happened to be washing their hands in the bathroom at the same time, let alone a snarky comment. But she was here for it nonetheless.

'How are the interviews coming along, by the way?'

'So good,' said Tia with a genuine grin. 'I've got a few more left to do but the rest are all transcribed and ready to edit down.'

'That's great! Cos Camilla wanted to have a chat with us today.'

'Oh, really?' asked Tia, through gritted teeth. 'What about?'

'Just about the photographer and location. We have a list of our go-tos that she'll probably want to finalise on, they're just so expensive . . .'

Nate's place instantly popped into Tia's mind. Well, technically it was the ceiling that popped into her mind first because that's where she'd been looking while his lips had been grazing her neck. *Okay, no, focus, focus,* she told herself, before looking up the studio on Instagram. Eloise paused her rant on the pervy photographer LCN had once commissioned as Tia passed her phone to her.

'How about here?'

Eloise scrolled a bit then started nodding. 'Ooh, now this is more like it!' Tia figured the exposed brick and the succulents Nate had added to the place would seal the deal for her plant-mum colleague. 'How did you find it?'

'It's my friend's studio actually,' Tia said hesitantly.

It's not weird to call him a friend, right? A kiss doesn't necessarily mean anything, right?

'And I reckon he'd charge us way less than whoever else is on that list.'

'So cool! And he shoots as well?'

'Yup. Most of those portraits are by him.'

'Awesome. And I didn't know you modelled!'

'What are you talking about?' Tia scoffed.

Eloise handed the phone back and Tia's stomach performed a somersault when she realised she was staring at a photo of herself that she didn't completely hate. In fact, she actually liked the way Nate had captured her. He had uploaded a candid of her pushing her pile of curls away from her face. She mentally cringed when she remembered frantically fanning the sweat that was starting to develop on her upper lip. She had never felt so unsexy, racking her brain how to suddenly become Bella Hadid for Nate's intimidating lens, yet you couldn't tell that in the photo of her. Tia smiled as she analysed the portrait, impressed by how relaxed she looked.

'Ladies!'

Camilla waved from the door of a meeting room, signalling them to join her. Tia's stomach did another somersault as she entered the clinical room and took a seat at the opposite end of the table.

'I haven't seen much of you, Tia, so I just wanted a little catch-up to settle my nerves.'

The chuckle she sprinkled on at the end didn't make her sound any less irritated.

'Well, I've been meeting up with a few contributors,' Tia started. 'I find that face-to-face interviews make them feel a bit more at ease?' she ended in an unnaturally high-pitched voice.

'I do understand, but all that running around can often waste quite a bit of time, you know?'

But going down to Greenwich to film a fucking cat isn't a waste of time, nah? Tia thought to herself while politely nodding.

'I also wanted to know where we're at with a location,' continued Camilla. 'Eloise, have you decided on a photographer yet?'

'Well, actually, Tia's found a photographer who has a great space already.'

'Adding someone new to the books can be such a faff though, Eloise.'

'I know, but his work is so fresh and real.'

'What about Eriksson?' suggested Camilla. 'He did a wonderful job with that "haircuts for the homeless" piece.'

'Yes, well, isn't Eriksson a little price—'

'My friend wouldn't charge an arm and a leg either,' added Tia in a bid to rescue Eloise.

She held out her phone and watched as Camilla scrolled through the studio's account, squinting her eyes at the screen.

'And has your *friend* got much professional experience?'

'Plenty. He's a rising star, in fact. He just shot a campaign with this clothing br—'

'Because this is LCN, Tia. Not some rowdy youth club!'

And there was that patronising chuckle again. It was the middle-class boomer's equivalent of adding 'lol' at the end of a shady text so they didn't come across as a total dickhead. Eloise looked just as baffled as Tia did. But Tia knew that if she wanted to make this happen, she'd have to remain focused on the goal and not hyper-fixate on Camilla's coded remarks. That was for the journey home after work.

Tia cleared her throat and started laughing too. 'I mean, I wouldn't suggest him if he didn't, Camilla!'

Eloise raised her eyebrows in warning.

'And, um, I've had a look at the list and, respectfully, most of the photographers on it aren't the best at capturing deeper skin tones, which is kind of imperative to the shoot's outcome.'

Like always, Camilla's unwavering glare rippled at the minuscule mention of race. Her readjusting her Cubitts glasses and fiddling with the tissue stuffed under her watch strap would've usually irritated Tia, but today she delighted in making her manager squirm a little. She could see the cogs in her brain turning, figuring out how she could quickly force into the conversation how much she loved Toni Morrison and Meghan Markle without making it too obvious and random.

'I agree,' said Eloise. 'It'd be a PR nightmare if the photos came out poorly. It's happened with *Vogue* and *Vanity Fair*,' she added to seal the deal.

The girls nodded and exchanged faux looks of deep concern with one another just to rub it in Camilla's stuffy face, who sat and pondered silently, until she cleared her throat.

'Well, it sounds like you two have your minds made up.'

They nodded as Camilla began to squirm in her seat.

'You think this friend of yours could come down for a meeting then?' She glanced at her watch. 'Say, before the end of the day?'

'Today?' asked Tia.

'I'd love to meet this rising star sooner rather than later.' She rose to her feet, signalling the end of this conversation. 'Just in case we need time to find someone else.'

'Sure, of course,' said Tia as the girls followed her out the room. 'I'm sure he'll be happy to.'

'Great,' said Camilla, stepping into the glass elevator. She gave a wry smile before the doors closed.

When she'd finally disappeared into the depths of the LCN building, Tia released a sigh and held her hand to her chest to settle her racing heartbeat. She couldn't tell if it was the adrenaline from implicitly telling her manager to go fuck her suggestions or the fact that she could be working with Nate for the next few weeks.

When Tia sat back down at her desk, she quickly opened her chat with Nate. They'd been messaging non-stop since their tryst in his studio, trying to plan when they could see each other next. Everything was going as perfectly as Tia could've hoped, but she couldn't help but feel a little apprehensive about bridging the gap between work and the guy she was into. She deleted and retyped the situation over and over, wondering if she was doing the most and coming on too strong – she didn't want to scare the guy away. She was about to close their chat out of pure anxiety until she started to remember the way Nate had spoken about his plans for the studio and how he was so caught up in his next move, and how much that resonated with her. *Fuck it,* she thought to herself before getting up to record a voice note.

As soon as she'd cleared her desk and thrown her coat on, Tia scurried back to the meeting room she'd escorted Nate to an hour ago, trying to get a peek of his face without Camilla noticing. He looked like he was *smiling.* That had to be a good sign, Tia thought, her heart still thumping as if it were about to burst out of her chest. The fact that he'd even got here at a moment's notice was a miracle, but to see that they were having a pleasant conversation felt unreal, almost making Tia feel uneasy.

Her colleagues began to trickle into the kitchen to dispose of their half-finished coffees when the door of the meeting room finally clicked open. Camilla let Nate out first, laughing at something he had just said, which filled Tia with even more hope.

'Brilliant, Nathaniel! Well, I'll see you in a bit then,' said Camilla before going back to her desk. 'Tia knows the way.'

Nate sauntered over to the kitchen, holding on to the straps of his backpack like a little kid on a school trip, glancing over at the open offices and glass meeting rooms.

'Knows the way where?'

'The Green Man?'

After spending more than forty hours a week actively listening to conversations about super-woke podcasts she just *had* to listen to, dodging questions about Cardi B, making sure she smiled enough into people's faces, and straddling the fine line between not being too loud or too quiet, the last thing Tia ever wanted to do was spend even a millisecond of her unpaid time sipping overpriced Disaronno at the pub after work. Her appearances were few and far between, meaning just the Christmas work do, when someone was leaving, or if Gbemi managed to bribe her into tagging along.

Today's bargaining chip came in the form of Nathaniel Clarke, watching as Camilla introduced him to everyone by the mahogany picnic tables outside the bustling pub. Tia sat on the corner of one, huddled with Gbemi and a couple of other colleagues who had her these-people-are-actually-normal-and-don't-have-a-house-in-the-South-of-France seal of approval. Everyone shared Tia's lighter as they all lit their respective cigarettes, until Gbemi cleared her throat and discreetly filled them in about Nate and how he'd come about. The group giggled together and began to flood Tia with questions. She watched from a slight distance as Nate wowed all of her colleagues with his charm and wit. He defended Arsenal against Arjun and Harry's digs; he later bonded with Harrison over the expensive backpack he had rested on the ledge of the pub's stained glass window, and he even managed to get a laugh out of Marc, who had blessed the outing with a guest appearance before heading straight back to the office. Petra seemed particularly enamoured by Nate, vigorously nodding and laughing extra hard at everything he had to say, slapping his shoulder as an excuse to touch him, almost screaming when she realised they were both wearing similar pairs of Docs. She kept twirling a lock of her artfully messy brownish-blonde bob and stared up at him with her icy-blue eyes, seeming desperate for him to give her even a smidgen of eye contact, though he didn't seem to notice, kindly paying equal attention to everyone else in the conversation.

'She's probably telling him how her best friend from boarding school was Ghanaian,' whispered Gbemi.

'Oh my days, do you remember how quick she was to tell us that?' laughed Tia. 'Like, I swear we just asked where the toilets were?'

As Gbemi and another colleague began to gossip about a camera operator leaving his wife for a journalist on the third floor, Tia noticed Nate's intense blinking towards her and got up to join the conversation he seemed to be trapped in. He started to place his arm around her shoulder but she wriggled away.

'Not at work,' she muttered.

He laughed and did it anyway. Petra cut short her debate with Harry.

'Tia! How do you guys know each other?' she beamed. 'Nate's told us how he's going to be shooting your hair thingy – so cool!'

Nate? What happened to Nathaniel?

'Oh, yeah, we're um . . .'

'Really good friends,' he said, his arm tightening around her. 'I'm actually a big fan of hers. So when she hit me up about this idea, I couldn't say no.'

Tia looked up at him and grinned, grateful that he'd spared everyone the embarrassing Hinge story and had actually bigged her up in the process. After Petra's third gin-and-tonic had started to kick in, she began talking Eloise's ear off about some Refinery29 piece that had caused a stir on Girlboss Twitter. Tia stood on her tip-toes and whispered, 'Thank you,' into Nate's ear. He smiled and looked as though he was about to pat the top of her curls until he pulled back and leaned down towards her face.

'D'you wanna get out of here?'

'Like, a whole hour ago.'

When they were finally away from the pub, Nate grabbed Tia's ice-cold hand and placed it in his pocket. She couldn't even react because he had already started walking, pulling her body in closer to get warm. They chatted throughout their entire journey through the backroads of Fitzrovia, until he begged her to follow him to a burger joint near Leicester Square. She wanted to be the cute kind of girl who only took nibbles of aesthetically pleasing sushi in front of him, but even she couldn't deny herself when he asked her for a second time if she was sure about not eating with him.

'I still can't believe you won her over.'

Tia folded her arms as Nate walked over with their tray of fries and burgers wrapped in silver foil. He went straight back to the counter for napkins and all the sauces he could carry, then popped a straw into Tia's milkshake before handing it to her.

'Won who over?'

'Camilla! Well, everyone actually. They love you already. Especially Petra.'

'I'm that guy, innit,' he laughed as Tia rolled her eyes. 'Gotta put your best foot forward and that.'

'I wish I was like that.'

'Like what?'

'Better at playing the game.'

He unwrapped a burger and handed it to her.

'I've always found it strange how people want to spend even more time with their colleagues,' she said.

'I think that's what happens when you actually like your job,' he replied. 'Are you familiar with the concept?'

'You dickhead,' she laughed. 'I like my job sometimes. I just hate the act I have to put on.'

Nate grunted in agreement as he began to wax off his fries.

'Like, I can't just go in and do my job without all

these expectations.' She took a bite out of her burger. 'You have to be chatty and bubbly so they don't think you're this aggressive prick, but if you're too loud—'

'They'll think you're doing too much. And if you're too quiet you're antisocial,' Nate added. 'Like, what if I just don't have anything to say, Darren?'

'Not Darren.'

'Or Holly. It's always one of the two.'

The pair laughed out into the air above them before shaking their heads and returning to their half-eaten meals, changing the subject to anything else but work. It wasn't long before they realised they were the only people still sat down. Nate walked Tia to Charing Cross station, offering to wait until her train arrived before he walked down to Embankment.

'You don't have to, it'll be here soon,' she said, looking up at his warm smile.

'Nah, I want to,' he said. 'And I want to thank you again for the job. You're the plug, I'm gonna kill this for you.'

'C'mon,' Tia grinned. 'What are friends for?'

'That wasn't weird, right?' he said, squinting his eyes, referring to what he had told her colleagues earlier. 'I only said that because, y'know, you said, "Not at work," and I don't want to make you uncom—'

'Nate, it's calm!' she laughed. 'I get it, don't worry.'

'Because . . .' He wrapped his arms around Tia's shoulders. 'I don't want to be just friends with you.'

'Oh?'

'Don't "Oh" me. I know you're feeling me too.'

'Yeah, you're growing on me or whatever.'

The South Londoner in her couldn't admit the fact that she was most definitely feeling him. Tia had always thought the idea of competing with a guy over who cared the least was dumb and tedious, but everyone said you had to do it. All the tweets and pretty typeface quotes on Instagram told her she needed to be mysterious and aloof. Self-proclaimed gurus preached about being chased because 'you're the prize!' Even her own friends would freak out over the thought of replying to a message too quickly. The kind of vulnerability everyone appreciated in R&B ballads and sappy Netflix films made great material for a catchy chorus or a monologue the high-school jock delivers to the quirky love interest – but in real life that scared the shit out of people. All too often, that kind of vulnerability resulted in the guy Tia had met on a night out suddenly ghosting at the mention of anything long-term. The last time she'd gone out on a limb for a guy had ended in him coming back with a brand-new girlfriend everyone had heard fuck-all about, so Tia wasn't in any kind of rush to fumble the bag that was Nate anytime soon.

Tia didn't even flinch when the announcement of her train's arrival blared through the speakers of the station. She was far too lost in Nate's eyes, as he was brainstorming ideas for the shoot, warning her about how she'd be sick of him by the time they were done, though she found that hard to believe. The speeding footsteps of office workers racing to get home pulled her back down to reality, and she looked at the departures board behind Nate's tall frame, realising she only had a few minutes to get into a carriage.

'Go on, go. I don't want you to miss it,' he said, patting the top of her head.

She looked reluctant to leave but he reassured her with a promise to FaceTime her, and she grinned before tiptoeing towards his mouth for a kiss.

12

'You look disappointed,' laughed Aaron.

Tia was startled to see him leaning against her front doorframe on a Friday night. She wished she was wearing one of those cute silky pyjama sets all the girls on *Love Island* wore instead of her old tracksuit bottoms and baggy Nike T-shirt.

'I am. I thought you were my Uber Eats,' she sighed, taking her curls out of their messy bun.

'Thought I'd come check you, innit. It's been a while since we've hung out.'

'You can't text first?'

'Would you have even replied?'

'Like we haven't been DMing each other music since you've been back.'

Aaron kissed his teeth. 'That's not the same, you dickhead.'

After hanging up his coat and bag, he dragged his feet into the kitchen. Tia poured freshly boiled water into the ceramic mug she'd made him buy her a few

Christmases ago. It was small, slightly impractical, and had caused the pair to bicker for most of their shopping trip together that day. He'd made fun of its brown speckled design, saying his niece could do a better job. Tia had dissed him for not appreciating its 'chic aesthetic'.

'There enough water for me?'

She was already back at her laptop, and was grunting as she typed away, far too engrossed in her notes to give Aaron a real response. He rolled his eyes and glided through the kitchen to sort himself out. Mug from the dish rack, bottle of Cravendale from the bottom shelf of the fridge, teabag and brown sugar from the jars in the cupboard above Tia's head, and teaspoon from the drawer by the microwave. Despite smelling like the floor of a grotty nightclub, a trace of Tia's favourite cologne on him wafted past her as he finally stood still to pour the remaining hot water into his cup.

'You stink,' she said, pinching her nose for dramatic effect. 'Where'd you come from?'

'Work do. Left early though cos I got gym tomorrow.'

'Yeah.' Tia paused, looking down at his calves. 'You need to do more leg days, still.'

Teasing him at any chance she got was a vital part of their friendship: an ego the size of Aaron's needed someone to check him, daily.

'Wowww. This is coming from the girl googling BBL prices?'

'Oh my days, it was once! I was just curious.'

He laughed while adding the finishing touches to Tia's brew: two sugars and a splash of milk. It felt routine because it was. Living only a few roads from each other was a particularly convenient part of their friendship that both parties appreciated. She always had someone to drop her home and he always had somewhere to sober up before returning to his very old-fashioned and very Jamaican parents. Aaron rested his bearded chin on Tia's shoulder to get a better look at all her notes sprawled across the kitchen counter. She froze as the hairs on the back of her neck immediately stood up.

'Looks like it's been a wild night for you,' he joked. 'What's this for, anyway?'

She kissed her teeth as she nudged him off before she could enjoy the feeling, and ordered him to put the milk and sugar back. When Tia finally lifted her face from her laptop and closed it, the tale of her triumphant pitch started pouring out of her mouth, as she re-enacted Camilla's poncy remarks and Petra's nasal voice, making Aaron laugh with every dramatic gesticulation. He followed her into the living room with both of their drinks and handed the ugly mug to Tia once she got comfy on the sofa.

'I just got off the phone with the schoolgirl's mum

and she was really sweet, so fingers crossed we get to shoot her as well.'

'I've never seen you this excited about work before.'

She scoffed before taking a sip of her drink and threw the Roku remote towards him. It landed on his chest, and he huffed, hating being tasked with finding them something to watch on Netflix that Tia would actually be satisfied watching.

'What's work saying anyways?'

'It's alright, still.' He huffed again but in that way Tia knew meant something was bugging him, and she waited for him to notice the look she was giving him. 'Nah, it's calm, but I dunno, man.'

'You not feeling it anymore?'

'It's not that.'

He rubbed the back of his head before giving a word-by-word account of a meeting he had had at work, something about being asked to optimise some features on an app to retain more users, until he saw the baffled look on Tia's face and laughed to himself.

'In English, please,' she said. 'I swear you do this shit on purpose.'

She sipped her tea and watched him scroll, until he landed on a terribly American-looking action film – she begged him for anything but that.

'Don't get it twisted, I like my job. But I can't help but feel like I'm doing all this work for someone else's dream. I've got my own ideas too, y'know.'

'Like what?'

He looked at her with a grin and sat up properly, putting down his mug, as if he'd been waiting for this chance forever, and began to retell how lonely he'd been in San Francisco before he'd met Olivia, much to Tia's disdain, and how much he'd struggled to find clubs and bars frequented by other Black people.

'Even in London, you wouldn't know where to go unless you were proper from here or knew people who knew,' he explained. 'So that's when Motive was born.'

'Wait, what's Motive?'

'My idea.' He took out his phone and pulled up a photo of a minimalist logo: a deep green location pin against a black background, above 'Motive' in a sleek typeface. He showed it to Tia with pride. 'A global database of Black nightlife. Made by us, for us.'

She smiled when she saw the sparkle in his eyes. He was glued to the screen in his hands as he began to explain his idea even more.

'Users will input their favourite spots and events in their city, and there'll be a section where people can vote whether they enjoyed it or not, and then the algorithm will be able to recommend you Motives once it learns enough about—'

He stopped when he saw the goofy grin on her face. It was the first time since he'd been away that she felt like she had Aaron, her friend, back.

'What? I'm listening!'

'I'm doing the most, I know.'

'Nah, this sounds so sick!' Tia laughed as he put his phone away and picked up the remote. 'I'm being serious.'

'There's just this part of me that feels guilty though. Like, I worked so hard to get there, into those kinda rooms. And now I want no parts.'

'Happiness was never guaranteed with these fancy jobs, that much I know,' Tia huffed as she leaned her head back on the sofa, thinking about her own struggles at LCN. 'You shouldn't feel guilty though, it's not your fault it wasn't what you thought it would be.'

'My mum and dad were so proud when I was out in the States. Literally rang everyone in Ochi to tell 'em,' laughed Aaron. 'Now I feel like switching things up would just be failing them – like I'd be going backwards.'

'A wise person once told me: "A change in direction isn't going backwards."'

Tia then remembered to check her phone, and was pleased to see a reply from Nate to something she'd posted on her Stories. She grinned and unlocked her phone to reply as Aaron continued.

'Maybe you're right. I should see what Liv thinks as well,' he huffed. 'Alright, it's between Sanaa Lathan or Nia Long. Pick one.'

After one too many seconds of silence, Aaron turned his face towards the other end of the sofa and saw Tia consumed by her phone. She looked up at the TV, wondering why a film hadn't been chosen yet, and was about to start cussing Aaron for taking so long until she saw him already staring at her.

'What?' she asked. 'Pick something, bruv.'

'Look at you cheesin', you dickhead! Who you texting?'

She immediately tried to hide her smile and looked up at the ceiling instead for a brief moment, before ducking her head back down to her phone, crafting the perfect reply.

'No one special.'

He laughed and waited for her to elaborate, but she was still too distracted to satisfy his curiosity. Aaron decided to take things into his own hands and threw a cushion at her. She laughed when she finally tore her eyes away from her iPhone to look at him.

'No one special, yeah?' he said. 'Cos that's not what Hannah told me.'

Tia sighed. She hated having these kinds of conversations with Aaron. Despite their closeness, actually speaking to him about other guys always felt unnatural to her, as if talking to him about them would sully this little bubble in which they'd built their friendship.

'And what did Hannah tell you?'

'Some photographer guy's got you whipped. No wonder you've been ghost these days.'

'Oh, please,' Tia laughed. 'Like you ain't spent all

your weekends doin' up tour guide. Afternoon tea, really?'

"Low it. Liv was dying to do it, I couldn't say no.'

'Whatever.'

'Don't try and change the subject.' Tia tried to hide her smile from Aaron's interrogation. 'What's this guy saying, though?'

'Nothing! He's cool. We're just chilling. Enjoying each other's company, innit.'

'Oh, so it's nothing serious?'

The way he asked her that got Tia's back up, as if he was trying to question the legitimacy of her and Nate's undefined relationship, but still a relationship nonetheless.

'I didn't say that.'

'Well, you didn't *not* say that.'

Her phone pinged. Aaron rolled his eyes when he saw the stupid grin on her face.

'Lemme see his game, then.'

'Move, man!' shouted Tia, swatting Aaron's hands away. He kissed his teeth.

'You gonna bring him to Hannah's birthday though, right?'

Aaron asking her that almost felt like a challenge. Though she was having fun with Nate, the thought of Olivia at Hannah's house was enough to make her want to throw up. There was no way she was going to watch them all over each other at her best friend's house. It felt too soon to introduce Nate to everyone, but Tia's pride wouldn't allow her to roll solo, especially since someone was technically in the picture.

'Of course I am,' she said, plastering on a wide smile. 'He wouldn't miss it for the world.'

Aaron looked at her thoughtfully. 'Can't wait to meet him.'

13

There was something about coming down from the liberating high of a lunch break that always crushed Tia's soul a little. She cherished every minute of the hour spent with Gbemi, usually walking to Pret and cackling about a thread that Oloni had tweeted the night before, coming back with pressed juices and expensive baguette sandwiches.

The thought of returning to the monotony of answering Camilla's incessant emails and transcribing interviews for other senior journalists always made Tia want to walk the extra-long way back to her desk, begging Gbemi to sneak in a cup of tea on the red sofa before begrudgingly going back to work.

'Should I be worried?'

'About the fact he was out all weekend? Or the fact he replied two days later?'

'Both,' said Tia, staring into her mug.

She scrolled through all the aesthetically pleasing lives on Instagram while trying to organise her thoughts out loud to Gbemi, who leaned back on the sofa and closed her eyes, in search of some clarity.

'Like, who says, "I wanna be more than friends," then goes MIA like that?'

She locked her iPhone then looked at Gbemi in search of agreement, but was met instead with a blank expression.

'Erm, someone who's single, babe.'

'Ugh, you're right!' Tia huffed. 'I'm buggin', man.'

'Nooo!' Gbemi started, pulling Tia closer to lean on her shoulder. 'Okay, maybe a tiny bit?'

'I need to chill the fuck out.'

'Yes, just a tad. He's probably just busy! Seriously, don't overthink. From what I saw at the pub, he's proper into you.'

As much as that comforted Tia, Gbemi was technically right. Nate *was* single. Tia couldn't believe she'd got herself into this state. She couldn't even work out why because up until several weeks ago, he hadn't even been in the picture. But the butterflies that came with every caress and forehead kiss was a feeling Tia didn't want to lose, and the way she felt like she could talk to him about anything, the way they connected about so many things, had already become too valuable to lose.

By 5.52 p.m., Tia had already logged off and skipped to the toilets while texting Nate. He had redeemed himself by breaking the ice with an apology – a reservation at the dumpling place he'd been going on about.

Though Tia had promised Gbemi she wouldn't get too caught up, she already found herself grinning like an idiot when his name appeared on her phone, replaying the sporadic voice notes he'd sent about his day over and over again.

'Someone's in a good mood,' said Eloise, inspecting her dark circles in the mirror. 'Hot date?'

'Something like that,' Tia grinned while rummaging through her make-up bag. 'What are you up to tonight?'

'Absolutely nothing. I just submitted my edit test and I'm fucking knackered.'

'But that isn't due till next week,' said Tia, dabbing her Glossier balm onto her pout. 'What's the rush?'

'Didn't you get the second email?'

Tia froze. 'What second email?'

She slowly turned towards Eloise, who suddenly regretted saying anything after seeing the horrified look on Tia's face.

'They need the edit tests by Friday because a bunch of editors are going on some team-building thing next week.'

'That's tomorrow.'

Eloise nodded.

'Fuuuck,' hissed Tia. 'Fuck. This can't be happening!'

'I'm guessing you haven't . . .' Eloise stopped herself from finishing the sentence, figuring that pointing out the obvious wouldn't be helpful. She slid her glasses up her nose bridge, looking unsure of what to do.

Before Tia could swear again, the door opened and Janine, the poshest writer on the team and probably the oldest person on the fourth floor, waddled in with her oak Bayswater handbag and Jigsaw coat, and politely smiled at the girls before entering a cubicle.

'Well, just like that toilet in about two seconds,' whispered Tia, pointing towards the door Janine had just locked. 'My day's about to get even shittier.'

Eloise wrapped her sleeve-covered hands across her mouth to hold her laughter in before they both scurried out of the bathroom. She followed Tia back to her spotless desk, where Tia collapsed into her swivel chair, letting out a dramatic sigh.

'Why are these edit tests so fucking long?' Tia whimpered. She gazed through the glass panels of the office, jealous of all the random colleagues turning off their desktops and zipping their backpacks closed for the rush-hour tubes and trains.

'Probably to suss out who can take on a dozen banal tasks without complaining.'

Infamous for its never-ending list of demands that would often span three to four pages, LCN's edit test was a ghastly combination of varied written tasks, each with their own specifications and a string of hypothetical questions, asking what you'd do if your tweets ended up in the *Daily Mail*, or who you'd speak to if your guest suddenly backed out right before a live interview. It was laborious and felt incredibly dramatic for a role Tia had basically already been doing for the past year or so. She scrolled to the very bottom of the document and found the all-important question 'How would you critique LCN's output and what would you do differently?' This one always felt like a bit of a trap to her. How could you tell a room full of old white people that LCN needed fewer of them without sounding like Malcolm Xtra?

She begrudgingly logged back into her MacBook when Gbemi waltzed up to her desk, coat buttoned and handbag swinging from her elbow, ready for the commute home. She shook her head when she saw Tia frantically typing, and was just about to cuss her until Eloise began to explain the crisis.

'Sis,' Gbemi began, 'I'm literally begging you to check your emails from now on.'

'I know!' Tia wailed. 'And I'm meant to meet Nate in a bit. Can't believe I'm cancelling over this shit.'

'Deadlines over dick and dim sum, hate to see it,' she said, patting her friend's shoulder.

Before she could go, Tia begged her to instruct what she should text Nate, while Eloise walked back to her own desk but came back just a few minutes later.

'Check your inbox.'

Tia found a forwarded email from Eloise with eighteen attachments and clicked on them one by one. Both she and Gbemi gasped in unison.

'Where the hell did you get these?!'

'This is a fucking goldmine,' added Tia.

The two looked up at Eloise with a look that demanded an immediate explanation. She looked over her shoulders, ensuring there weren't any jobsworths lurking around, before leaning closer to the girls.

'I may or may not have overheard Petra bragging about this folder at the pub not too long ago,' Eloise began. 'So I had a word with my old classmate in HR and he managed to send me these.'

'I'm never saying no to 'Spoons ever again,' said a gobsmacked Gbemi, as she read through the carefully crafted answers over Tia's shoulder. Tia was equally chuffed with Eloise's intel. They were old applications from previous successful interviews, hailing from before TikTok was even a thing.

'There's a bit of an unspoken formula when it comes to nailing an LCN application, which I never quite got until I saw all of these,' she continued. 'They're a tiny bit old but the harder questions are still the same, so just rework your answers a bit and that should do the trick.'

'You could get in so much trouble, Lou,' said Tia.

'And if I do, Petra's is the first name I'm dropping,' she said as Gbemi slapped her knees and shrieked. 'Besides, why is it one rule for them and another for us? I'm sick to death of these toffs.'

Gbemi patted Eloise's shoulder. 'Oh, I like you!'

It had never occurred to Tia that anyone besides the

people who looked like her and Gbemi also felt out of place at LCN. She'd kind of assumed all the white people here were more or less cut from the same middle-class cloth, and if they weren't, at least they could pretend with a Daunt Books tote bag and a detailed knowledge of *The High Low*. Though she treated Eloise with the same kindness she had received from her, Tia felt a little bad for having lumped her in with all the other people she and Gbemi loathed so much.

'Thank you for this, honestly,' said Tia. 'I owe you big time.'

'How about a round at 'Spoons after you smash this?'

'Yes, but only if it's the one furthest away from this building.'

Eloise laughed. 'Deal.'

14

After catching herself staring at the grey ceiling panels
for way too long, Tia sat up from her seat and stroked
the mousepad of her MacBook to appear productive.
She logged in and lazily searched through her inbox for
any feedback on the research she had compiled for
Petra's reworked gentrification story. It was instead
going to focus on the self-made trust-fund girl bosses
transforming inner-city London, one blush-coloured
boutique at a time. There was still no word on the edit
test she had submitted almost two weeks ago, which
made her sighs and groans even louder these days. She
looked over her screen at the other teams dotted
around the open office space. Clusters of mild-
mannered thirty-something writers, comparing
headlines and subheadings. Some were on the phone
and scribbling notes, others were perched on top of
desks, engaged in conversation. To Tia's left, a couple
of camera operators in their unofficial uniform of
cargo trousers and mismatched band shirts were

faffing about with lenses they were about to take on a shoot. Right beside her sat Harry and Arjun, sharing a computer screen as they watched an edit of their sure-to-be next viral hit, an interview with some local football club's oldest member.

Although she didn't necessarily rate the Petras and the Harrys of the office, at least they were doing something they seemed to be proud of. At least they were being heard and taken seriously, no matter how stupid and unserious Tia thought their stories were.

Last night, before falling asleep, Tia had read somewhere that her hero Elaine Welteroth had already been an editor at *Ebony* before the age of twenty-five. It had felt like a personal attack on her lack of career progression, setting in motion the imposter syndrome that had already been clouding her mind. It had jolted Tia into a panic-search on LinkedIn for literally any doable job that sounded remotely sick enough to add to her Twitter bio.

Scrolling through job listings on dreary recruitment sites and the mere thought of having to grovel through a cover letter, explaining why she'd love to exchange forty hours per week of her life in order to pay her phone bill and eat something other than the rice at home always stopped Tia from jumping the LCN ship sooner. Having to muster up enthusiasm for 'fast-paced environments' and 'new challenges' made her want to physically throw up, and having to prove her worth by masking her anxiety under sexy terms like 'perfectionist', 'dedicated' and 'hardworking' just so they could get past the fact she'd never gone to university, felt like Mission: Impossible. While she kind of hated her current job, job-hunting itself was enough to make her shut the fuck up and just get on with it. The never-ending celebratory posts from her old classmates on LinkedIn didn't help either, as they announced their next 'thrilling' move up the career ladder with a chummy photo of them suited and booted on a rooftop overlooking St Paul's Cathedral. Tia would typically tap the 'like' button semi-grudgingly and let the autocorrect function on her iPhone finish the second half of the word 'Congratulations!!!' She didn't mind clapping for others, but her hands were beginning to feel a little sore, and she wondered when it'd ever be her turn. Suddenly, a message from Gbemi popped up on her screen.

gbemisolakikelomo@LCN.co.uk:
have you heard about the edit test yet?

tiamartin@LCN.co.uk:
nah not yet . . . why?

gbemisolakikelomo@LCN.co.uk:
i heard someone screaming in the
toilets saying they got through

tiamartin@LCN.co.uk:
oh shit, lemme check one sec!

gbemisolakikelomo@LCN.co.uk:

yes pls cuz i already know what i'm ordering at spoons xx

Tia saw an unread email from Camilla near the top of her inbox. Her chest tightened as she double-clicked the subject line. She breathed a sigh of relief immediately upon reading the opening line, congratulating her for passing the edit test, mentioning how pleasantly surprised Camilla had been by Tia's answers and her 'new-found perspective'. Tia smiled at this through gritted teeth, unsure whether to be chuffed about receiving a positive comment from Camilla or embarrassed she had received ratings from her least favourite person in the whole building.

Further down the message was the time and date for the final interview, with a list of names of the senior journalists who'd be interviewing her, Camilla included of course. The other two were senior journalists Tia had only spoken to in passing during the Christmas pub quiz, who seemed pleasant enough. In an effort to stop her overthinking, she went to the red sofa and made a call to her mum, who praised God and credited Tia's success to the T. D. Jakes sermon she had kindly forced her to listen to the other week. After hanging up, she quickly texted Nate and eagerly waited for his reply, while the group chat kept pinging, with Hannah attempting to book a Dancehall Brunch to celebrate and Luca sending Pinterest photos of interview outfits, threatening to kill her if she showed up in another graphic T-shirt she'd bought from Depop.

When she walked back through the kitchen, Eloise was standing by the sink washing her Tupperware. Tia tapped her shoulder, profusely thanking her for the goldmine of edit tests she had sent. Eloise's expression looked entirely at odds with the Molly Goddard-esque dress she was wearing. It was pretty and very pink, with a lace Peter Pan collar and frilly sleeves that floated with her arms' every move. Tia grinned at the dirty pair of biker boots that stood to attention beneath the delicate hem and began to clap.

'This is giving me life, by the way.'

'Oh, thanks, it even has pockets.'

'Love that, but I'm not loving this,' said Tia, pointing towards Eloise's furrowed brows. 'What's wrong?'

Eloise immediately began to chew her bottom lip, while violently yanking tissues from the dispenser to quickly dry her small hands. She kept starting and restarting her sentence until the smile on Tia's face began to quickly fade.

'Oh my days, you're actually scaring me.'

'Sorry, it's just, um . . .'

'Go on.'

'I just got an email from the schoolgirl's mum,' said Eloise. 'Which reminds me, you were also CC'd in but you probably missed it, so you should try and get on top of your inbox a bit more bec—'

'Eloise! What's happened?'

'She's pulling Shannon out of the shoot.'

Tia shook her head and smiled. 'But that's impossible. I spoke to Cheryl last week, they were both so excited.'

Before Eloise could speak, Tia asked her to stay put and ran back to her desk to retrieve her laptop, so she could see the message for herself. When she returned to the kitchen, Eloise popped her head out of a nearby meeting pod, a ghastly glass box that could fit no more than a single armchair and a table. The buzz of the office floor was muted as soon as Tia squeezed herself in and closed the door behind her, sliding down the glass until her bum hit the carpet. She whipped the laptop from her underarm and raced to type in the password. Eloise looked down at her concerned face from the armchair, tapping the ground with her boot out of nerves, hoping Cheryl might have suddenly reconsidered.

'I don't get it.' Tia closed her laptop after reading the email four times. 'All this stuff about Shannon's future being jeopardised? Where the hell would she get that from?'

'I have no idea.' Eloise stared at the floor intently, as if she was trying to decipher what had happened right there and then. 'But it'll still be really strong without her.'

'I dunno, man,' Tia sighed. 'The whole thing was

kind of built around Shannon, plus all the other subjects had such similar experiences. She connects everyone.'

'So what do we do? I tried ringing her earlier but she didn't pick up. Should I try her again?'

'Leave it for now,' said Tia in a low voice, her hands cradling her burning face. 'If we piss her off and she blocks us or something, then we're really fucked.'

Eloise nodded and was surely about to say something sweet and encouraging, Tia was certain of it, until the sound of a calendar alert went off.

Eloise had to disappear to another meeting, but Tia stayed put in the tiny meeting pod, slumping into the armchair with her arms spread out on either side. The glass pane in front of her overlooked the other floors of the office, as well as the sprawling newsroom on the lower ground floor that served as the heart of LCN. Everyone below looked like ants and everyone else sitting at their desks looked like the *Sims* characters she'd used to play with, mindlessly completing a never-ending list of tasks. Some were typing away at their keyboards, others were taking notes over the phone, a group of damn-near-identical salmon-coloured men in the unofficial LCN uniform of slacks and pressed T.M.Lewin shirts were laughing, looking as if they had just finished a meeting. Though she couldn't think of anything worse than spending her youth chained to a desk, she envied how busy they all looked. They were probably just answering emails or trying to find a guest for a debate programme, which never exactly thrilled Tia, but they were being productive and probably tolerated the monotony of it all far better than she ever could. She didn't have the energy to get up but was unceremoniously kicked out by a politics journalist who had booked the pod, tutting as Tia scrambled her things together to leave. He slammed the door shut as Tia dragged her feet back to her desk, feeling even more deflated and defeated than ever before.

15

That night, Tia relayed everything to her mum as they ate dinner together in the living room, her little sister periodically interrupting to show them a TikTok dance. Tia's mum told her to pray on it, and reminded her to walk by faith, not by sight. Tia quietly sighed and twirled the spaghetti in her bowl with her fork, knowing full well her mum would launch into a mini sermon if she caught even a whiff of her scepticism. She later forced her body into the shower, breaking the cast of gel around her edges and the rest of her flattened hair. Her complex routine consisted of an apple cider vinegar cleanse, detangling her curls with copious amounts of conditioner, then raking through her sweet-smelling leave-in, plus two other pricey styling products. She painstakingly brushed the coconut-scented creams through her sectioned hair one by one, ensuring each and every curl took on the perfect shape, overcompensating for the lack of control she currently felt in every other aspect of her life.

It wasn't until she finally finished blow-drying her

hair that the sudden silence of her room invited back all the thoughts and back-up plans she had tried to conjure up while scrubbing her scalp in the shower. She threw on the first clean T-shirt she could find and climbed into bed to scroll through Twitter, when Nate's name finally popped up on her vibrating phone's screen.

Other than a couple of emails about paperwork he had to fill out for some LCN admin, they hadn't spoken properly since she'd flaked on their dinner plans. Tia let it ring for a few more seconds to seem busy, before finally answering the call.

'Hey, stranger.'

'Don't say that.'

His voice was deep and sounded a little hoarse. Despite the fact that Tia was trying to be a little annoyed at him for going MIA, she couldn't help but crack a smile when she heard his tired, breathy little laugh.

'You'll make me feel bad. How you been, trouble?'

'I'm actually in a lot of trouble,' Tia sighed, wriggling under her duvet. 'Or rather, we're in a lot of trouble.'

'Talk to me. What's happening?'

Tia didn't realise how fast she was talking until she had finished relaying everything that had happened at work that day. She gave Nate the complete run-down on Shannon's sudden departure and how confused she was at her mum's 180.

'Okay, first of all, imma need you to take a deep

breath,' he started. Tia could hear his smile through the phone. 'I can't hear you. Are you doing it?'

She kissed her teeth then took a dramatically loud deep breath to satisfy his request.

'Good,' he said. 'These kinda things happen all the time, okay? So don't torture yourself over it. You're doing the best you can, right?'

'I mean, I guess.'

'Don't do that!' He kissed his teeth. 'I wouldn't be working with you if you weren't the shit. This idea that's going to blow everyone away came from you!'

She smiled as he carried on telling her to chill the fuck out, quietly listening to him.

'After seeing her daughter go viral overnight, she's probably scared. The internet's a fucked-up place and my guess is she doesn't know much about it beyond her Facebook feed.'

'You're probably right.'

'I'm always right.'

'Ugh, shut up!' laughed Tia. They bickered for a moment before Nate returned to mentor mode.

'Nah, but on a real, I think we need to try and help her understand how this could be good for Shannon. Beneficial even.'

'She's such a cool kid, man.' Tia sat up in bed. 'So bubbly and weird. She reminds me of me. And she wants to be a writer as well.'

'Yeah, you are kind of weird,' Nate joked.

'Fuck you!' Tia laughed, until the cogs in her brain began to slowly turn. She stared at the ceiling for a moment until Nate checked she was still on the phone.

'Yeah, I'm still here,' she reassured him. 'Wait . . . What if we got Shannon to write her own piece for the feature?'

'That's . . . actually a sick idea,' said Nate. 'Give her full control of her own narrative.'

'Exactly. And her first byline too. For LCN, no less.'

Tia stretched to the end of her bed for her laptop and began to type away, emailing Eloise the idea, then drafting another message for Cheryl. Nate's adorable chuckle stopped Tia mid-sentence.

'What?' she asked.

'Your keyboard. I like hearing you hard at work.'

'And it's all thanks to you,' she said, before deleting and rewriting the second line of her message. 'Well, it was my idea, but your pep talk really helped.'

'Hmm, we make a pretty good team,' he said. 'I don't mind being your cheerleader.'

He started freestyling a *Bring It On*-worthy chant, that would've cringed Tia out if Nate hadn't been so fine. She was appalled at how much she was willing to stomach from someone she was so attracted to, his deep voice making her wish he was right beside her, talking into her ear instead of through a phone.

She decided to leave the work for when she was actually on the clock and in the office, closing the laptop and giving her undivided attention back to their phone call. She asked Nate when he'd be free for their dim sum dinner that never happened, then heard chatter in the background.

'Oh, I didn't realise you were with people.'

'Yeah, literally just finished wrapping a shoot,' he said. 'I only just saw your text so I thought I'd shout you.'

The chatter and laughter of what sounded like quite a few girls got a little louder, with one of them calling for Nate.

'Well, thanks for squeezing me in.'

He laughed then said goodbye to someone.

'What was it for?' asked Tia.

Nate started laughing, which threw her off until she realised he was talking to someone about something they were showing him, slowly erasing Tia's grin. She'd been about to suggest a day for their next date, but she didn't want to beg it when he clearly sounded occupied. He asked her to repeat what she had said but the chatter around him only grew louder, putting Tia off even more.

'Anyways, imma let you get back to work,' Tia said in her most upbeat voice. She could've talked to him for at least another hour but didn't want to move all clingy. 'Thanks for letting me vent.'

'Rah, locking me off so soon? Was about to ask what you're tryna get into.'

'I'm about to get into my bed!' She winced at how unsexy that sounded. 'I gotta get Shannon back ASAP before Camilla finds out.'

'Ite, I hear it.' Nate sounded disappointed. 'Let me know what Shannon's saying then, yeah?'

'Yeah, of course.'

'Cool. Goodnight then. You better dream about me.'

'Man, whatever.'

They laughed some more before Tia ended the call and lay back on her bed, wondering if she should've linked Nate. She imagined the kinds of things Luca and Hannah would say: prioritising boring old work over a buff baggage-free guy who was clearly into her. But he'd sounded like he was with a bag of girls, much to Tia's disdain. She kissed her teeth before rolling over to her side. She forced her eyes closed.

The next day, Eloise approved of Tia's final call-out strategy and sat beside her while she carefully typed out an email highlighting how this shoot could not only change the school's uniform policy but kickstart Shannon's writing career. Tia mentioned that she could arrange a tour of LCN's world-famous newsroom, and peppered her message with the names of a wide network of senior journalists who would probably love to take Shannon under their wing. She beautified every single sentence, praying it'd be enough to convince Cheryl to come back. Eloise nodded as she read through the final draft and said, 'There's no way she could refuse this!' Tia clicked the 'send' button.

However, their hope dwindled more and more as days went by without no response from Cheryl. With the shoot just a mere few weeks away, they both began to worry about how they'd break the news to Camilla, who would surely run to Marc and slag off Tia, ruining her hopes of ever being made a staff writer. In an effort to avoid bumping into Camilla, Tia had taken to sneaking her laptop down to the cafe on the office's ground floor. It overlooked the newsroom and was open to the public, in an effort to improve LCN's image, trying to prove to everyone they weren't a bunch of stuck-up toffs. Camilla much preferred the private employee-only club that was situated beneath a different LCN-owned building, away from the Muggles.

Tia slid her headphones over her ears, drowning out the sounds of clinking mugs and saucers, and elderly visitors complaining about the rock-hard cookies they had purchased with their teas. She began to resume a mind-numbingly boring research task given to her by Harrison, until she heard her email notification sound go off. Tia's stomach plunged when she saw Cheryl's name in bold at the top of her inbox.

Hello Tia. I'm sorry I haven't been in touch, I just needed time to think. My husband and I are putting our trust in you and Nathaniel. See you in a few weeks.

Tia closed her eyes and took a deep breath after reading the short but gratifying message. She immediately forwarded the email to Eloise, who replied, 'OH THANK FUCK OMG,' with a GIF of Patsy Stone dancing with a bottle of champagne. Tia smiled that they were now on the meme-messaging level of friendship, sending back a GIF of Rihanna dancing with gun fingers. She went back to reread Cheryl's message, as if she needed to see it again to believe it, and paused at the mention of Nate. She'd been so quick to email Eloise that she hadn't even registered his name properly. She decided to phone him.

'How and when did you convince Cheryl?'

'A magician never reveals his secrets.'

'Nate!' He laughed and took the piss out of the way she yelled his name. 'Stop playing, man.'

'Alright, I'll tell you everything – under one condition.'

'Anything. I owe you big time.'

She grinned at the keyboard in front of her and began to twirl a lock of hair around her finger before realising what she was doing, smiling to herself even more at the sound of Nate's calm voice, convincing her to see him as soon as possible, not that he needed to beg.

16

The next day, after spending the morning subtitling one of Arjun and Harry's latest masterpieces about a therapy dog changing the lives of office workers in a start-up based in Dalston, Nate's name popped up in bold letters at the top of Tia's inbox, a welcome sight for her sore eyes. He had scheduled a meeting in Outlook for that entire afternoon, under the guise of finalising some 'incredibly important' details for the shoot that 'just had to be seen in person'. He'd italicised all the words that sounded the most urgent, letting Tia know he was fucking around, and she laughed to herself as she clicked to accept the invitation. Seeing as the shoot was just around the corner, and Camilla was becoming more overbearing by the day, it didn't take much for Tia to agree to his plan and skive.

She cradled her phone between her ear and her shoulder as she rummaged through her bag for her Oyster card, stomping down the worn-out stairs of

Peckham Rye station, all while trying to listen to Hannah's lecture.

'I'm not playing, T.'

'I know you're not.'

She rolled her eyes as she tapped out and stood by the barriers, concentrating on their discussion and adjusting the heavy laptop bag that was dragging her shoulder down.

'Don't you think it's too soon to meet friends, though?' asked Tia. 'And it's your birthday – like, that's a big statement.'

'So? Wasn't he the one who said he wanted to be more than friends?'

'Yeah. Like two seconds before shoving his tongue down my throat.'

'Listen, you like him, right?' asked Hannah, already knowing the answer. 'And he obviously likes you. What's wrong with acting on that? We're bound to meet him one day.'

She struggled to disagree with Hannah, who could tell by Tia's response or lack thereof that she was slowly but surely winning this argument.

'Besides, it's just a drink-up, it's not that deep. Hardly meeting the in-laws.'

Tia laughed. 'You and Luca act like my parents, though.'

'Because we care and want you to get some dick!'

'Ah, yes. Spoken like a truly responsible mum.'

'I'm not a regular mom, I'm a cool mom,' Hannah said in a nasal American accent.

Tia laughed into her phone until she spotted a familiar figure smoking by the main entrance's noticeboard.

'He's here, I have to go now.'

'D'you guys need anything?' Hannah continued, committing to the role. 'Some snacks? A condom? Let me know.'

'Fuck off,' Tia cackled.

After saying their love-yous and goodbyes, Tia walked out to the station's courtyard and was immediately pulled into an embrace.

'Hey, trouble,' said Nate, ruffling the back of her curly hair.

Tia closed her eyes and grinned. She took in the comforting washing-powder scent of his sweatshirt and they walked, fingers intertwined, through the dingy markets and modest stalls that dotted the high street.

The two sat side by side and worked on their respective tasks on the wooden table they'd had their first kiss on, a memory neither of them seemed to have shaken off, judging by the number of kisses Nate tried to sneak in between his Zoom meetings with clients and Tia's transcribing. She tried to mention Hannah's birthday drink-up but couldn't work out how to do it without making it mean something. Sounding like she really wanted him to come would probably put too much pressure on him, even though she really wanted him to come. Would it scream 'commitment'? Would it reek of clinginess? Would it feel too coupley? Would it be too much too soon? All these questions floated in her mind as she tried to rehearse how she was going to ask him, trying to perfect her too-cool-to-care-girl voice, because anything else that even remotely hinted at her giving a shit would surely make him do a runner.

Luca would have been proud that Tia was finally regurgitating the nuggets of wisdom he'd been force-feeding her all these years. She hated how dating often felt like a competition of who could care less but she didn't want to lose again like she had done with Aaron.

'Tia,' said Nate, getting her to come back down to earth. She shook away the haunted memories of her past dating mishaps and smiled back at him. 'You hungry?' he asked.

The sun had started to set and the streets below the windows of the studio were starting to glow and fill with life again.

'Always,' said Tia as she stretched her arms and back. Nate laughed while tapping away at his phone. 'Could you pick up our dinner then?' He texted her the order confirmation before grabbing her coat and handing her his keys. 'I need to jump on a call real quick, but it's just across the road.'

After finishing a cigarette and collecting the greasy

bag from the hole-in-the-wall takeaway, she finally figured out the perfect way to mention the drink-up without compromising her Cool Girl facade.

When she opened the door, Tia noticed the ceiling lights were switched off. The glow of a floor lamp drew her to the wooden table, which had been cleared of their laptops and the scattered piles of magazines. It was instead draped in a heavy linen tablecloth with pillar candles lit and placed in the centre. A SiR tune quietly played in the background as Nate emerged from the backroom with a pretty-looking bottle of rosé in hand. Tia quickly picked her jaw up from the floor and shrugged off her coat.

'What's all this?' she asked, noticing the smell of incense wafting in the air.

'Well . . .' Nate cleared his throat. 'I still didn't thank you properly for the booking. It means a lot.'

The biker jacket-clad Cool Girl inside her brain started to shake her head, disappointed at how much this was melting Tia's usually icy disposition. How was she meant to be too cool to care when he did stuff like this? She ransacked her mind for a witty remark.

'With a takeaway I had to collect?'

That's right. This low-key romantic gesture hasn't fazed me, she said to herself.

'I had to get you out of here somehow so I could set up, innit!' Nate said as they laughed together.

'Well, I should be the one thanking you, to be

honest,' said Tia. 'If you hadn't spoken to Cheryl, we would've been fucked.'

'Listen. Enough about Cheryl and the shoot.' He ushered her to the wooden bench by the table. 'I know you've been working mad hard, so let's just relax tonight. You deserve to chill for a minute.'

She took a sip of the wine he poured her and watched him carefully lay out their dinner between them, explaining how he'd ordered extra chilli oil because he remembered her love of spicy food from one of their first conversations on Hinge.

'This is . . . really sweet,' she finally admitted. 'Do you thank all your clients like this?'

'Only the pretty ones,' he joked, taking a seat beside her.

'Oh, all the models and groupies?'

'Mm-hmm,' he laughed. 'Suttin like dat.'

He saw the unimpressed grin on her face and popped a dumpling into her mouth. Her eyes widened as her tastebuds were overwhelmed by the piping-hot garlicky goodness of it all.

'Oh my days.'

'Don't say I never put you on.'

'Whatever.'

She ignored him and continued chewing, savouring all the meaty juices and hints of fiery ginger as he stared at her.

'What, bruv?' Tia asked, trying not to crack a smile.

She tried to reach for another with her chopsticks but Nate pulled the foil container back towards himself. 'Oi!'

'Not until I get my ratings.'

Tia tried to reach over his body for the food he kept moving away, shrieking as he grabbed hold of her waist with his other arm, sneaking little kisses on her cheek and neck.

When they'd finished stuffing their faces, Nate took Tia by the hand and guided her to the sofa on the other side of the room. She sat on the furthest end and pulled her legs up towards herself to get comfy with her glass of wine, embracing this perfect night with Nate as he sat down in the middle, resting his hand on her thigh. In the low lighting, the pair continued to drink and bicker and banter over the dumbest things. It was the flirty kind of bickering that kept you on your toes as you searched for the next clapback, hoping your next line would make them laugh even harder than before. The kind best accompanied by a little alcohol to fuel the tension. The rosé tasted like shit but it did the job in loosening the tight knot in Tia's stomach.

Too caught up in Nate's boyish charm, and rubbing her aching sides from laughing so hard, she didn't pop the question until her third glass. He'd just promised to take her to another spot in East for more Chinese food, when Tia decided it was now or never. All the green lights were there. The kisses, the romantic takeaway, him suggesting future plans: she ticked the milestones of her mental notepad and decided it felt safe to go out on a limb, so she brought up Hannah's birthday party.

'It's calm if you can't make it though,' she coolly concluded.

Nate studied Tia's face as she returned to her glass for another sip, avoiding eye contact.

'Are you gonna be there?'

'Well, obviously.'

'Then that's where I'm gonna be.'

And there he went again, sounding all cool and resolute.

'Great. Sick.'

He smiled and laughed at her coy smile, her head resting against the sofa's backrest.

'What?' she asked.

'You're such a lightweight.'

'Am not.'

'Are too.'

'I'm just tired, that's all.' She put her glass down on the floor and wriggled back into the corner of the sofa, folding her arms. 'This drama with the shoot has proper taken it out of me, I swear.'

'I bet.'

'You still haven't told me how you got her mum to agree.'

'Oh, that.' He leaned his body against her legs and

took a sip of his drink. 'I was just honest with her about the whole thing, innit. LCN is a bit of a beast and they've never really got it right when it comes to representing us.'

'She probably really appreciated that.'

He nodded. 'So I was just saying to her, "From one outsider to another, I won't let you down." And I told her how much I trusted and believed in you too, that you're not like the rest of them.'

Tia smiled, her head leaning on the backrest of the sofa. Being tipsy had always made her far more expressive than she'd usually be, but her heart couldn't help but flutter at hearing how much Nate backed her. His lack of hesitation when it came to declaring what he thought about her always threw her off in the best way possible. It frightened her sometimes. Her past made her seek comfort in the trepidation of dating, because being clueless about someone's feelings towards you often felt much better than the irrevocable conclusion of being rejected and unwanted.

'Thank you.'

'For what?'

'Believing in me. Getting Cheryl back. The dumplings. Everything,' said Tia. 'I'm so glad I'm working with you.'

'I feel like the dumplings really sealed the deal.'

'Oh, hundred per cent.'

She grinned to herself as Nate laughed, until the

room fell silent. They locked eyes, and Nate placed his glass on the coffee table in front of him. Her heart began to thump more and more the closer he moved towards her. She closed her eyes when Nate's soft lips pressed against hers, and she smiled into his gentle kiss as he cupped his warm hands around her flushed cheeks. He slid his hands around to the back of her head and nestled his fingers in her curls as she returned each and every kiss while holding on to his wrists, not realising how much she had wanted him to do this to her, happy for him to take the lead. She softly bit his bottom lip, giving him the green light to pull her body closer to him. She embraced the feeling of his firm chest against hers and wrapped her arms around his neck, as he began to push her down onto her back, their faces still fused together, his hand running up and down the sides of her body. She ran her tongue around his lips, compelling him to open his mouth and meet her tongue with his own.

He took her hands from around his neck and held them above her head, pinning them against the sofa's armrest. His tongue grew stronger as did the motion of his hips between her legs. She met his pace until he couldn't seem to handle it anymore and pulled his face away, kissing and biting a trail down her neck. He sat up a little and masterfully undid the first few buttons of her cropped cardigan until her black lace bra was revealed. Tia looked away, resisting the urge to cover herself with her arms, until he began to adjust the straps of the bra, slipping his fingers between them and the skin of her shoulders. She could do as she had always done and crack a joke to diffuse the sexual tension, knowing Luca and Hannah would shake their head and cuss her for being so lame. But tonight was different. Nate made her feel different. She wanted him and she wanted this to happen.

17

Tia shut her eyes tight when she felt him tug at the lace of her bra. He lowered his head and began kissing the stretch marks on her breasts, as if he wanted to ease her of her apparent shyness. She cradled the back of his head and looked down at him as the warm feeling of his tongue making slow circles around her nipples started to feel too good to be reserved about. He looked up at her and brought his hand up, gently pinching a nipple between his fingertips. She arched her back and accidentally let out a moan, letting him carry on his exploration of her body.

He came back up to kiss her and she held his face as he slipped her bodycon skirt up towards her stomach. His fingers began to graze over the moisture between her thighs, again and again, and she writhed at his every movement between their slow, passionate kisses, until that wasn't enough for him.

He sat up and began running his fingers down the sides of her underwear, the unsexiest pair of black cotton briefs she'd fished out of the pile of washed clothes that lived on a chair in her bedroom. She mentally cringed that they didn't match the energy of her bra, though Nate didn't seem to care. Tia pushed her hips firmly against the sofa when she realised she couldn't remember the last time she had shaved. He caught the panicked look across her face and laughed a little.

'I don't care about that, man. I just want to make you feel good.'

Tia looked unsure, until Nate began to kiss the around the tiny ribbon bow of her briefs.

'Can't I do that for you?' he asked in a hushed tone.

She looked into his gaze between her legs and relaxed her body into the sofa, a signal for him to continue. He pressed her legs together and slipped off her underwear, throwing it onto the coffee table. Too shy to look at his face, Tia stared at the ceiling and shut her eyes tight as he began to kiss her hips and inner thighs and gasped the second she felt his warm tongue press against her clitoris. He tightened his grip around her thighs and kept them apart, ensuring she felt every carefully considered motion of his mouth, flicking his tongue back and forth over the spot, making Tia arch her back and wriggle around helplessly. She held the back of his head, half wanting him to carry on, half wanting him to stop because she couldn't handle the feeling anymore, and looked down at his forehead. Nate looked up without stopping and smized at the desperate look on Tia's face;

her whimpering only seemed to encourage him. She grabbed hold of her mouth, almost unable to process how good this was feeling, and he slid his hands up her torso, reaching for her hands, lacing his fingers between hers, as if he wanted to experience every bit of her reaction to his touch. She began to writhe against Nate's face, between his syrupy kisses and moans until the sensation between her thighs was too intense to clench on to, the throbbing feeling so severe it was almost painful, and she finally let go, the tingling ecstasy running like waves throughout her entire body.

Nate sat up with a satisfied look on his face and pulled Tia's body up for a tender kiss. She wrapped her frame around him and kissed him back, planting more kisses on his jaw and down his neck, preparing to return the favour. Her reserved nature instilled by her churched-up childhood didn't usually allow her to take control and wield her prowess when it came to getting physical with anyone, but Nate wasn't just anyone to her, not anymore. This felt safe. Nate made her feel sexy, and desired, and he took care of her in all the ways she'd hoped Aaron would've wanted to and more, fuelling her desire to please him right back.

Nate's stare was filled with fire as she tore herself away from his mouth and firmly pushed his torso against the backrest of the sofa, easing her quivering body down to the wooden floorboards and reaching for the button of his jeans. He wasted no time in helping her undo the zip, sliding his jeans and boxers down as she began to kiss his abdomen and groin. She slowly worked her hands up and down his shaft before gently sliding her mouth over the tip, gradually pushing her head up and down the length of him. Being so out of practice, she grappled in her mind for type of the advice Luca would often bestow or that TikTok Hannah had once sent in the group chat about getting rid of your gag reflex, though it was much too late for all that.

Tia was pleased to look up and find Nate's eyes closed, savouring the pleasure and swearing under his breath. It comforted the anxiety she had about her lack of experience, and she made her hands and tongue work faster and more rhythmically until he opened his eyes. He scooped up her messy curls into his hands and looked into her eyes, moaning her name over and over until he finally came. Before she could do anything more, he leaned forward from the sofa and pulled her up for a kiss, his arm around her waist and the other hand firmly holding the back of her head. His gratitude was palpable, as he started pecking her cheeks and neck so much she began to laugh, still in a daze from what they had just done.

When their bodies parted, she felt a chill and looked down at her unbuttoned cardigan and scrunched-up skirt, suddenly acutely aware of how dishevelled she was probably looking now that she was coming down from their shared high. Still kneeling on the floor, she turned around and gasped at her underwear beside a wineglass, snatching it from the coffee table. Nate laughed as she got up to adjust her skirt and instinctively told her where the toilet was before she found her bag and scurried off.

She leaned against the closed door behind her and stared at her reflection with an ear-to-ear grin. It took the remaining discipline Tia had left in her body to not shriek at a volume Nate could hear. *Luca and Hannah are going to DIE,* Tia thought to herself while peeing, already imagining how proud they'd be of her in the group chat. After washing her hands, she rinsed her mouth with running water and wished she had come more prepared, before finally dropping a cryptic message in the group chat, teasing them before they inevitably begged her to spill. She then inspected her curls, or what was left of them, poofy and fuzzy from all the fraternising her hair had been subjected to, and tried her best to arrange them into a shape that was not so lopsided. Being unable to stretch her wash-and-go for less than three days would've pissed Tia off on a normal day, but today it was lost for a good cause. She grinned to herself.

Her phone pinged and vibrated on the sink's countertop while she was trying to slip her briefs back on. She hopped over on one leg to get a better look at all the notifications popping up, cheesing to herself at all the eyes emojis and messages typed in capital letters. Distracted by her phone's screen, she missed the hole her leg was meant to go through and knocked over a small wastebin in the corner of the toilet, the force pushing the door ajar.

Tia winced and immediately crouched to the ground, hoping Nate hadn't heard anything, and her stomach dropped when she overheard him laughing and heard further murmuring, realising he was on the phone to someone. *Was he already telling his friends too?* Tia smugly thought to herself as she began throwing the bits of scattered rubbish back into the bin. It was mostly clothes tags and used paper towels, until she saw a half-ripped square wrapper on the floor. Tia froze for a moment and convinced herself that it wasn't what she thought it was, before picking it up by its corner with her fingertips. She flung it into the bin and stood up as soon as she saw the absence of its contents, the rounded shape still moulded into the foil.

She stared at it until the sight of the bin blurred into one big blob, then tried to swallow the lump that had suddenly formed in the back of her throat. She didn't know how to feel or how to process the thought of Nate doing what they had just done with another person. Her mind then flashed back to his joke about thanking his pretty clients and Tia started to feel a bit queasy.

Though they hadn't exactly discussed what they

were, he'd been waving those green flags that Tia had assumed would lead to exclusivity. She hadn't been talking to anyone else since they'd met but it had never occurred to her whether it had been the same for Nate. He laughed again and her heart skipped a beat. She checked the time on her phone. *Who'd be making him laugh like that past 1 a.m.?* she asked herself, already knowing the obvious answer.

She smoothed down the sides of her skirt and checked her reflection once more before slowly walking back out.

'Hmm, I bet,' he was saying, sitting on the armrest with his hand in his pocket, grinning at the floor.

Her stomach flipped at the sound of his deep sexy voice being put on for whoever was on the other end of the late-night phone call. When he heard her nearing footsteps, the speed at which he ended the conversation made Tia feel even more tense, as she strutted past him to finish the rest of the wine in her glass.

'I'll see you tomorrow then, yeah? Cool. Bye.'

She felt his arms come from behind and wrap around her waist, but she couldn't shake the uneasiness she felt, thinking back to all the other girls who had probably been in this exact same position.

'Who was that?' Tia asked

'Oh, just some work stuff. You were gone for a while, thought you got lost.'

She nodded and cleared her throat, trying not to get caught up in the kisses he was planting down the side of her neck.

'Yeah, um, it was Eloise,' she began to lie. 'Camilla wants a meeting first thing tomorrow morning.'

'No, let's not talk about work anymore.' Nate turned Tia's body round and cupped his hands around her face. 'At least not until we finish what we start—'

'I actually have to go now.' She held his hands and took them down from her cheeks. 'I didn't realise how late it was.'

'Oh, rah. For real?'

Nate looked stunned but tried his hardest to play it cool, turning his dropped jaw into some sort of half-smile. He folded his arms and perched himself back on the sofa's armrest as Tia scrambled her things together, avoiding any kind of eye contact. She didn't have the guts to look at his face properly. He offered to drive her home as she was putting her coat on but she cut him off mid-sentence.

'My Uber's like two minutes away,' she lied again. 'But I'll see you at Hannah's yeah? It's this Saturday, I'll text you the details.'

She let him kiss her goodbye, barely forming a pout with her lips. Tia gave him a faint smile as their faces parted.

'Calm.' He wrapped her coat around her and tied the belt for her. 'Text me when you get home, yeah?'

'Mm-hm.'

She turned around and headed for the door, still feeling his awkward gaze burning a hole into the back of her head.

'Make sure.'

'I will.'

18

'What do you even want from this?' asked Luca.

Tia lay beside him on the double bed as he swiped through an invitation-only dating app no-one had heard of, while Hannah sat cross-legged on the carpet in front of her mirror, laying down her edges in intricate swirls, despite the fact they'd probably get sweated out a few hours into her drink-up.

'What do *I* want from this?'

'Yeah. Because if it's more than sex, you should let him know how you feel,' said Hannah.

'What?' piped up Luca. 'And let her be the dickhead who starts the "What are we?" convo? No way.'

'But she'll never know unless she actually chats to him about it.'

'He's so hot-and-cold, I wouldn't even know how to start that convo. Like, one minute he's MIA,' explained Tia, checking her notifications in case Nate had decided to reply to her texts. 'The next minute he's saying and doing all the right things.'

'Like letting you use his face as a seat?'

'I am fucking dead!' Hannah cackled.

'He definitely looks like he'd talk you through it.' Luca turned to Tia for confirmation. 'Did he talk you through it?'

'Nah, he deffo did,' added Hannah. 'Next to getting pussy, there's nothing them artsy man love more than the sound of their own voice.'

'I beg! Can we refocus?' Tia clapped her hands in the air. 'Maybe I should just slow it down. Like, he's clearly seeing other people. Should I be doing the same?'

'It wouldn't hurt. Don't just put one dick in your basket.'

'Nah, see, this is what I hate,' said Hannah, putting her toothbrush and Eco Styler back onto her vanity table. 'She obviously likes him, so why play this game? T, you should just tell him how you feel.'

'The last time I did that, the guy came back with a whole girlfriend,' Tia groaned, covering her face with her arms as her mind replayed the first time they had met Olivia. 'I'm not gonna make myself look like a dickhead again.'

'Exactly!' said Luca, triumphantly. 'If he's moving like that, you can too! It's not like you're in a relationship.'

As always, Hannah and Luca stood on opposite ends of the spectrum. 'To give a fuck or not to give a fuck?'

was the question that had been roaming through Tia's mind ever since her tryst with Nate. She wanted to do a Luca and not care. She rolled around on the bed like a frustrated baby while her friends continued to bicker over what she should do. Luca said that if Nate wanted them to be something more, he would've made it happen already, but Hannah countered this by pointing out all the wonderful ways Nate had been there for Tia.

'Who does all those things with someone they don't want to be with?' she asked.

'Men,' Luca said flatly.

'Well, I think you should just chat to him, T. He's coming tonight, right?'

'Who knows.' Tia sat up and threw her messageless phone down onto the mattress. 'Probably nose-diving in another girl's fanny for all we know.'

It came out of Tia's mouth with more vim than she'd intended, judging by the stunned looks on her friend's faces.

'Mad ting.'

'You know what, I think that calls for a drink.' Luca poured a generous amount of the Echo Falls they had started on earlier into Tia's plastic cup and handed it to her. 'No drama tonight. Let's just get lit.'

'That's the best idea you've had all night,' laughed Hannah, readying her cup for more of the fruity rosé.

After more pre-drinking and selfie-taking, Hannah's guests finally began to trickle in, long after the time

Hannah had instructed everyone to arrive of course. Don Toliver's 'No Idea' blasted through the speakers as obligatory welcome shots of tequila were forced around. The crowd was a mixture of their old sixth-form friends (some Tia would've preferred to keep in the past), Hannah's kooky fashion schoolmates, and the odd co-worker she felt she could trust to keep tales of her debauchery out of the office.

Between checking her phone for any word from Nate, Tia mostly floated in and out of conversations. They ranged from the latest baby on the way to what someone had done in Croatia last summer. A few consisted of bragging about graduate jobs and cushty commutes, while others spoke about flat-hunting and finally moving away from their parents. Tia had nothing new to say. She was still thrown by the fact that the former classmate who had asked her for a pen every day for at least a year, and would return it with the lid all chewed up, was now bringing new life into the world. She smiled and nodded and asked all the leading questions you were meant to ask in these grown-up conversations, hoping it'd distract everyone from asking her anything at all. If they did, she'd reply with the same script she always stuck with: 'Work's great – can't complain! Yeah, still single. Not really seeking, but I'm open to whatever. I'm just really focused on my career right now, y'know?'

She had to add that last part to ease everyone's visible

discomfort about her still being single. Even though she felt like she had someone, he didn't feel like hers to claim. Everyone else's lives seemed to be moving towards something real; everyone seemed to have it all figured out. And while she currently had no interest in babies or saving for a deposit, she envied the smug, self-assured smiles on everyone's faces. The satisfaction of having a solid life plan and actually sticking to it always felt like a bit of a hopeless boomer fantasy, until she was face to face with people her age who were really doing it. There had been a time when it had felt like everyone was in the same boat; when they were all single and hopelessly seeking; when hearing that someone was pregnant always ended with wondering whether they were going to keep it or not; when everyone happily admitted that they didn't know what the fuck they were doing. But now it felt like Tia was on the *Titanic* while everyone else was sailing off into the Instagrammable sunset.

After having her ear talked off by an old classmate wanting to spread the gospel of Forex, Tia eventually escaped the sweaty living room and was reunited with a tipsy Luca in the kitchen.

'You good, babes?' he asked, stuffing crisps in his mouth.

'Yeah, literally had to run away from Emmanuel and his—'

'Oh my gosh, don't! If I hear the words "passive income" one more time I'm gonna throw up.'

'I should've taken a shot each time he said it, you know!'

'You'd be fucking paralytic before midnight.'

'That's not a bad goal,' laughed Tia, reaching over for a handful of crisps.

'Is Nate on his way yet?'

Tia looked at her phone to see if she had missed a call or a text but there was nothing. In fact, there hadn't been much of anything in their chat since her abrupt exit from his studio two nights ago.

'Maybe,' she said coolly. 'I'm sure he'll be here soon.'

Hannah then waltzed in with an adorable little bottle of Hennessy in hand, waving it around in everyone's faces and grinding against her giggling friends, mouthing the lyrics to a Burna Boy song flooding the kitchen.

'So cute, right?' she said, holding it up with pride. 'Aaron just got here and gave it to me.'

'Of course he did,' answered Luca, snatching the bottle.

Tia felt a familiar tap on the shoulder and turned to see Aaron dodging to the other side. She rolled her eyes before he began to ruffle her curls, much to her dismay. 'Not the hair, you prick!' she yelled as he took a step back to examine her outfit. He chuckled a little before pretending to try and pull down the black miniskirt she had borrowed from Hannah's wardrobe, which only irked her further. She swatted his hands away and said,

'Do you mind? You weirdo!' before smoothing the tight material over her chunky thighs.

'Does your dad mind?' asked Aaron. He took out his iPhone and pretended to make a phone call. 'Cos we both know he'd rinse you right now.'

'What he doesn't know won't hurt him!' bellowed a voice coming into the kitchen.

'Jamal!' Hannah shouted. 'What are you doing here?'

Jamal had been lurking in Aaron's shadow since the first day of sixth form, so the three were hardly surprised that he turned up here tonight as well.

'I think my invite got lost so I tagged along with Aaron,' he said with a toothy grin. He walked to the dish drainer by the sink and helped himself to a glass rather than taking a plastic cup from the towers of them right there on the table. He pulled out an obnoxiously large bottle of Cîroc from the inside of a Gucci puffer jacket neither Hannah, Luca nor Tia had ever seen online before.

'But I knew you wouldn't mind,' he added.

Luca offered a fake laugh while Tia punched Aaron's arm, which ended up hurting her knuckles more than it did him.

'Tia, Tia, Tia,' said Jamal as his eyes raked up and down her body. 'Have you missed me, babes?'

She folded her arms and said, 'Not really,' with a wry smile. Aaron chuckled and put his arms around her and the unwanted guest, swaying their bodies along to the beat of the music as if he could force everyone to behave like one big happy family. He stopped to look around the room, then looked back down at Tia.

'So where's the lucky guy? The one you've been ghosting me for.'

'Wow, you been drinking already?' she asked, squishing his cheeks with her hand.

'No,' Aaron shook her hand off. 'But I can tell you have.'

'I can't see Olivia anywhere either,' added Tia, trying to look over his broad shoulders. 'Finally giving her tour guide a break, I see. Good for you.'

The two stared at each other for a second before bursting into laughter until a group of sixth-form friends entered and immediately surrounded Aaron. Girls giggled with each other after greeting him, guys shouted about how they were trying to be like him, and Jamal got in everybody's way, trying to savour the left-over crumbs of attention and hype.

Though it had been years since they'd left school, Aaron still had that wonderboy aura about him that instantly made you want him to like you. The Nike Tech tracksuit Aaron was currently wearing would have looked so basic on anyone else in the room, but his impressive physique always made even the simplest of items look irresistible. His palpable charm and charisma meant he didn't need to try or overcompensate, and he knew it. Aaron lapped up the praise while someone forced a tequila shot into his hand. His faux-grimace was followed by his Colgate smile as the crowd cheered and egged him on to do another. After he rejected a third shot, the group moved Aaron away from Tia and migrated to the living room to reload a Drake song at Jamal's request.

Tia, Luca and Hannah eventually dragged them-selves away from the snacks and bounced their bodies along to the beat of 'Madiba Riddim', joining the rest of the sweaty guests in the centre of the dim living room. With one hand, Tia held her hair in a messy pile on top of her head, while Luca's fingers were inter-twined with her other. Hannah swayed her hips between their gyrating bodies before being pulled away by her boyfriend for a private dance of their own.

It took another cup of the poorly mixed rum punch, two videos added to Luca's close-friends Stories, and half of Hannah's dancehall playlist for the drink to finally hit Tia's system. She peered around the room for an escape and teetered towards a vacant armchair, but before she could turn around to sit, Aaron jumped into it, manspreading his muscly legs.

'Gotta be quicker than that, B,' he said through his signature grin. 'Beg you grab me a drink, since you're up.'

'You're so lucky I need a refill!' shouted Tia, kissing her teeth. 'You better jump as soon as I come back.'

She snatched the half-empty cup from Aaron's hand,

but suddenly crashed into an unidentified torso, spilling the backwash over the person's trousers. She was too waved and the room was too dark to make out the face properly, but Tia gasped and apologised profusely while Jamal cackled in the background, doing nothing to help the situation as per usual. When she looked up to apologise another ten times, the person's hand reached down and held her chin.

'You're so lucky I needed a drink,' Nate laughed. 'Though that wasn't the way I'd imagined.'

19

Before she could apologise again, Nate took Tia's wrist and pulled her in for a hug and swayed their fused bodies from side to side.

'You're here,' she said into his ear.

Though it only lasted a couple of seconds, Tia could already sense the whispers and glares coming from her old classmates who surrounded them, trying to decipher who the guy was that Miss Too-Stush-For-Anyone was allowing to feel her up.

As they parted, she noticed the cornershop bags he picked up from the ground, and quickly guided him to the kitchen. She sat on the countertop, watching him fish out cans of Red Stripe from one, a dark bottle of wine and some vodka from the other. She couldn't help but smile at the sight of him flitting around against the backdrop of her friends and acquaintances. Finally having someone who was there just for her almost washed away the doubts she'd had about him earlier that night. She looked his outfit up and down with an approving gaze:

his dark green corduroy shirt layered over one of his many white Ts, black trousers, a black baseball cap, and a pair of trainers that complemented the rest of his colour palette. His choices seemed a lot more deliberate and considered compared to all the other guys she'd grown up with who were at the party, but that only made Tia like him more for putting in the effort.

'You are gone,' he said, kissing his teeth. 'Why are you such a lightweight?'

'You took too long, I had to start the party without you.'

'My bad, you're right,' he laughed. 'I need to get on your level and make up for lost time, still.'

Tia grinned as Nate's face neared hers for a kiss, until the aroma of a sticky Wetherspoons floor filled her nostrils.

'Smells like you're already on my level,' she said, gently pushing him away. 'I thought you had a shoot today.'

Nate began to sniff his clothes in jest before filling their cups with shots of vodka.

'Oh, yeah. We wrapped early, so we all grabbed a drink afterwards. That's why I'm a bit late.'

'Oh.' Tia nodded and looked away, her overactive imagination already concocting scenes of Nate downing drinks with Bella Hadid wannabes. *You're not meant to give a fuck, remember?* she coached herself, thinking back to Luca's preaching from earlier.

'Woah, woah, woah, wait!' He gently tugged at a curl before moving in closer to her ear. She had never been so grateful for such a crowded kitchen. 'It's bad luck to toast without looking at each other,' he said. 'Something about seventy years of bad sex?'

Corny as fuck! Tia thought to herself. But she was tipsy enough for the cliché line to run, and he was buff enough to pull it off without looking like a total dickhead.

She replied, 'I think it's only seven, you know,' and quickly regretted it.

Her mind was quickly flooded with flashbacks of her friends lecturing her about how unsexy it was to be a know-it-all. She distinctly remembered the PT she'd dated who'd stopped talking to her after she'd corrected his pronunciation of 'prosciutto' in front of a waiter.

'Seven?' said Nate. 'Well, still, we wouldn't want that now, would we?'

When she looked up at Nate's face, he was already staring down at her. His plump lips rested against the rim of his cup for a moment before the two sipped their drinks together. She scowled at her cup while Nate laughed and continued staring.

'What d'you want, man?' she said, jokingly.

He rested his hand on her thigh. 'You're just proper cute when you're like this,' he said, pushing her hair behind her shoulders.

'Ugh, cute? No one wants to be cute,' she retorted. 'Babies are cute, puppies are cute . . .'

'What would you prefer then? Sexy? Beautiful?'

'Gorgeous, stunning, out-of-this-world . . .'

'All of the above,' he laughed and leaned in closer to her ear. 'Like, I don't want you to leave my sight tonight.'

Nate's hand slid up her thigh and towards her hip and Tia leaned back to see the look on his face. She couldn't help but smile when she saw the fiery glint in his eyes, and bit the bottom of her lip, trying to resist the urge to kiss him then and there. Before she could whisper something back, Hannah stumbled back into the kitchen. This time she was much drunker and was accompanied by a group of equally smashed girls.

'GET A ROOM!' she yelled, before running a tap and filling cups of water for everyone around her. 'It's nice to finally meet you, Nate.'

'Hannah, right?' he said, handing her the wine he had brought. 'Happy birthday!'

'Ooh, I like you already!' said Hannah, as someone backed into her.

She turned around to cuss them while Nate and Tia laughed at the hot mess of a group, until Aaron shouted from the door, asking for his drink. His eyes darted from Nate's face to his hand around Tia's lower back, and he walked over with his chest held high and a smug grin.

'So you're the reason why T's been ghost!' he laughed. 'It's good to meet you, man. I'm Aaron.'

'Shut up, bruv,' said Tia.

'What? I'm playing, man,' chuckled Aaron, fixing himself a drink. 'Nah, but I've heard a lot about you, still.'

'All good things, I hope.'

'Of course. Heard you're doing bits with the whole photography thing, man. Sounds sick.'

'Ah, 'preciate it, man. I'm tryin'!'

'Must be lit, though. I peeped your work – you got all kinda gyal around. I think I may need to switch careers.'

Tia rolled her eyes as Aaron tried to get Nate to laugh along with him, nudging his shoulder with his fist.

'It ain't even like that, bro.' Nate smiled and shook his head. 'Gotta stay professional.'

'Yeah, not everyone thinks like you, Aaron,' said Tia, kissing her teeth.

'What! All those models and that? Shit's bound to happen sometimes, right?'

Tia flicked Aaron's ear and begged him to shut up, as Nate laughed it off, watching the two bicker. She was about to suggest they go into the next room to find Luca, until Jamal staggered in, abusing the lyrics to a J Hus song that was playing. He leaned against Aaron's shoulder, waiting to be introduced to the new face.

'What's good, bruva?' Jamal extended his hand and Nate shook it. 'I'm Jamal, but everyone calls me Money 'Mal.'

'No one calls you that,' said Hannah flatly.

The group sniggered as Tia whispered into Nate's ear about how Jamal had made a couple of grand off crypto and basically thought he was the black Bezos, making him laugh even more. Jamal tried to laugh along, telling everyone how much they needed to jump on NFTs, until he saw Nate say something back into Tia's ear with a devilish grin.

'Rah, so, Tia, is this you, yeah?' asked Jamal.

'What's with all these questions today, please?' she asked, looking to Hannah, who shook her head and smiled, not wanting any part of a conversation involving Jamal.

'What? Man can't be curious?'

'We're friends,' she replied with little enthusiasm.

'Ah, calm. So what you saying then, T. Can man get your Snap or . . . ?'

'Are you blind?' asked Hannah.

'Who asks for Snap post-2010, bro?' laughed Aaron.

'Ay, don't get involved, fam. She's not your problem anymore, you're all boo'd up now.'

Aaron's smile disappeared as Jamal carried on and on, dragging up memories of their puppy-love days, despite everyone telling him to shut up. Tia didn't know what she was waiting for, but Aaron's lack of protest kept her feet welded to the kitchen tiles.

'I think she's my problem now,' Nate loudly declared.

He threw his arm over her shoulder and gazed into her widened eyes. 'And I don't like sharing.'

Before Tia could pick her jaw up off the floor, Nate ushered her out of the kitchen. Her heart was beating so fast it felt as though it was about to leap out of her chest. She was furious at how, even after all these years, Aaron could never back her properly. Memories of his friends' piss-taking and his ability to dance around the topic of what she was to him came flooding back as if it were only yesterday. She hated how being around him long enough could transform her into feeling as small as she had when they'd first started this grey, blurry dance back in sixth form.

As she and Nate weaved between the sweaty dancers in the crowded living room, he perched himself on the sofa's empty armrest and pulled Tia close to him.

'I'm sorry about that. Jamal is such a dickhead. Don't lis—'

Nate cut her off with a peck and smiled at Tia.

'Let's just have a good time.'

He took a sip of his drink and tightened his grip around her waist, swaying her body along to the base-line of the music, as if he wanted to shake the tension out of her body. The room suddenly erupted when someone took hold of the aux and Juls's 'Wicked' started blaring through the soundbar. The two looked over and laughed at all the two-stepping, skanking bodies, with everyone from the kitchen returning to join in, Aaron included.

His eyes locked with Tia's straightaway, but her drunken pettiness took over, as she wrapped her arms around Nate's neck. She giggled as he nuzzled his face into her ear, encouraging her to let loose and have fun. Tia decided to go along with it, ignoring all the thoughts and questions that clouded her mind, relishing in Nate's ability to make her feel like the most important person in the room.

20

The party began to wind down at around 3 a.m. with the majority of the guests too drunk or high to carry on having a coherent conversation. Sean, Hannah's boyfriend, didn't look like he was planning to leave anytime soon, judging by the devilish grin he kept giving her when people started saying their goodbyes. Luca and a girl from their old form group were passed out on the two comfortable surfaces in Hannah's living room, and Aaron had left earlier than anticipated, though Tia had had no intention of asking him for a lift this time.

'Just come back to mine,' whispered Nate as Tia took the cigarette he was holding out towards her. 'No funny business, I swear,' he added with his arms held up in the air.

She laughed the smoke out of her chest and raised her eyebrow at him, trying to gauge how genuine he was being. He looked down at her with a screwface, pretending to be serious for just a moment, until it quickly melted into a smile. *Why can't I say no to you?* she thought. Before she could talk herself into sleeping on Hannah's kitchen counter, the raindrops she felt on her forehead quickly convinced her to just go home with the boy.

The rain began to pour as Nate's Uber drove them through the quiet, glossy backroads of Camberwell to his place in Greenwich. The hot air blasting from the car's heater made Tia's eyes feel even heavier; she drew random patterns in the condensation on the window beside her as Magic FM played quietly in the background. It wasn't until they had got out of the car that they realised the driver had in fact dropped them at the bottom of Nate's road, meaning they had to sprint through the rain all the way to his front door. He carefully draped his varsity jacket over Tia's curls, despite her protests, and they ran together hand in hand under the light of the dingy streetlamps. She shrieked as they inadvertently stomped in puddles, and he laughed at how much of a princess she was being. They giggled and shivered together when they finally reached the entrance of his basement flat, all sweaty from what had felt like a marathon, as Nate fiddled with the many sets of keys he had in his pocket.

The familiar but comforting scent of Dettol brushed past her nose as Nate quietly guided her through the dark corridor and into his bedroom, his index finger placed over his mouth, letting her know to tread lightly in case his mum was asleep. The bare walls and wooden laminate flooring made his bedroom feel colder than it was, and it didn't look as if he was totally settled in.

'I'll be right back,' he said in a hushed tone, excusing himself, though she was too distracted by the bits and pieces of his personality scattered throughout the room to reply, fascinated by this mini-museum of Nate. A collection of art and film books were carefully lined up on his IKEA desk. Beside them stood a novelty cup that looked like a massive DSLR lens filled with ballpoint pens and Sharpies, and his chair was draped in a chunky-knit cardigan Tia had never seen him in before. She was comforted by the toiletries that were prominently displayed on top of his dresser: deodorant, a tub of cocoa butter, another tub of Vaseline, an unopened bar of black soap, some Cantu hair creams, and a couple of bottles of cologne that weren't 1 Million by Paco Rabanne, much to Tia's delight.

Nate returned to the room while putting on a T-shirt, flashing the side of his lean, brown torso.

'You're soaking wet,' he said.

Tia widened her eyes then quickly realised he meant her outfit. 'Oh, yeah, right!' she said. 'Yeah, that rain was a joke.'

He pulled out the third drawer of his dresser and stared at its contents, before walking to his wardrobe and opening the doors, peering into the darkness. He crossed his arms and looked back at Tia, as if he was trying to suss something as she stood there, awkwardly staring back at his squinted eyes.

'What?'

'Hoodie? T-shirt?' Nate pulled Tia towards him and his clothes, resting his stubbly chin on her shoulder. 'Take your pick. What's mine is yours.'

'How generous.'

Goosebumps appeared on the back of her neck as he stood behind her, wrapping his arms around her torso as she deliberated what to slip into. She both loved and hated how her body instantly reacted to the littlest stimulus catalysed by his touch. It sometimes embarrassed Tia how apparently starved she had been of something as basic as the feeling of another person. But she couldn't help but relish his ceaseless endeavours to always be touching her in one way or another whether gripping her hand or his whisper tickling her ear in the corner of a dark, bustling room. She almost felt the feminism leave her body, the way she delighted in feeling so desired and wanted. Tia cleared her throat and shrugged him off, her attempt at playing it cool, as she reached for a green flannel shirt.

'You might not get this back,' she said, holding it up towards Nate's face, who didn't appear to mind Tia already threatening to steal his clothes.

'That's a risk I'm willing to take,' he laughed under his breath. 'I want you to be comfortable here.'

'Hmm. Hostess with the mostest.'

'So I've been told.'

Tia's eyes darted from the inside of his shirt drawer and found Nate's mischievous grin looking right back at her, always leaving her unsure of how serious he was being.

'Do you want to change in here and I'll leave? Or the bathroom maybe?' he asked, handing her a towel. 'Turns out my mum's at work, by the way, so don't worry about being quiet,' he reassured her.

She opted for the bathroom and scurried through the hallway following his directions, closing the door with the weight of her body. She stood there in the dark for a moment before pulling the light's string cord that dangled beside her, attempting to calm herself down, still in disbelief that she and Nate were about to be alone in his room all night. She peeled her damp clothes off of her body and inspected her goods in the mirror in front of her, readjusting her breasts so her bra straps would cut off her circulation a little less, and grabbing a handful of her ass as a way to convince herself that she did in fact have a sufficient amount of cheek. *Wait, what am I doing?* she asked her reflection. *No funny business!* She repeated this over and over as she threw her curls up into a pineapple.

When Tia returned to his room, dry and enveloped in that fresh laundry smell, she found Nate sitting by his desk, sprinkling tobacco into the crevice of a long light brown rolling paper, and humming along to the melody playing from his speaker.

'Nightcap,' he said without lifting his head.

She laid her clothes on the radiator before looking out of the window above it. The murky sky covered the bedroom in a deep periwinkle tinge, the kind that greeted you whenever you had stayed up for far too long.

'You can get into bed, you know. I'll be over in a sec,' he said.

'Oh, cool.'

Tia cleared her throat and crawled across the mattress, slipping herself beneath his grey jersey duvet. She tried to think rationally, reminding herself that this didn't have to mean anything. *But he's so cute,* she thought as she looked at the back of his head. *Just stay in the moment, T!* she begged herself, fearful that her overthinking would ruin what had been a pretty cool night.

In an effort to kill any bit of sexual tension, she decided to sit cross-legged on top of the duvet in the centre of the bed. Nate joined her, ashtray in hand, with the zoot hanging from his mouth, the tip of it glowing an orangey-red colour. He made himself comfortable once he'd handed it to Tia, and he started to play some more music from his phone, which was resting on the bedside table, lying down and singing a few lines of the bridge. It didn't take long for the weed to touch her, relaxing every muscle, quietening every irrational thought with each exhale.

'Glad you came back here? You probably would've had to sleep on top of Luca.'

'Either that or sneak into Hannah's mum's room,' she said, passing the zoot back to him. 'Actually, no. She and her boyfriend are pretty loud, I would've been traumatised, still.'

He grinned and shook his head. Tia stared at him, his mouth readying to say something.

'Nah, but your friends seem cool. That guy in the puffer was doing the most though.'

'That's Jamal for you.'

'You mean Money 'Mal,' said Nate, exhaling the smoke without trying to laugh it out. 'So, what – were you and that other guy a thing or . . . ?'

'Not really,' Tia cleared her throat. 'We're just friends.'

'Oh, swear. Like how we're "just friends" or . . . ?'

'What are you trying to say?'

She squinted her eyes at Nate who looked back at her with an equally mischievous grin.

'Just seemed like there was more to it.'

Tia looked at him to elaborate.

'Just the way he was looking at you. You women wouldn't get it but mandem know these things.'

Tia laughed and Nate did too. The look on his face seemed relaxed and nonchalant, like he always was. Too cool, too chill to ever seem like he was jarred or jealous in the slightest, but his tone said otherwise. Perhaps the drink from earlier had worn off, Tia thought, as she took the joint from his fingertips. She was frankly too mash-up to try and be three steps ahead of the conversation and work out where it was leading to, like she always did. How was she meant to tell the guy she currently liked that his assumption was accurate and there was more to it with Aaron?

'And what do you know?'

'That he probably hated the way I was all over you.'

'Ah, so that's why you were doing the most,' Tia said, passing the joint back.

'So there is more to it?'

'I didn't say that.'

'You didn't have to.'

'We're friends.' Tia rolled her eyes. 'He's not the relationship type, anyway.'

'Look, you don't owe me an explanation. I get it, trust me.'

But why don't I owe you an explanation? Tia thought to herself. Though Nate was technically right, she wanted him to demand an explanation, to give a damn, to be upset over the idea of someone else being in the exact place in her life that he was currently occupying.

'Things just get so messy when you try to put a label on it.'

'How so?' she asked.

'Like, all the rules and expectations that come with labelling it. Rather than just being, and enjoying the moment.'

Tia nodded. Nate rested his head against the head-board while she gathered her thoughts.

'There's nothing wrong with getting a clearer picture of what you mean to someone though, nah?'

'Hmm. But how does calling it something affect what you mean to them, if they're with you now?'

'I dunno. Sometimes it's just nice to know you belong to someone.'

'But why do we need to belong to anyone? Even saying that out loud, it just sounds so restrictive.'

Tia didn't know what to say. Nate wasn't wrong but she didn't think he was right either.

'Yet you were happy to call me "your problem" in front of everyone?' she retorted. 'What happened to "I don't like sharing"?'

Nate laughed as Tia finished smoking, taking the roach from her and putting it in the ashtray on his bed-side table.

'You didn't seem to complain.'

When the music had stopped, a silence washed over the room and Nate unlocked his phone to play some-thing else, until Tia rested her hand on his knee and pointed to her ear, her eyes closed. She always became extra sentimental whenever she was high. He smiled when he realised she meant the rain beating against the window and slapping the concrete that surrounded the quiet flat. It had got so heavy that it almost blurred into a constant but muffled hush, which was making Tia feel even sleepier. The muscles in her eyes and body felt heavy. She could've stayed in the same position forever, wrapping her arms around herself so she could force out a whiff of whatever fabric softener Nate used, until she felt a slight chill. She loosened her hair from her scrunchie and got on her knees to crawl back towards the pillow, when Nate tugged at her sleeve and sat up, his face just a few inches away from hers.

'Can I help you?' she asked.

The famished look in Nate's eyes caused a flutter in the pit of Tia's stomach, her indica-induced body suddenly awakened by anticipation. Her spine shivered as she felt his stubble graze her neck as he tried to search for more of the faded scent of her perfume, starting a trail of kisses from her jaw to her chest. She began to feel lightheaded, unable to tell whether it was from the zoot or the fact that she was turned on, and sat back on the soles of her feet, her hands down on either side of her, giving him full access to her body. Before he could plant another kiss, Tia lowered her face and their noses collided clumsily. She giggled as he laughed and kissed his teeth, placing his hands around the nape of her neck and pulling her in for a tender peck that ended way too soon. When their faces parted, she looked at his eyes gazing down at her plump lips, as if they were the last bite of his favourite dish. He studied them for a moment before pulling her back in for another and another, his hands sliding down to the back of her thighs, prompting her to get up and sit on his lap, which only intensified the heat between their adrenaline-fuelled bodies. His touch was soft but stern, the way he gently guided her legs around him, as if he couldn't bear to be even a centimetre apart from her, pulling her hips towards him as much as he possibly could. Part of her wanted all of this to stop, still ruminating on how little he seemed to care for defining whatever they were, something that had always been paramount to Tia. But the other part of her was too intoxicated by knowing just how much he wanted to consume her in this very moment. She was addicted to this feeling of physically belonging to him, even if just for a night.

Tia sank into Nate's embrace and wrapped her arms around his neck, her frame powerless to the feeling of his shaft pressing against her, his loins guiding her hips along to a rhythm that ensured she felt every hardened part of him, the thin strip of lace between her thighs getting wetter with every motion. She kissed his lips back even harder, until a moan escaped from her mouth – she was unable to hold it in any longer. With one hand still firmly guiding her body, he used the other to push her curls to one side and whispered into her ear, asking if it felt good, if he should keep going, but she was too entranced to give a coherent reply, nodding into the side of his assured face.

'Can we finish what we started?' he sighed while unbuttoning her shirt, his voice all croaky and parched, as if Tia were the only thing he wanted to drink. 'I want you so bad right now.'

The last time he had said that, Tia had bolted out of his studio in under two minutes flat after overhearing his cosy phone call with God-knows-who at one in the morning. Though she had no concrete proof, flashes of him being like this with a bunch of randoms started to trickle into her mind, until a sharp gasp escaped her. The feeling of Nate's fingers caressing her ripped her away from her anxieties, sending tremors of pleasure throughout her entire body.

'Is that a yes?'

She grabbed on to his shoulders to steady her weakened frame and nodded while writhing against his hand, following the feeling of him teasing her. 'Yes,' Tia breathed. She was tired of overthinking her way out of the happiness and excitement her friends always seemed to have so much more of. Whatever her and Nate were, they'd figure it out together in their own time.

21

The Bakerloo line journey from Charing Cross station to Oxford Circus was the same one Tia had taken most mornings over the past three years. She'd squeeze herself into the sweaty tube carriage full of recycled air and existential dread and mentally kiss her teeth at the receptionists and PR babes who used an extra seat for their gym bags. She'd roll her eyes at the toffs who insisted on fully extending their arms to read their subscription copies of the *Daily Telegraph* and give a lowkey screwface to people taking up too much space with their folded-up Bromptons and electric scooters. The eight-minute journey was usually so agonising that she'd try to mask the sinking feeling in the pit of her stomach with whatever Spotify recommended that day. She'd drag her feet up the stairs of the Underground and pull them across the pavement leading up to the office, begging the weight wrapped around her lungs to let go and disappear, as it always seemed to tighten itself whenever she looked up at the massive LCN letters above the glossy entrance doors.

But today was different: her breathing slowed down as she readied her ID badge, and her heart didn't race as much as usual while preparing for the morning meetings. She was somehow on top of her research tasks, and with help from Eloise she managed to keep a lid on all things related to the shoot. It was only two days away, and though the backdrops had twice been delivered to the wrong address and interviewees had been late to get back to her with their clothes sizes and dietary requirements, this was the first time Tia had actually felt excited for work – and it was for a story she had pitched. She finally felt as though she belonged to this place that had made her feel like an imposter for so long.

Even Gbemi noticed a difference, as they walked out of the analytics meeting together and beelined for their precious red sofa. There was only an hour or two left before the end of the day, and the office around them was abuzz with the promise of after-work pints and dinner reservations.

'You look knackered.'

'Cos I am,' sighed Tia. 'And I've still got more work to do.'

'Still, this shoot is gonna be so sick.'

'Hopefully. Camilla's been acting mad weird, though. I've hardly seen her about.'

'Ain't that a good thing though?'

'It is. It's been nice not having her on my back, still.'

'Petra's been on one though. She's been seeing this new guy and hasn't shut up about it since.'

'Oh my days, is that why she's been more peppy than usual?'

'She's deffo getting her back cracked on the regular.'

Tia cackled into her mug. 'Who's the lucky guy then?'

'I dunno. Probably some other journo from around here. You know how she stays, forever mixing business with pleasure.'

'Speaking of new bae . . .' Tia sat up and slapped Gbemi's legs. 'What's yours saying?'

Gbemi struggled to keep a straight face, as she grinned into her mug. 'I don't know what you mean,' she said, trying her hardest to avoid Tia's mischievous glare.

'I saw an elbow in your Story last night. I know a soft launch when I see it, bitch!'

Gbemi giggled into the air before unlocking her phone and showing Tia the latest restaurant her new ting had taken her to. She had met David at a mutual friend's baby shower, not long after her hellish date with the weirdo from church, and they'd immediately hit it off. He ticked all of her parents' boxes, meaning he was Nigerian, had a decent job and knew the Lord, but he was also tall, leng and had banter for days, ticking all of Gbemi's boxes. Since then, it had been weekends of fun dates and sweet late-night phone calls that almost made Tia forget all about Gbemi's often-cynical ways. She rambled on about his latest 'good morning' text between toothy grins, as she swiped through photos of edible-gold starters and Boomerangs of cocktails puffing out clouds of smoke – and it suited her, being so happy and loved up and doted on.

'So LCN's City Girl is no more?'

'I am dead,' laughed Gbemi. 'We still got you out here, nah?'

'I wish.' Tia kissed her teeth. 'I'm down bad. And I don't even know how it happened.'

'You say that like it's a bad thing.'

'It is when you don't know what the fuck is going on.'

As much as Tia wanted to let go and be in the moment, basking in the glow of what had been an amazing night with Nate, she couldn't shake off the weight of not knowing what they were or what they were doing. She hadn't heard from him since the morning after their first night together, and she wasn't sure what to make of it all.

'Have you guys *ever* spoken about what you are to each other?'

'Not really. I mean, he said he wanted to be more than friends *once*. But that was ages ago – does that count?'

Gbemi shook her head. 'You know you have to talk to him, right?'

Tia groaned before taking a gulp of her tea. 'I hate initiating. Like, surely he's wondering the same things too?'

'He either hates initiating just as much you—'

'Not when it comes to being in bed though.'

'Or he has no idea what he wants and doesn't know how to say it.'

'Then where does that leave me? If he doesn't know what he wants.'

'It leaves you in charge. You want someone to be sure of you, that's, like, the bare minimum. And if he can't even give you that, you cut.'

'Do I have to cut?'

'Yes, you have to cut. No matter how fire that head was.' Tia squealed into her hand as Gbemi began to laugh. 'But on a real, this will remain a situationship unless someone makes the first move.'

It jarred Tia how they could make out in front of strangers at a party, or pull off each other's pants in the middle of his workplace, but when it came to their real feelings they both walked on eggshells and held their cards close to their chests, disguising their thoughts in between debates and hypotheticals. But Gbemi was right, Tia thought, annoyed, on the walk back to her desk: the only way out of this grey area was to tell Nate how she felt, though the mere thought of that made her want to throw up.

Work was a welcome distraction, as Tia whizzed

through the edits Petra had wanted on a piece they were finishing up. She had always tried her best to avoid conversations bordering on anything remotely personal, as much as Petra tried to take it there. It wasn't until Petra had asked Tia what she was up to after work that she fell into the trap and had to ask her back.

'What about you?'

'Oh, I've got a hot date.' Petra grinned while brushing her hair out by Tia's desk. 'D'you like spicy food?'

'Yeah, love it,' Tia answered.

'I thought so! This guy's taking me to some Chinese restaurant and everything on the menu is spicy – I just don't think I'll be able to hack it!'

'Oh, I'm sure you'll be fine. What's a hot date without a little spice?' Tia laughed off.

'Oh my gosh, that's hilarious,' giggled Petra. 'I'll have to steal joke that for tonight!'

'It's all yours.'

Petra continued babbling about the other things her and this guy were gonna get up to as she continued getting ready at her desk. She carefully applied her signature lipstick, an orangey-red shade that always seemed a little too bright for Petra's oat-milk complexion, and loudly smacked her lips in front of her handheld mirror. Tia smiled and nodded at whatever Petra was saying until she finally said her goodbyes and disappeared off to the crowded toilets to finish primping.

Tia's last task of the day before she could head home

consisted of ringing all the contributors for a final chat before the shoot, confirming their arrival times and talking them out of any nerves. She left Cheryl till last, who thankfully sounded excited for the day ahead and had hardly any questions.

'Though the interview portion will be touching on important topics, I just wanted to reassure you that the shoot itself is going to be super chill. We just want you and Shannon to be comfortable.'

'Thank you, Tia. I really appreciate that,' said Cheryl.

'You're so welcome.'

'Because I can't lie to you, when that Camilla rang it did get my back up a bit. Which was why we pulled out in the first pl—'

'So sorry to cut you – when Camilla rang?' Tia's stomach clenched as she whipped her feet off her desk and sat up in her chair. 'When did that happen?'

'It was after our first interview with you. She was very pleasant, don't get me wrong!' Cheryl explained. 'But when she started chatting about what could happen to Shannon for taking part, I guess it just freaked me out a bit.'

'No, I can imagine.'

'But after hearing you and Nathaniel explain it, I felt much more at ease. I'm glad we're doing this now.'

'Well, I'm happy to hear that,' said Tia, trying her best to remain upbeat until they said their goodbyes.

Tia sighed as she put down the desk phone's receiver,

playing with its spiral cord, trying to breathe in through her nose and out through her mouth. The confidence she had felt that morning suddenly became a distant memory, as she asked herself why Camilla would speak to a contributor without even telling her first. She wondered whether Eloise had had any idea, but recalling how equally sick she'd looked when they were trying to win Cheryl back, she decided there was no way she could've known. Tia prepared to log off, until she saw the green icon by Yvonne's name for the first time in ages. She knew no one else could advise on her on how to deal with Camilla better than Yvonne, and quickly messaged her to see if she was free for a chat. Yvonne immediately rang Tia's phone, ordering her to come to her desk.

22

Tia arrived on the seventh floor and scurried to its furthest corner by the windows that overlooked Regent Street. Despite it being an open-plan office, Yvonne's corner was clearly distinct from the rest of the desks that surrounded it. She shared a row that would typically fit about four members of staff with just her long-time producer, meaning she had ample space for all her trinkets and finery. Beside her desk stood several pots of orchids and whatever extravagant bouquet of flowers she'd been gifted that week, be it from her latest beau or a PR executive trying to win her favour. Her landline phone was nestled among a lavish bottle of hand cream and framed pictures of herself with memorable interviewees, such as Michelle Obama, Karl Lagerfeld, Whitney Houston, Ai Weiwei and Kermit the Frog. Beneath her desk you could always find a Jimmy Choo shoebox or three, as she was forever running from a press luncheon to a premiere and then back to the office again.

Yvonne sat in her chair with her knees pulled up to herself, scribbling red ink onto a stack of stapled papers. In front of her sat her trusty Eau de Nil teapot accompanied by two matching cups and saucers. Though it had been decades since she'd stepped on a catwalk, her style and eternal chicness never left her. Yvonne's personal uniform of a blouse tucked into wide-leg trousers always had these special touches that made her stand out. Today's silky edition comprised poet sleeves and a lavallière tie, its ivory colour making her deep-brown skin tone glow even more than it usually did. Her heeled pumps lay sloppily on the floor below her, as if she'd stepped right out of them and had fallen into her seat, and her thick glasses were perched on the tip of her nose, as she crossed out a word and circled another.

When she realised Tia had arrived, Yvonne immediately threw her papers down and stood up in her pop-socked feet, pulling her in for a long, hard squeeze, enveloping Tia in the smoky, pomegranate Jo Malone scent she always wore.

'Oh! How are you, my darling?!'

When they parted, she gestured with her chin towards a metal cabinet, a signal Tia understood all too well, and she immediately fetched a Charbonnel et Walker box from the second drawer, before sitting in the empty

chair beside Yvonne, who was already pouring chamo-
mile tea into the delicate cups in front of them.

'You look amazing, as ever,' said Tia.

'I don't bloody feel like it,' Yvonne huffed. 'This
script is doing my head in. Loved it a few nights ago
and now I can't stand it. Typical!'

'Is this for the BBL documentary?'

Yvonne nodded and began divulging horror stories
and details of botched surgery victims and fraudulent
doctors across the globe, then stopped herself before
she spoiled the ending, urging Tia to watch it the
second it was out.

'I also have another bit of big news but you have to
promise to keep it to yourself?'

Yvonne held out her little, manicured finger and Tia
met it with her own to confirm the binding pinky
swear.

'You could be looking at LCN's next Arts editor.'

Tia gasped. 'No way! Yvonne, that's huge. What happened to Rupert Spencer, though? I didn't think he'd
leave that role until he dies, which . . . with the way he
looks, seems like it'd be pretty soon.'

'That relic's days were numbered ever since he
stopped being a functioning alcoholic.'

'Well, congratulations! This is amazing news.'

'It's not official yet!' She laughed. 'I've heard they're
considering two other people but I've had some great
conversations with Simon Boden lately. He can't get

enough of all the work I've been doing with LCN Lead.'

'And now it's paying off.'

'Precisely.'

'I mean, that sounds pretty official to me,' Tia said excitedly, though Yvonne tried to dismiss it. 'Plus there's no one of your calibre here, it's a no-brainer. When do we find out officially then?'

'Hopefully by the time I'm in Saint Barts. I'd love to celebrate in that sea and sunshine; I'm literally counting down the days!' Yvonne folded her manicured hands in her lap. 'Now, enough about that. Give me an update, what have you been up to?'

Tia started on a good note and spoke about having made it to the final round of the interviews for the promotion. Then she told her about the shoot, and how, even though she was filled with anxiety, she had never been more excited about work. When she moved on to reveal the real reason she was there, detailing Camilla's -isms and schisms, and the way she'd nearly jeopardised the shoot, Yvonne started side-eyeing and nodding, as if she had heard and seen it all before. It filled Tia with a strange calmness that reassured her that she wasn't going crazy or blowing things out of proportion, that her frustrations were valid.

'Oh, darling,' Yvonne sighed. 'I mean, it's definitely unorthodox. Especially to do that without telling you – it's your story and she should respect that.' Tia could feel a 'but' coming on. 'But unfortunately, I can't guarantee this kind of behaviour won't happen again at a place like this.'

'So it doesn't get any better?'

Yvonne smiled. 'I'd be lying to you if I said it did.' Tia sank in her chair a little and continued listening. 'Don't get me wrong, once you climb through the ranks there'll definitely be less of these petty battles. But again, I'd be lying to you if I said there wouldn't be any battles, period.'

'So what do I do?' asked Tia, staring into her cup.

'Choose them wisely. Despite that nightmare of a manager's meddling, you got Cheryl back and everything's on track, right?'

Tia nodded.

'Then I'd say it's best not to rock the boat, for now.'

'What? And roll over and let her win?'

Yvonne placed her cup back on its saucer and leaned in closer to Tia, looking deep into her brown eyes. 'For us, it's always about the long game. It may feel like you've let her win now, but it won't feel that way once you've bagged that promotion.'

Tia gulped her drink down at the thought of her final interview in a few weeks, having to sit across from the witch who had tried to sabotage her project. Yvonne got up from her seat and walked towards the window, wistfully looking out at the black cabs and double-decker buses whizzing up and down the road.

'After twenty years at this place, it breaks my heart how some things still haven't changed.' She looked down at the window ledge, overcrowded with an array of glass awards and golden plaques, her name and her programmes' titles engraved on each and every one of them. 'You'd think by now I could just waltz into any job I'd like around here, but no: still vying against someone's random mate from Bullingdon,' she added in a hushed tone.

Tia shook her head as Yvonne sat back down by her desk. 'How do you do it?' she asked. 'There's literally no one better for any job.'

'I don't even know sometimes.' Yvonne laughed to herself and looked around at the empty office floor. 'I've been here for so long. It'd feel strange to say good-bye and leave it all behind.'

She was right, Tia thought to herself, an LCN report without Yvonne would feel unnatural. An exclusive interview or a primetime documentary without the sight of her iconic bob haircut or the sound of her rich laugh would be downright dull and lifeless. She was the face of LCN – or rather, the face LCN liked to use despite the glaringly different shades of their directors and board members. And yet even she was susceptible to the bullshit politics that went on throughout the place. Tia hated that Yvonne was still so gracious about it all, even though she had every right to be angry.

'You deserve all the flowers, I hope you know that. A lot of us wouldn't even be here if it wasn't for you.'

'And that's why I'm still here! Working my arse off in all this leadership lark,' Yvonne cackled, and leaned back in her chair, popping a chocolate truffle into her mouth. 'I can't let you girls down now, can I?'

23

Tia had already starting rubbing dollops of cocoa butter into her freshly washed skin when the sound of her phone's alarm began to blare through its speaker. She quickly ran over to her bed to turn it off, before swiping the screen down to see if there was a notification from Nate. *It's not like he could forget about today – he's probably prepping as we speak,* she told herself, tapping on the Spotify icon.

She played some music on a low volume and threw on a grey hoodie, then sat down on the floor in front of her mirror with all her tools and creams laid out beside her. She brushed her damp curls up into a pineapple bun, concentrating on the back and sides to ensure she smoothed out any kinks, before taking a toothbrush and dipping it into her green tub of hair gel. She smoothed down her edges as best she could, still never able to get the perfect swoop and swirls she desired, no matter how many tutorials she watched. Tia dotted and blended concealer over her under-eye circles and dark marks, keeping the rest of her make-up minimal: she flicked a few hair strokes into her soap-laden brows, dabbed a tint over the apples of her cheeks and her pout, and coated her non-existent lashes with a cheap black mascara (which was nearly drying out so made them look a bit clumpy, just how she liked them). She shimmied her thighs into her khaki cargo trousers with all the extra pockets – her favourite for shoot days – and slipped her feet into a pair of Vans, before looping her trusty pair of gold hoops into her ear lobes. She gave herself a final approving gaze in the mirror.

During that morning's routine, Tia tried to rationalise herself out of an anxiety attack, reminding herself that she'd been on plenty of shoots before, and that every item she had written on her checklist was already packed in the suitcase she'd prepared the night before. Today's shoot was the first piece of work she was finally proud of producing in all her three years as a researcher. It was her baby and her fantasy melded into one, and she also knew how important this project was to Shannon, Cheryl and the rest of the women who had graciously put their trust in Tia to tell this story properly: she didn't want to let them down. Today had to be perfect.

When she got to Hannah's, Eloise had just arrived, and waved at Tia from the doorstep.

'Today's the day!' Hannah beamed, welcoming the girls into her living room, its floors covered in glossy branded bags that Hannah was putting into laundry bags to transport to the shoot. Eloise still couldn't believe FUNKI were letting them use so many nice things, and asked Hannah how she'd managed to pull this off.

'Oh, they don't know about this,' she laughed. 'I've been teefin' these all week for this shoot, babe.'

'Oh my God, won't you get into trouble?'

'Yeah, Han. I ain't tryna get you fired, bruv,' added Tia.

'Listen, once they notice their shit on a whole LCN feature, they'll have no choice but to give me a real job.'

Hannah zipped the last laundry bag and handed it to Tia, noticing the way she was chewing on her bottom lip and fidgeting with the sleeve of her hoodie. She nudged Tia to stop and wrapped her arms around her shoulders.

'Today's going to be amazing. You've got this.' Tia relaxed herself into Hannah's small frame and exhaled. 'I'll be down before it's over, 'kay?'

She nodded as they parted and looped the remaining bags over her arms before air-kissing Hannah goodbye and hopping into the Uber with Eloise. On their way to the studio, they went through the order of events for the day twice, discussing what to order for lunch and whether they had adequate vegan options for one of their guests. The girls arrived at the studio a little after 8.30, which gave them a solid hour-and-a-half of prep time before their first guests were due to arrive.

The steel street door to the studio was already opened, the thumping bass of a Kaytranada song echoing down the stairwell. The girls piled inside with the clothes and accessories and threw the bags down by the empty rails in the corner of the room, before looking around at the airy space. Though Tia had been there on multiple occasions, it felt like a totally different place when it was rearranged for work, almost a world away from all the memories she had already made between the brick walls.

'It looks even better in person,' said Eloise, walking over to the plants on the windowsill.

A dressing table was positioned near the rails, its surface emanating a lemony-bleach scent, and the dazzling lightbulbs around the mirror were already switched on. She began to walk towards the other side of the room to see where Nate was, when he emerged from behind a door. The stunned expression on his face confused her a little but she smiled at him, and he eventually grinned the closer he got to her.

'Hey, stranger.'

'Morning,' he said.

'Didn't realise today was still happening – you've been mad ghost lately,' she joked.

'My bad,' he laughed and rubbed his eyes. 'You know how I get when I'm working.'

Why is he being so . . . off? Tia asked herself. It's not like she was expecting a declaration of how much he'd missed her or anything, but his disposition was strange, distant even. They had barely spoken since the morning after Hannah's birthday, yet he was acting so blasé about it.

'Tia?'

'Sorry,' she mumbled, stopping herself from staring at him. 'What were you saying?'

'Do you guys need anything?' he asked. 'I just need to go to my car real quick.'

'Oh, um. Maybe a steamer, if you have it? Or even an iron will do. Hannah's one was way too heavy to bring.'

'Sure.'

He walked past her to a large cupboard by the kitchenette and dragged out a clunky-looking grey machine. He saw the look on Tia's face and immediately reassured her that despite its ancient appearance, it was pretty reliable, and warned the girls how hot it got.

Before she could thank him, a girl holding a large mug emerged through the door, moaning about a headache. Her face was bare and her dark fluffy coils were teased out into a mini afro. Bamboo hoop earrings hung from her lobes and matched the multiple rings she wore on her fingers, and it looked as though she had got the memo about dressing comfy: she was wearing a baggy T-shirt, jogging bottoms and a pair of Air Forces.

'Oh shit, sorry. Didn't know other people were here!' she laughed, revealing her pierced tongue, and extended her hand. 'Hi, I'm Jada. Tia, right?'

'Hi, yeah. It's nice to meet you.' Tia smiled, shaking her hand.

'She'll be assisting me today,' Nate added.

'I fucking love your hair, man. What do you use?' asked Jada, looking up at the curls piled on top of Tia's head. 'Because I've been tryna do this natural thing, but it is long as fuck!'

Tia laughed and immediately began listing all her favourite products and potions, when Nate interrupted their chatter. 'Just remember, we're here to work, yeah?' he joked. 'I'm gonna get some more stuff from my car.'

'Erm, where was that energy last night?' she shouted as he walked out of the room, laughing. She turned to Tia and let her in on the joke. 'Coming from the guy doing shots till three, you know.'

'Oh, so that's why he's quiet today,' said Tia, to which Jada nodded, rolling her eyes before walking over to Eloise to introduce herself properly.

As soon as Nate came back, two large rolls of fabric in his arms, everyone got to work, while the bassy music continued to blast throughout the studio. Jada followed him to the set next door, helping with the lighting and backdrops, while Tia and Eloise laid out their laptops and folders containing all their essential documents: details of everyone's allergies, health and

safety assessment forms, and the all-important schedule for the day. Soon after, they unpacked the rest of
the garments and hung them on the steel rails, dividing
them into sections for each of their guests, and steamed
all the oversized shirts, flowy dresses and satin pieces.
Tia smiled as she worked the wrinkle out of a pair of
trousers, mentally reminding herself to thank Hannah
until the end of time for nailing the brief. She'd wanted
the clothes to be comfortable but soft and elegant-
looking, in a creamy, natural colour palette that would
make everyone's skin pop, seeing as Nate was so skilled
at capturing complexions. Tia had sent them both a
screenshot from a Solange music video that she badly
wanted to recreate for the shoot, knowing it'd be
achievable even on the measly budget Camilla had
allotted for the project. Tia checked the time on her
phone before noticing Jada putting on her jacket. The
door she'd come through was ajar, giving Tia a glimpse
of Nate pacing up and down the room.

'Just going shop – d'you guys need anything?' she
asked.

'Ooh, can I tag along?' said Eloise, before turning
to Tia. 'Just gonna get some snacks. Everyone will be
arriving soon and it'll be a while till we break for lunch.'

'Good idea,' she nodded. 'LCN's card is in the
folder.'

Though the music kept playing, the room felt quiet
to Tia, as she ran the steamer over the sleeve of a shirt,

resisting every urge she had to bounce over to Nate and see what he was doing. Despite his apparent hangover, she still thought he was behaving oddly. Even the various questions he'd asked while everyone was busy preparing had been directed mainly at Eloise, as if he was trying to avoid Tia. She glanced over at the sofa and shook her head, remembering how her legs had been up in the air the last time she was on it. *How does he do this?* she thought. One minute they were waking up together, the next he was drawing a line. Tia closed her eyes and shook her head in an attempt to refocus. *I've got this,* she told herself. *May the spirits of Elaine and Edward guide me,* she recited, hoping to channel her favourite fashion mavens, until she heard her name being called from the set.

'We're almost ready,' Nate said as Tia walked through the door. 'Just wanted your final approval. What do you think?'

A swathe of heavy oat-coloured linen hung over the backdrop stand. Parts of it were pinched in certain places, creating a pleated effect that Tia loved. The excess material that spilled to the ground was artfully laid out and bunched up beneath a few floor cushions. A wooden stool had been placed in the centre, and beside it stood a glass vase with feathery pampas grass sprouting from it. She smiled, seeing all the details she had mentioned to Nate in emails and sporadic texts laid out in front of her.

'It's perfect.'

He began to ramble on about other fabrics and rolls of satin he had, pointing to the ones he had rested against the brick wall behind them. For the first time since she had known him, he sounded a bit nervous – it was his first real commission after all. It comforted Tia, knowing he was just as anxious as she was about pulling this shoot off successfully.

'No, no. I love it, seriously. It looks amazing.'

She folded her arms, still gazing at the fruits of their labour, and let out a sigh of relief.

'You good?' he asked.

'Mmm.' Tia nodded. 'Are you?'

'Why wouldn't I be?'

'I dunno.' She cleared her throat and looked at the floor. 'You're just bare quiet today. Making me feel like I've done something, or whatever.'

Nate looked into her eyes for a moment before cracking a smile she knew all too well, and he pulled Tia's arm for a hug, wrapping her arms around his waist. She couldn't help but nuzzle her face into his neck as the firm feeling of his embrace and the smell of his spicy cardamom cologne began to immediately ease all the nerves she was feeling for the day ahead. Tia wanted to stay like that for ever, until he squeezed her sides harder, roughly swaying her body from side to side.

'What are you doing, bruv?' she gasped, barely able to get a word out.

'I'm tryna get you out of your head.'

'By suffocating me?!'

'Is it working?' he laughed.

'Just move from me, man!'

He groaned as she squeezed him back, until they finally parted, his arms draped over her shoulders, his eyes fixed on her gaze.

'Today's gonna be sick, okay? You've got this.'

There was something about Nate's earnest way of encouraging her that made Tia feel uneasy. Partly because she had no idea what they were, so she didn't know what to expect from their relationship. She had never really had anyone, bar Luca or Hannah, who'd wanted to be there for her so badly. In theory, it felt good, having someone to lean on, but she feared getting used to the feeling, in case it might disappear one day. However, today it felt so good that she couldn't help but embrace it.

'We've got this.'

He grinned at her and lowered his head to hers, readying his lips for a kiss, when they heard someone by the door. The two turned and immediately sprang back from each other when they saw Eloise, who was desperately trying to hold back a grin. She playfully looked away, then looked back at Tia's blushing face.

'Sorry to disturb!' Eloise cleared her throat. 'But, um, our first guest will be here in a sec.'

'Right, yes!' Tia stared at the ground while marching out of the room. 'Cool. Let's do this, team.'

'Cool. I'll be out in a sec,' said Nate, sounding like he was dying to laugh.

'Cool, cool. Great!' Tia shouted as Eloise began to tease her.

'I fucking knew it!' she hissed. '"Just a friend" my arse.'

'Can we not do this right now?' begged Tia, rifling through the documents beside their laptops in an attempt to maintain some professionalism.

'I wanna know everything!'

Tia burst out laughing and swatted Eloise away from her, when their first guests came through the doors. She beamed at Shannon, guiding her plump, cardigan-wrapped mum into the studio. Shannon's hair was styled into two juicy-looking afro puffs, which almost matched the size of her cheeks, still shiny from the cream she had rubbed into her face before leaving her house that morning. She looked adorable, and a far cry from the video of her that had circulated the internet – but all that would be a distant memory by the time their project had been published, Tia hoped.

24

All the worries and anxieties Tia had started the day with faded as more of the women she had been speaking to for so long arrived at the studio, the room abuzz with their chatter and excitement. Their conversations ranged from how nervous they were about being photographed professionally for the first time to whether the camera really did add ten pounds, sharing woes over being interrogated at work over their wig choices and hair lengths. On the sofa, one of the country's only Black female university lecturers, who wore her locs in an intricate updo, was giggling with a twenty-something influencer about the havoc she used to wreak back in her heyday as a British Black Panther member. Leanne the PhD student was marvelling at all the clothes on the rails with an activist art student Tia had met last year at an event Yvonne had brought her along to.

Once Shannon had changed into her outfit, she slowly walked out of the bathroom, everyone waiting with bated breath. She immediately walked over to the full-length mirror by the window and smiled at her reflection, playing with the fluffy layers of tulle that made up her baby-pink skirt. She was still wearing the grey hoodie she had arrived in, even though Cheryl had begged her to change into some of the fancier things that hung on the rail. Tia and Nate approved of the contrasting combination though.

'You look so sick!' said Tia from behind her. 'Do you feel good?'

Shannon nodded.

'Do you feel comfy?'

She turned to Tia and nodded again, playing with the drawstrings of her hoodie.

'Good. That's all that matters. We wanted to keep things simple because we want you to be the focus. We want everyone to see just how beautiful you and your hair are – is that cool with you?'

Shannon gave a loud and resounding, 'Yes!', making everyone laugh. 'That's cool with me.' she added.

She looked at herself once more in the mirror and teased her afro puffs a little more, then stood to attention. Tia guided her and Cheryl onto the set, where Nate and Jada welcomed the two with massive smiles and praise for Shannon's courage. Nate guided her to the stool and took a few test shots, then told everyone they were about to begin. Shannon was a little stiff at first, posing as if it were a school picture day, until Jada got involved, shouting random quotes from *America's*

Next Top Model and hyping Shannon, making everyone laugh and loosen up until they began to get the money shots. Even Cheryl jumped in for a few photos, her matching afro puffs too good not to photograph.

A little before midday, Eloise and Tia headed for the high street, and returned with stacks of brown oil-stained boxes filled with freshly baked pizzas, courtesy of LCN's company card. Tia scribbled the toppings onto the lids, clearly labelling which one was vegan, and laid out them side by side on the kitchenette counter, buffet style, while Eloise tore open packets of paper plates and serviettes.

Some guests began helping themselves, but then Tia noticed she couldn't see Nate or Jada, so she walked over to the set to call them in. Nothing could've prepared her for what she walked in on. Their backs were turned to Tia while they were being talked at by Petra, who stood between them. She covered her orangey-red lips with her hand, trying to contain a laugh, slapping Nate's shoulder like she had done the first time they had met. She stopped when she spotted Tia standing by the door and the other two turned around.

'Hey, girl! I was wondering where you'd gone off to.'

'Well, this is a surprise.' Tia plastered on a grin. 'What are you doing here?'

'You need to check your emails, babes!' Petra joked, closely following Nate and Jada out to the kitchen area. 'I'm totally kidding. Camilla just wanted someone to check in on you guys.'

'Oh. That's um . . . nice of her. D'ya hear that, Lou?'

Eloise nodded, though she looked just as baffled as Tia.

'So if you need any help today, do give us a shout. I brought my laptop to do some work but I'll be around.'

'Oh, you don't need to be stuck here babysitting!' laughed Tia. 'It's been great. We're about half an hour behind schedule but other than tha—'

'Listen, it's your first commission. Don't beat yourself up for running over slightly!' said Petra, resting her hand on Tia's shoulder. 'Besides, I'm sure Nate won't mind if we run a little late, right?'

She grinned in his direction as he picked up a plate, ogling the array of pizzas. *Who's we?* Tia thought to herself. She smiled and nodded Petra away, unwilling to drag the conversation out any longer, and grabbed her coat on her way out of the studio doors, patting down its pockets to feel for her lighter and cigarettes. She popped a cigarette into her mouth on her way down to the street and shook her Clipper before igniting the tip. A few seconds later, the door creaked open and Jada slid out with a cigarette of her own. She beamed when she saw Tia and joined her by the ivy-covered brick walls.

'You are hilarious,' she said.

'What d'you mean?' Tia laughed.

'Your face when you saw that girl? If looks could kill, boy.'

'That obvious, huh?' Tia took a pull of her cigarette as Jada started laughing. 'She's just a lot. She's calm, but in small doses, innit.'

'Nah, I feel you. She's a lot calmer today though. Maybe she's still hung-over too.'

'What do you mean?'

Before Jada could answer, her coat pocket began to vibrate, and she excused herself to take the call. She threw her remaining cigarette on the ground before going back into the building, leaving Tia alone, baffled at what she had just heard. When she returned upstairs to the studio, Petra was stood by the sink as Nate was filling the kettle, chatting with her between getting everyone's drink requests in. It wasn't unusual for Petra to beg friends, especially if they were remotely Black-looking, Tia told herself. But their closeness still made her feel uneasy.

Despite Petra's presence, the rest of the day flew by, as Tia flitted between the set and the other room with the rest of contributors, ensuring everyone was happy and had enough to eat and drink. She often stood by the tethered laptop, looking between its screen and the set in front of her, already loving everything Nate was capturing. Together they had already decided on their favourites between preparing for the next person to shoot, as Eloise shrieked at how good everyone looked. Some photos were full of toothy grins and belly laughs, others were of the women lounging on the cushions among the lush pampas grass looking serene or moody, everybody's varying brown skin tones glowing beneath the studio lights that shone above them. It was everything Tia could've hoped for, and she couldn't remember the last time she was this happy at work.

After saying their final goodbyes and walking everyone down to the street, Eloise and Tia gave each other a high five as they returned to the empty-looking studio, and collapsed onto the leather sofa. Tia let out a huge sigh, still in disbelief that the day she had waited so long for was finally done. They helped each other off the seats and began to gather the laundry bags from the corner of the room, then carefully removed the clothes from the hangers and folded them away. Halfway through tidying the room, Tia felt someone hug her from behind. When she turned around, she was relieved to see Hannah's face, who joined the girls loading up the laundry bags.

'How you gonna get home with all this stuff?' Tia asked. 'I can book an Uber with my work's card if you wa—'

'Nah, you're good. I already called Aaron to meet me here.'

'Aaron?'

'Yeah. He wanted to see you on your big day. Plus, he hasn't got much going on these days so I was like, why not?'

'What d'you mean?'

'He quit his job, remember?'

'What?! He only told me he was thinking about it.'

'Rah, I thought you'd be the first to know,' laughed Hannah.

'Wow. I didn't think he'd actually follow through with it though.'

'And he had a huge argument with Olivia,' added Hannah. 'He didn't tell her until he'd handed in his resignation letter, and she flipped.'

A few months ago, news like that would've delighted Tia, but now she didn't know what to feel. The times she had already spent with Nate had almost caused whatever attachment Tia had left for Aaron to fade away.

Eloise and Tia zipped up the last bags and dragged them over to the studio's entrance when Hannah pulled a dark green bottle out of her tote bag, waving it at the girls and shaking her hips as they giggled at her. Tia took it from her hands and inspected the goods: Aldi's finest Prosecco.

'To celebrate your first big feature – hello!' Hannah winked.

The three walked over to the kitchenette as Tia shouted for Nate, Jada and (reluctantly) Petra to come over and join them, who all looked ecstatic to see some alcohol. Everyone cheered at the popping sound of the cork, and Tia began pouring the bubbly liquid gold into the few plastic cups they had left from the shoot, as everyone chatted, when she noticed they were three cups short.

'I'm happy to drink from the bottle!' Tia laughed, and turned to Nate. 'But we're still gonna need more – got any?'

Before he could nod, an arm from the other side of Nate shot up in the air.

'Oh, I'll get them!' Petra declared. 'Since I'm already so close.'

She strutted to a cupboard and fished out a pair of glasses, keeping one for herself and handing another to Nate with a smile that felt like they shared a secret, an inside joke no one else knew. Tia could feel the stares and side-eyes from Hannah and Eloise as she poured what was left of the Prosecco, before clearing her throat and lifting the bottle.

'Thank you, guys, for today,' said Tia. 'I couldn't have done it without you all and I can't wait to see what we've done on big LCN!'

She took a swig as everyone toasted and began chatting among themselves, and Tia overheard Petra's sniggering. She was on her tiptoes talking into Nate's ear; the rim of Nate's cup was resting between his teeth and his other hand was placed firmly in his pocket as he was half-heartedly listening.

'What were you saying last night about seven years?' Petra giggled. 'Was it seven years of bad luck?'

'Bad sex, actually,' Tia piped up without even thinking, her face beginning to burn.

She looked up at Nate who quickly replaced the stunned look on his face with a forced grin, his jaw tensing. His natural urge to bulldoze a conversation with random facts he knew and segues about a famous client he'd once worked with suddenly wasn't there anymore. Petra giggled even more and grabbed hold of Nate's arm.

His inability to meet her eye was all the confirmation she needed. Tia knew something had happened. The sudden realisation felt like a punch to the stomach, and she took another swig of Prosecco as Petra digressed about the time she'd randomly moved to Berlin for a summer. Nate continued to feign interest in her babbling. Everyone's chatter and the music that thumped from the speakers began to blur into one dreary sound as Tia stared at the girls in front of her, trying her best to concentrate on whatever they were talking about. But she couldn't stop connecting the dots over and over again in her mind, asking herself all sorts of questions that only Nate would know the answer to. Questions she didn't have any real right to ask him.

Hannah took hold of Tia's shoulder, as if she'd been calling her name for ages. 'You good, sis?' she asked. Tia grinned and nodded before excusing herself to go the bathroom. After washing her hands four times, she opened the door and saw Nate leaning against a wall.

'I know you're vex.'

'I'm not vex,' she said, walking past him.

He rubbed the back of his head and followed her out to the wider studio space. Tia looked around and noticed a few people were missing. Petra sat at the wooden table, typing something on her laptop and looked up.

'El had to leave but your friend's waiting for you downstairs.'

'Oh, cool. You're not leaving yet?'

'I actually need to discuss something with Nate.' Petra gave a smug grin that made Tia recoil. 'Some upcoming projects we'd like him to shoot.'

Tia laughed to herself and nodded while packing the rest of her things and putting on her coat, unable to fathom the audacity of everyone in the room. She marched towards the doors of the studio and shouted a goodbye, barely looking over her shoulder, when she heard footsteps behind her.

'Tia.'

She carried on walking down the steps of the echoey stairwell, the cold air already numbing her face and the faint smell of paint filling her nostrils. She concentrated on putting her left foot in front of her right, out of fear she would burst into tears if she actually stopped to deep the fact that Petra and Nate had most definitely fucked.

'Can we just talk about it?' asked Nate, following her down.

'What's there to talk about?'

His sigh was deep and made Tia stop in her tracks, tensing her jaw to try and calm herself down. She turned around and looked at him; his eyes widened.

'What?' she asked.

The way he looked at Tia made her feel like he could see right through the nonchalant act she was so badly trying to pull off. It got under her skin that she'd allowed him to know her this well, that she'd given him some expertise about herself. *Does he know Petra like this as well?* she asked herself, until couldn't avoid the elephant in the room any longer.

'You can do whatever you want,' she said before continuing to walk down the stairs.

'Is that really how you feel?'

'Yeah. That's how I really feel.'

Nate rubbed the back of his head and sighed again. 'I don't get you, man.'

'What do you want me to say, Nate? That I'm angry? Jealous?'

'I don't know.'

'Would that even make a difference at this point?'

'I don't know.'

Tia marched down the steps as he continued rambling.

'No, of course it would,' he continued. 'Look, I

thought we were both on the same page, just figuring each other out, having fun.'

'If that's what you think then why are we even having this conversation?' Tia stopped again.

'Because I feel like I've hurt you.'

'Do you, innit. Or do Petra, I don't fucking care anymore.'

'Is that what you really want?'

She kissed her teeth as Nate sped past her down the stairs and blocked her way down, his hands holding on to the iron handrails.

'Just be real with me for once.'

'For once? Are you dumb? All I do is talk to you about everythi—'

'Nah, not about the shoot or what some prick at work said. About us.'

They stood almost chest to chest, as Tia stared into his dark eyes, almost lost for words, but too angry to back down and cower away.

'You know you've never once said how or what you actually feel for me?'

'And when was I meant to do that, Nate? Before or after you fucked Petra?'

'For fuck's sake, man. Look, I didn't know what we were an—'

'Did it have to be explained?'

'I'm not a fucking mind-reader, Tia!'

It was the first time she had ever heard Nate raise his

voice, and it infuriated her, as the sound of his echo bounced between the ice-cold walls of the stairwell and rang in her ears. He shut his eyes for a moment before rubbing the back of his head, immediately regretting his outburst. She barged past him, but Nate still followed her down to the ground floor where they saw Hannah holding the door open for Aaron. Neither of them knew where to look, but their faces said it all. Tia just wanted the concrete stairs to open up and swallow her whole at the thought of Aaron overhearing them. Her heart began thumping so hard it felt as though it was about to burst out of her chest when Aaron looked at her, and Hannah just scurried out to the car.

'T, you good?'

Tia nodded, though it didn't convince him. Aaron glared at Nate.

'She said she's good, bro.'

'Who's chattin' to you?'

'Allow it, please,' Tia said to the both of them. She turned to Aaron. 'I'll be out in a sec.'

He kissed his teeth and reluctantly walked off. The steel door slammed shut and plunged her and Nate into darkness with nothing but a dim wall light flickering above them. She stared at the scuff marks on her trainers, unable and unwilling to look into his eyes. He stood in front of her with his hands in pockets. Not a word between them was exchanged, yet her affinity for him, like a loosened thread, kept her dangling around him, in case he had anything else left to say. She wished he'd apologise and kick Petra down the stairs; she wished he would wrap his arms around her and tell her everything was going to fine like he always did; and she wished he'd throw away the facade and just admit how much he cared about her. But the longer they stood in silence, the angrier Tia became. She struggled to hold back her tears back but she knew it was now or never. If she didn't say how she actually felt now, she never would.

'I wanted us to be something,' she said. 'But not if I have to ask you to want it too. I don't want to be— I'm not. I'm not an option.'

He began to mumble something when her phone vibrated. She saw the missed calls from Aaron and a text about a double yellow line.

'I have to go,' she said bluntly. 'Holla when you're done with the photos.'

25

'You got work tomorrow?' asked Aaron.

'Sort of. Gonna go in after lunch, do a half-day. Get a head start on some things.'

'Cool, cool.'

Tia could feel his stare whenever they stopped at a traffic light. She couldn't look him in the eye after he and Hannah had overheard her and Nate, and was firmly keeping her eyes fixed on whatever she could see out the window. Her stomach kept twinging at the thought: the embarrassment of another failed relationship, or whatever it was, unfolding once again in front of her friends – and worst of all, in front of Aaron. He was being nice about it though, offering her his precious aux cord and asking for song requests, which never usually happened when you were a passenger in his car. He hummed along to the melodies, tapping his fingers on the steering wheel, trying to lighten the mood, until they stopped at another red light.

Aaron cleared his throat. 'Since you got a late start tomorrow, you got time for a lil . . .'

When she turned to him, his thumb and forefinger were pinching the air in front of his full lips. He pretended to take an inhale and began to laugh when he saw Tia shaking her head.

'I've got bare work to do, bruv—'

'You've got bare overthinking to do.'

'I haven't got much of a choice, have I?' she sighed.

'Nah, not really,' he said, looking in his rear-view mirror with a smug grin. 'I'll have you home in an hour, tops.'

Before Tia could respond, Aaron had already pulled out of the queue of cars and taken a U-turn. He weaved through the leafy backroads of Nunhead and Brockley and arrived at an unassuming cul-de-sac in Ladywell, parking his car outside a house on the corner. He disappeared into it for a bit while Tia waited in the car, the engine and music still on. He only did that when he knew the exchange wasn't going to take longer than a quick 'hi' and 'bye'. When Aaron jumped back into the driver's seat, he threw several pop-top containers into Tia's lap, and buckled his seatbelt before driving back towards the main road.

'Don't they usually come to you?' she asked.

'He has his kids over, innit,' said Aaron. 'You got chip?'

She patted her pockets down, felt her box of

cigarettes, and nodded, as Aaron continued driving, rapping along to the lyrics of a Knucks song that blared through the car's sound system. When they arrived at their destination, he rested his hand on Tia's headrest as he parked. She couldn't work out why such a meaningless gesture felt so intimate and tender, and resisted every urge to look in his direction, staring down at her thighs instead. As soon as he turned the engine off, he opened the glove compartment by Tia's knees and retrieved his grinder and rolling papers, and she handed him a cigarette. She glanced at the car's interior while he billed up, seeing if anything had changed since the last time she'd ridden shotgun, since it'd been so long. The opal rosary his grandma had given him after his graduation still dangled from the rear-view mirror, and the cupholders beside the gearstick still housed loose change, a tin of cocoa butter Vaseline and half a packet of spearmint chewing gum.

They got out of the car and followed a concrete path between swathes of green grass, until they reached a tired-looking bench. Aaron sat down on his usual side and placed the zoot between his lips, flicking Tia's shitty lighter until it was finally lit. A pungent cloud emanated from its glowing tip and the sharp breeze blew the smoke all the way out towards the skyline in front of them. Blythe Hill was nothing special, but it was quiet, not too far from the cornershop, and had a surprisingly decent view of Canary Wharf – a world away from the south-eastern suburbs and streets Tia and Aaron had grown up in. He passed her the zoot and she took a few pulls while looking out at the glittering lights of the skyscrapers in the distance. It was the closest thing they'd got to stargazing as students, coming to the hilltop to blow some off steam after exams. Tia smiled to herself, remembering how they'd use to get gassed off Drake's *Take Care* album playing from someone's BlackBerry, plotting how they were going to leave ends and take over the world once they were done with school. She looked over at Aaron, unable to remember the last time they had just sat and hung out in a comfortable silence. But the quiet bliss was soon ruined by a grumble from Tia's stomach. She tried masking the sound by coughing and wrapping her arm around her belly but that only made Aaron laugh.

'Don't try it, bruv,' he said as she returned what was left of the zoot. 'Heard you loud and clear – let's go.'

She kissed her teeth and laughed back at him, too unbothered to argue or save face. He slowly got to his feet and pulled Tia up by her hand, throwing his heavy arm over her shoulder as they marched back to the car.

After a pit stop at Morley's, they arrived at Aaron's a little after midnight with boxes of fried wings and chips. Aaron headed for the kitchen and Tia tiptoed up the carpeted stairs to his room. She hung her coat on the hook behind his door and spread the grey sherpa blanket from his bed out on the floor before sitting down to eat, the munchies fuelling her drive to tuck in as quickly as possible.

'Why you so craven, bruv?' Aaron asked as he came into his room, two glasses in hand.

'Fuck off, man. I haven't eaten since, like, one,' said Tia, waxing off a chicken bone.

'Swear you been using that same excuse since colly?'

'I'd fly-kick you if I wasn't so hungry.'

'Whatever, man . . .'

When she tore her eyes away from her food, she saw Aaron stretching his arm towards the top of his wooden wardrobe, reaching for a half-empty bottle of Hennessy. He poured a shot into one of the glasses before diluting it with one of the canned drinks that had come with their meals.

'Oh, so it's that kinda night?' she asked, licking burger sauce off her thumb.

He laughed and grunted before turning round to see if Tia was game. She shrugged and begged him to only pour her a little. He sat down next to her and the two exchanged his box of food for her glass of drink, Aaron taking a bite out of a fried chicken leg, Tia taking a sip and shuddering at the concoction. He laughed at her inability to drink anything that wasn't a sugary rum punch, but she returned to her food, telling him to shut up. Hanging out with Aaron like this almost made Tia forget all about the hellish end she had had to what was meant to be a dream-come-true day at work.

Long after they had finished eating and were well onto their second glass of drink, they lay on his bed, as if they'd just come back from double psychology. Tia's eyelids felt heavy and they began to close, worn out from all their bickering and laughing, until Aaron cleared his throat.

'I don't wanna ask what's happened between you and my man.'

'Then don't.'

'I won't.'

'Good.'

'But ... don't let some prick rob you of your moment, innit,' he said, tentatively. 'Hannah went on like it was sick today.'

'It was cool, still,' admitted Tia. 'Finally seeing everything happen.'

'Exactly. Gotta celebrate every little win, kid.'

'You're right.'

'I'm always right.'

'Whatever,' she tutted. 'What you saying though? Hannah said you quit.'

'I had to, man. I'm dead serious about Motive.'

'That's huge. Have you told your parents yet?'

'Soon,' he said, resting his hands over his stomach.

'I've got a meeting the week after next with a potential investor. Once I've got some money and a bit of traction, I'll tell them everything.'

'You'll get there soon.' She nudged him with her leg before shutting her eyes again.

'Thanks.'

'And what does Olivia think?'

It wasn't until the question had slipped from her mouth that she remembered what Hannah had said about the two.

'It's over.'

The news jolted Tia into opening her eyes wide. She tilted her head to get a look at his face but he was still staring at the ceiling.

'Wow.'

'Yeah,' he said. 'She was cool but I dunno. We didn't see eye to eye on a lot of things. But her reaction to Motive was, like . . .'

A couple of weeks ago, this kind of news would've absolutely delighted Tia. She would've alerted the group chat; she would've tweeted something petty; she would've posted a hot selfie to show Aaron what he could have; and she would've thanked God for answering her prayers. Could all those times with Nate really have erased everything she had felt for Aaron? Her stomach twinged again at the thought of having to speak to Nate again, still reeling from the words they'd exchanged after the shoot, still unsure of where they even stood. She reached into the pocket of her trousers and took out her phone, checking it for even a speck of activity from him, but there was nothing. He still hadn't read her text messages from that morning, pissing her off all over again.

'"You know, like, ninety per cent of start-ups fail, right? You'd be freaking insane to leave Google!"' said Aaron, mimicking Olivia's American accent as Tia began to laugh.

'That's shit, man.'

'Like, you immediately got it. But Liv? She didn't show any . . .'

'Support?'

'Exactly! Shot it down immediately, like I don't already know the risks. I'm not a dickhead.'

'Well, not completely,' said Tia. Aaron flicked her leg. 'But it's true. Everything we want is on the other side of fear.'

'You get it? Can't spend my life behind a desk, at least not yet anyway. I need to at least try a ting.'

'Yeah, cos that office life ain't it. I learn that more and more every day.'

'Trust me,' huffed Aaron.

Tia lifted her fist towards Aaron and he met it with his, spudding her back.

'You've got this, okay?' They unfolded their fingers and held on to each other's hands, turning their fist-bump into a handshake. 'I believe in ya.'

He kept hold of Tia's warm hand as she pulled herself up from the bed to sit up. She covered her yawning mouth with her other hand, then checked her phone for the time: it was almost 3 a.m.

'You wanna cut now?' he asked and she nodded. 'I'll drop you, innit.'

'I'm only down the road. I need the fresh air anyways.'

He kissed his teeth at her stubbornness and stood up to give her a hug. She laughed at the impact of his heavy arms around her shoulders and patted his back.

'Thank you for today.'

'I've got you, man,' said Aaron.

'I've got you too.'

He slid his hands down her body and wrapped them around her waist, making Tia's heart tremor. She closed her eyes for a moment and savoured the faded scent of his spicy bergamot cologne, until she could feel him pulling away, his beard brushing past her burning cheeks. She loosened her arms and looked at the floor, almost embarrassed that a mere embrace had suddenly made her feel so many things, until she felt his firm grip still around her body. When she looked up at him and saw that he was already staring at her, a silence fell over the two of them that was different from all the comfortable ones they had been sharing all night long. The air between them was thick with heat and a palpable tension that made it hard for

Tia to look away. The look in his dark brown eyes was replaced with curiosity, sparkling with all kinds of possibilities Tia hadn't really seen since the night before he left London. He glanced at her mouth until she couldn't possibly handle any more what-ifs, and he put a hand behind her neck, pulling her in for a kiss.

26

They inhaled each other deeply as Tia wrapped her arms around Aaron's neck, surrendering herself to a long-awaited desire she didn't want to overthink. He kissed her lips over and over again before sliding his tongue into Tia's mouth to meet hers, intensifying the passion they had both suppressed for so long. He smoothed his hands over her curves as if committing the feeling of her body to his memory, before sitting down on the edge of his bed, trying to pull Tia on top of him, their faces still fused together. She lifted her leg, placing a knee on the left side of his body, a symbol of her willingness, though a part of her still felt cautious. When she managed to pull her bottom lip away from his mouth and come up for air, his large hands cradled the back of her head, as if he didn't want her to be even an inch away from him. She smiled into his eyes and placed his hands around her waist again, reassuring him that she wasn't going anywhere. He looked up at her in

awe as she gently gripped on to his neck and straddled him.

She began to plant little kisses all over his face: the
corners of his pronounced pillowy lips, the peaks of
his enviably high cheekbones, the part of his jaw that
tensed whenever he was concentrating. He laughed a
little when she got to his chin, realising that she was
purposely avoiding his parched mouth that kept pout-
ing for attention. Tia knew what she was doing, wanting
to make the man she'd waited on yearn for her, for her
own selfish satisfaction. But mostly she wanted to
savour every bit of the forbidden fruit she had admired
from afar for so long. She was abruptly interrupted by
the feeling of his hand between her thighs, rhythmically rubbing her crotch.

A moan escaped her mouth between his fierce kisses
and he finally pulled her body onto the bed with him,
laying her back down on the mattress and quickly
standing up to slide his T-shirt over his head. The
liquor they'd shared and the satisfaction of finally getting to this point with Aaron made it easier for Tia to
follow his lead, letting him slide her trousers off and
removing her own hoodie with less trepidation than
during her first tryst with Nate. *Why are you thinking
about him when everything you've ever wanted is about to happen
right now?* she asked herself, squirming beneath the
weight of Aaron's muscular body. She wrapped her legs
around his waist and continued kissing him back,

coaching herself to enjoying the feeling of his bulge grinding against her, when they suddenly heard a thud from outside his room.

Aaron quickly got to his feet, standing over Tia in his boxers, his index finger over his guilty-looking smirk. She slapped her hands over her mouth as a laugh tried to escape, and nodded, watching him walk across the bedroom to switch the light off before throwing on some tracksuit bottoms and slipping out the door to investigate. Tia heard Aaron call out for his dad and the sound of his feet carrying him down the creaky carpeted stairs. While she waited for him to come back, she felt around on the mattress for her phone and felt a cold, weighty block by her ankles. She picked it up and the screen glowed, almost blinding her sleepy eyes. She quickly realised it wasn't hers.

The message from Olivia jolted Tia into sitting up properly. She tapped the dimming screen again to make sure she wasn't seeing things, but lo and behold: Last night didn't feel like a mistake . . . in bold white letters beneath a missed-call notification from her. Tia suddenly felt a knot in the pit of her stomach, as she threw the phone back across the mattress before getting to her feet and taking a deep breath. The reminder of the random bitch Aaron had decided to bring back despite everything they had shared and had been through suddenly made Tia very aware of the fact that she was damn near naked in his bedroom, and she felt around on the floor for her trousers, desperate to cover herself as quickly as possible.

The anguish that was gnawing away at her insides and making her heart tremor was different from what she had felt when she'd first been confronted with Aaron's girlfriend. It wasn't a feeling of heartbreak, or of guilt – because as far as Tia was concerned, Aaron was now technically single. It was more like indignation: she was disappointed at herself for having almost let him have her without so much as a conversation or a smidgen of clarity on this frustrating dance they'd been doing for so long. Tia barely flinched when Aaron returned, continuing to put her hoodie on in the dark room. It wasn't until he switched on the LED lights beneath his TV that he realised that Tia had all of her clothes back on.

'Rah, was I gone that long?' he asked with a faint grin. 'What happened?'

'Uh, nah,' she said, tying the laces of her Vans. 'But I should go, it's late.'

'You really tryna leave now? Right before it got interesting.'

'Interesting, you know,' she huffed to herself. Aaron walked up to her and brought his face towards hers for a kiss until she held her hand out against his bare chest. 'By the way, you got a missed call.'

Tia began to put on her coat while he checked his phone, looking around the room for her bag until she spotted it in the corner near his trainers. She suddenly felt his hand around her other wrist.

'Is this why you're leavi— Look, me and her are done. It's over.'

She stared at the earnest look on his face, not knowing how to feel or what to believe, or what to say back. He took her bag from her and dropped it on the floor, taking both of Tia's hands in his own.

'She's not you,' he reassured her. 'It's always been you, T.'

A couple of months ago, there was nothing Tia would've wanted to hear more. But now, it didn't feel like enough. It didn't answer all the questions that had run through her mind the moment she first saw his fingers, the ones that were currently gripped around hers, laced into Olivia's.

'I know you know it too,' he added, desperately searching for something, any bit of confirmation in her eyes.

'What does that mean?'

'Why d'you think it's never worked out with anyone else?'

Because I've always wanted you, she thought to herself.

'Back in the days, in college – that kiss before I left . . . Shit, even right now. Don't you see? We both keep coming back to each other.'

'That wasn't us coming back to each other, Aaron. I was always around, like a dickhead,' said Tia, shaking her head out shame for her past self. 'It was you, coming back to me.'

He kept going on and on about the past, but it only made Tia angrier. To her, those memories of their first kiss in the computer lab when they should've been revising, or their impromptu picnics in Greenwich Park when they were too broke for actual dates were precious, sacred even. They were the shreds of historical hope she'd held on to while he was away, because if those moments meant that much to her, then surely they were just as important to him as well. But to hear him use their shared history in this rushed confession of his felt insulting to Tia, as if he was only mentioning these moments to win an argument, not to prove his devotion to her. Tia ripped her hands from his grip.

'This was a mistake.'

'A mistake?'

His repetition of the word made Tia feel like she had struck a nerve and bruised his ego. It paled in comparison to the embarrassment she had felt the night he'd waltzed in with his shiny new plant-based girlfriend in front of everyone, but she pressed on. She had to. This was the furthest they had ever got in the what-the-fuck-are-we? type of conversation, and she didn't want to lose her chance of finally confronting the person who had kept her in limbo for so long. He was never going to free her from this torture, so she had to do it herself.

'Is that what you think this is, between us? A mistake?'

'Yeah, I do,' she said shakily.

Tia always imagined The Talk with Aaron happening over a candlelit dinner by the Thames under a starry sky, as he finally declared his love for her while she sipped on the Prosecco he'd paid for. Arguing in his bedroom couldn't have been further from the fantasy. The fairy tale she'd spun for herself for so long had always given her butterflies, but these days the uneasiness was making her feel sick and anxious. She couldn't keep pretending anymore.

'It's not enough. I want more than this,' Tia finally admitted. 'I want better than this.'

'I want the exact same.'

'No, you don't, Aaron.'

'How are you telling me how I feel?' he asked in a stern voice.

'Because if you wanted to, you would've done it already.'

'What does that even mean?'

'It means how the fuck do you bring a whole girlfriend home then tell me it's always been me? Are you mad?' she shouted before wincing at her own volume.

Aaron looked stunned, staring into her glazed eyes looking right up at him. It took everything in Tia's power to hold back her tears. When she finally looked away, he put his arms around her until she pushed them off.

'Would tonight have even happened if you hadn't met Olivia?'

He opened his mouth to say something but couldn't get a word out.

'I'm not some fucking back-up plan.'

'I'm sorry. For bringing her back, for everything. I was dumb,' he began. 'But all I want is you. No one gets me like you.'

He searched her eyes for a chance, for some hesitation, for a glimmer of hope he seemed certain he was going to find there, until she looked at the floor and shook her head.

'I can't do this, Aaron,' she said. 'It's too late.'

27

Tia flashed her teeth to a pair of women by the paper-towel dispensers before walking past them to the furthest sink and setting down her washbag on the counter. She slid her fingers into her scalp and fluffed out her deep-conditioned roots and curls, the tropical scent of her hair cream affording her a comfort that made her wish she was back under the safety of her duvet. She inspected the thin flicks of eyeliner she'd drawn on at home and applied a single coat of mascara, figuring it was best to keep things polished and clean-looking for her big day ahead. The women standing on the other side of the bathroom continued chatting about a charcuterie board one of them had posted on Facebook. On any other day Tia would've tuned out their discussion, too consumed with a looming deadline or overthinking a comment someone had made about her never smiling enough, but today she welcomed their lengthy discussion about which gluten-free crackers didn't taste like cardboard. Their chuckles bounced off the tiled floors and followed them out of the bathroom. Tia took a deep breath as the door shut behind them, drowning out the sounds of the constant office chatter and ringing landlines.

She crouched to the ground and looked for any pairs of brogues behind the cubicle doors, checking she was alone, and stood back up in front of the mirror. She forced another smile at her reflection and placed her hands on her hips, trying to power-pose her anxiety away, but she couldn't stop focusing on the feeling of her heart pounding. She ensured the zip of her dark jeans was closed and undid the top button of her white shirt, allowing the nameplate necklace that rested on her décolletage to be on full display, before shaking her head and doing the button back up, figuring the thick golden hoop earrings she'd looped into her lobes already read as too 'urban'.

Making her way back to her desk, she dug her hand into the pocket of her blazer and whipped out her phone to double-check her time slot, and saw notifications from the group chat, and from her mum and her aunt, all wishing her good luck in their own unique ways.

Aunty Yasmine
Love you my beautiful niece xxx

Destiny's Child(ren)
Lulu: YOU'VE GOT THIS BITCH.

Han: Good luck sis, we love you!!

Mum

Let go and let God. I love you x

She lowered herself into her chair and scrolled and swiped around her phone's screen in search of another message, but she didn't find what she was yearning for. Other than a WeTransfer link to the photos from the shoot, Tia and Nate hadn't been in touch since their exchange at the bottom of the stairs, a memory that still made her shudder. She tapped onto their chat and glanced through their last few conversations, peppered with Spotify links and flirty emojis, almost in disbelief at how quickly their daily correspondence had come to this sudden halt, as if none of it had ever mattered. To her, that was the scariest thing about whatever they were: the lack of labels and expectations meant that this person to whom she'd opened up and had talked to almost every day for months could just vanish without owing her a damn thing. They could merge and intertwine so many different parts of their lives then go their separate ways without so much as an explanation offered. And sure, Tia benefitted from this too – she didn't owe him anything either – but she didn't want to get caught up in the old game of who could care less. She paused on a screenshot of his calendar he had sent her a week or so ago. He'd set himself a reminder for the date of her final interview, and she'd laughed at him promising he'd call her afterwards so he could be the first person to congratulate her on the promotion, even though she wouldn't hear back from Camilla until at least a week later. Tia loved how much Nate believed in her and she hated how much she was missing him, despite the sight of Petra still making her blood simmer through her veins.

She kissed her teeth and shoved her phone back into her pocket when she suddenly heard Camilla calling her name. Tia turned towards the wiry head of hair poking out of a meeting room and plastered on her widest smile before getting to her feet. She marched down the corridor in her most confident stride, her arms at her sides and her fingers wrapped around her thumbs in an effort to centre herself. She entered the chilly room and was ushered into a single empty chair tucked on one side of an intimidatingly large boardroom table. Camilla joined the two other women sat on the opposite side, who were just ending their conversations before turning their attention on Tia. One was Liz Baker, a Scottish Shorthair-obsessed sub-editor who worked closely with both Camilla and Marc. She had straggly brown hair that was always pulled into a messy bun, and was often draped in some kind of Merino poncho, and today was no different. The other was a random senior journalist from a completely different department, to keep things unbiased Tia guessed, though she looked no different from Liz and Camilla, still in some variation of the standard middle-class uniform. Her interpretation took the form of a Bella Freud jumper and very loud bauble-y jewellery pieces that resembled the work of a toddler who probably attended a Montessori nursery. Tia firmly shook the hand she held out.

'I'm Josephine. From World News.'

'Nice to meet you.'

Tia cleared her throat and straightened her back, making sure to return everyone's squinted-eye smiles and nod enthusiastically at whatever small talk they were forcing. Camilla slid over a few documents to the other two women before clearing her throat to get everyone's attention.

'Right,' said Camilla with a sickly grin. She slid her glasses up her nose bridge and folded her arms. 'Shall we begin?'

Tia breezed through a lot of their questions, sharing that perfectionism was her biggest weakness and that her passion for telling stories from LCN's most underserved readers made her a great candidate for the job, on top of all the years of experience she had. They nodded and scribbled in their notebooks, apologising for not always looking at her because they were busy writing *all this brilliant stuff* down. Tia noticed every raised brow and curled lip, trying to decipher what they could be thinking about as she reeled off her carefully considered answers, all while trying not to trip on the thin line between showing passion and reeking of utter desperation.

'And what do you think LCN could do to change for the better?' asked Liz.

'Oh!' Tia huffed. 'Ooh, erm . . . Let me think.'

She smiled and looked at the ceiling, pretending to think of her answer on the spot, though she already knew what to say. There was no way in hell Tia was going to tell them what she really thought: how LCN should do a *Teen Vogue* and fill up their newsrooms with people that didn't resemble any of the women currently sat across from her. She had to play the long game, Tia thought to herself, remembering Yvonne's words, before spinning some nonsense about increasing LCN's environmental coverage. She relaxed into her chair a little as Liz nodded and wrote something down, until Camilla asked the final question.

'Can you think of a time you overcame a challenge at work?'

Camilla adjusted the sleeves of her Breton top before folding her arms, her beady eyes still fixed on Tia who couldn't stop playing with her fingers under the table. She breathed out through her nose and stared at the wood grain on the table then looked back up at her manager's smug grin. *To hell with Yvonne's long game,* Tia thought to herself before clearing her throat.

'Um, actually, yeah. Not too long ago, a contributor pulled out of an upcoming shoot at the last minute,'

Tia began, digging her nails into her lap. 'She was pretty important to my project and it couldn't have been done as well without her, so I knew I couldn't let this happen after weeks of planning.'

'Oof, that is tough,' Josephine remarked.

Liz chimed in that she'd be a millionaire if she had a penny for every time a key contributor had gone rogue and disappeared, while Camilla just stared, totally unaffected by Tia's anecdote.

'It was,' Tia continued. 'But after finally getting hold of her, I was able to dispel her concerns and got her to trust me. And the shoot was brilliant – her and her daughter really enjoyed themselves.'

'And how exactly did you gain her trust?' asked Liz.

As Tia looked at her lap, she could almost remember the feeling of Nate's thumb stroking her knee, on the sofa in his studio as he'd smugly explained how he'd convinced Cheryl to come back to the shoot. She remembered how chill he'd been about the whole thing, like he was about everything else. Tia still couldn't work out whether she loved or hated that about him, but now wasn't the time to get caught up in reminiscing, she thought to herself, looking back up at the women across from her.

'Well, I knew where she was coming from. LCN hasn't always got it right when it comes to representing certain groups, and I couldn't shy away from that while talking to her.'

She inhaled the chilly air through her nose and into her chest before speaking again.

'And after a while, she began to see that I wanted to change that with this story, that what we were trying to say was bigger than just being a pretty puff piece.'

They all nodded and began writing things down and Tia's throat began to feel a little tighter than before.

'And I think that's our job as journalists, right? To give a platform to those we don't hear from a lot. And in turn, those stories help us understand each other better.'

Tia felt like this would've been her mic-drop moment if she were a strong female lead in a film, but then she remembered she was sitting in the icy meeting room of a dreary office in Central London, and not on a movie set in Hollywood with Meryl Streep playing her boss.

She remembered how her words meant the difference between being seen as sassy or too outspoken, and how the British stiff upper lip and boardroom politics ruled the building she currently sat in. She slipped her hands under her thighs as the women continued nodding and scribbling into their notebooks.

The office seemed livelier than usual when Tia returned from her post-interview cigarette, everyone around her either lost in their phones or gossiping. After spending the previous hour fake-laughing at Camilla and Josephine's anecdotes, there was nothing Tia wanted more than a bit of silence. She immediately slid her headphones over her curls and logged into her laptop, figuring everyone's palpable giddiness was over an MP being caught in a lie or some cousin of the Royal Family dying. As she logged into her laptop, she suddenly felt a hand on her shoulder and was relieved to see the knitted sleeve of Eloise's argyle jumper.

'So how did it go?' she asked with a cheesy grin.

'I think it went really well, actually.'

'Why do you sound so shocked?' laughed Eloise. 'This is great!'

'Yeah, I dunno. You never really know how these things go, innit.' Tia sighed. 'Thanks for your tips, by the way. I still owe you a round at 'Spoons.'

'How about tonight?'

'Tonight it is then! Also, did you see Marc's email?'

Eloise nodded with glee. After being so impressed by some of the photos he'd seen from the shoot, Marc had wanted to publish the feature over the weekend, promising Tia it'd get ample real estate on LCN's homepage. Initially, Tia was a bit miffed by the decision, seeing as weekends were a notoriously difficult slot for stories to do well on, but being given a prime spot on the homepage was an opportunity rarely given to anything pitched by a mere researcher. It filled the girls with both fervour and fear, but to Tia, it made all the time she had spent obsessing over typefaces and photo dimensions and re-working interviews feel very much worth it.

'I actually have some things to run by you before we hand it over to Social. D'you have some time?'

Tia nodded and picked up her laptop, and followed Eloise over to a free table in the kitchen. She looked around and noticed even more people around the office floor hissing at each other in hushed tones, some pointing towards their laptops and others huddled together under a television screen that Tia couldn't quite make out from where she was sitting.

'D'you know what's going on today?'

Tia pointed at everyone around them as Eloise sat beside her.

'Oh, probably the Arts editor thing. He's apparently got a bit of a sketchy reputation, hence the backlash.'

'*He?*'

Tia's stomach lurched, hoping Eloise had got it wrong. She immediately unlocked her phone and went to Twitter for confirmation. A statement from LCN's press office sat at the top of her timeline. Underneath was a portrait of the new recruit, who looked like a greasier hybrid of Colin Firth and Hugh Grant, which basically translated to every other man in the building.

'What was his name again? Nigel something?'

'Nigel Saunders.'

'That's the one.'

Tia continued reading his credentials while Eloise mentioned his affair with a nineteen-year-old V&A

intern, his stint in New York's art scene, and something about him being a distant relative of Thomas Gainsborough. 'I'm just gonna grab a coffee before we start,' she said. 'You want anything?'

'Nah, I'm good. Go ahead.'

When Tia had had enough of trawling through everyone's tweets on her phone, she logged into her laptop and immediately drafted a message to Yvonne. She didn't know what to say or where to begin. As much as she wanted to tell her how furious she was on her behalf, Tia figured it'd be best not to point out the obvious or rub it in. But she just wanted to let Yvonne know she was thinking of her. After writing and deleting at least four different sentences, Tia finally settled on something short and sweet, and clicked 'send'. She was startled to get an immediate reply, but it was only Yvonne's out-of-office, apologising for her absence and stating she'd be back from her holiday in a few weeks' time.

28

Still on a buzz from the poorly mixed fish bowls she and Eloise had consumed earlier, Tia wasn't quite ready to go home when she got off her train. She texted the group chat to see what everyone was doing but they both quickly replied with their excuses. Hannah was having a night in with Sean and Luca was working till late. They promised to convene over a fry-up the next morning, though the promise of hash browns and salty bacon didn't curb Tia's disappointment.

The main road was charged with that electricity that can only come from a Friday night, full of possibility and impromptu drinks. The pub in front of the station was bustling with groups pouring in and out of its doors and onto the pavements, people swigging beers and lighting each other's cigarettes. The second-hand smoke made Tia crave one herself, so she dragged her feet to the Turkish Food Centre down the street and begrudgingly bought a box. She shook her head as she tore open the plastic wrap, removed the silver foil and slid out a cigarette, reminding herself about how she'd made herself a promise that she'd never let her little sister find out she smoked, just in case she grew up thinking it was cool. This self-imposed precaution forced her to loiter around Catford Broadway before circling back to her block. She turned up her music while walking past the Black hair shop owned by old Asian men, inhaled at the hidden gem of a Japanese restaurant, exhaled at Tony's Butchers, tapped off the excess ash near a tiny nail salon, and finally threw the butt into an overflowing bin by the grocers, which had mounds of spring onions, plantain, red peppers and yams piled outside their window.

Though she had reached the end of her ghetto pilgrimage, she still didn't want to go home. Between her final interview, the news about Yvonne's Arts job, and at long last completing what would be the biggest feature of her career to date, Tia felt restless and antsy. So much had happened and it had suddenly dawned on her that she no longer had anyone to talk to about it all. There was an acute loneliness that sometimes pinched her so hard it felt like she could hardly breathe if she sat and ruminated on it long enough. That's why she was always so busy, with work, with brunches and nights out, with endless scrolling and double-tapping. Anything to distract herself from the fear of never having someone interested in her and the little details of her day without having anything to gain.

The sudden wails from a group of drunken men stationed outside a shabby cornershop snapped Tia out of her thoughts, as they diverted their attention away from their game of dominoes and onto her. She ignored their catcalls and, without thinking, walked towards the main road at the end of the market strip, taking her even further away from her house. She kissed her teeth when she realised she'd have to walk a big circle just to get back home without bumping into them again, when her phone vibrated.

The notification stopped her in her tracks. It was Nate. He'd replied to Tia's Story of her drinks with Eloise.

Looks like today went well . . . how the interview go?

So he did remember, she thought to herself. She half grinned at the phone, then immediately loathed herself for even reacting to this crumb of attention – she was better than this. In the midst of wallowing in her bitter disappointment in herself, Tia accidentally opened the message and swore under her breath. Her thumbs floated above the screen for a minute or so as she tried to quickly think of what to say. It was bad enough that it would show up as 'read' so soon. She didn't want to look like she'd been desperate for a message from him, though she kind of was – but he couldn't know that. She had lost the game of who cared the least a long time ago.

She replied: Good, thanks.

If he was going to act like nothing had happened, Tia would do the same. Her pride had been trampled enough. It would seem like he was also doing away with the prideful hour-long replies since he began typing back immediately. That's great. I'm glad. He started typing again.

How's work been otherwise?

Not too bad, thanks.

Lol so is this what we're doing now?

What?

The dead replies

Dunno what else you want me to say
I'm not a mindreader.

She locked her phone and shoved it into her bag out of anger. She couldn't fathom how he could expect any kind of normalcy when their last conversation had been the first and worst argument they had ever had. The buzzing of her phone stopped her in her tracks again.

I deserve that.

Can we talk? Tonight, if you're free?

When Tia approached Nate's studio building, she saw the ground-floor door was ajar and slipped inside. She stared at the exact spot she'd stood in during her and Nate's last conversation before shaking off the memory and began to climb up the concrete steps. As Tia reached the top of the stairwell, she could hear the familiar jingle of Nate's keys. He had his back turned to her and was locking the doors to his studio with only one of his arms through the sleeve of his jacket. It looked like he was in a hurry. When he turned around and saw Tia, the startled look on his grizzly face soon settled into a smile that still put some part of her at ease. She grinned back, quickly glancing at the stubble around his mouth. It looked thicker than usual, as if he hadn't shaved in a while.

'I was, uh, going to wait for you at the station,' he said, rubbing the back of his head. 'Guess I was too late.'

'It's cool.'

She took a cautious step closer to him, her arms firmly crossed. Not immediately wrapping them around him felt weird to her. She suspected it felt a bit offbeat to him too, given the expectant look in his eyes. She shifted her eyes onto the door behind him.

'Right! My bad. Let's go— I'll unlock this.'

Tia followed Nate over to the wooden table where he placed his jacket and keys, looking over her shoulders to get a clue on what he might have been up to since the last time she'd visited, but there was nothing out of the ordinary, just a couple of extra plants and the garment rails pushed to one side of the room. The warm glow of the paper floor lamp in the corner made it feel as cosy as it had been the first time he'd brought her here, but recent events kept her from feeling at ease. Unsure of her place, she put her bag down and perched herself on the edge of the table and stared out of the mottled windows. Nate walked over to his laptop to restart a song that was playing through the speakers of the airy studio space. He began to make conversation while tidying the art books and magazines that were scattered around.

'I like the blazer.'

'Thanks.'

'For the interview?'

Tia nodded.

'I like it. How did it go?'

'You kinda asked that alrea—'

'Right! Right. I did,' he said. He fetched himself a bottle of water then stopped in his tracks. 'You thirsty or . . . ?'

'Nah, I'm good.'

'Cool, cool.'

This is painful, Tia thought to herself before clearing her throat.

'So, you said you wanted to talk?'

'Yeah. I thought we should.' He looked out of the window Tia was staring at before leaning against it. 'I've missed you.'

The look in his dark eyes as those three words fell from his mouth was enough to make Tia's legs weak.

She hated how powerless she felt to his undivided attention, though she wasn't sure how long she'd get to have it all to herself.

'Really?'

'You sound shocked.'

'Well, I couldn't tell. Haven't exactly heard from you in a while.'

'I just thought you needed space after the whole . . . you know.'

'So considerate.' Tia laughed a little.

'I never meant to hurt you, Tia. That's the last thing I wanted to do.'

A part of her believed that, but it didn't make the whole thing any less embarrassing or painful. She looked at the floor, her head weighed down with so many questions she was too proud to say out loud. But she had come too far to let the fear of being honest hold her back from getting the answers she needed.

'Everything you said about wanting to be more than friends,' she slowly began. 'Was that all a lie?'

'No. I meant that, for real.'

'How though? When you've been with Petr— Have you been seeing other people this whole time?'

He sighed and rubbed the back of his head.

'Just say it. You be real with me, for once.'

'Look, I didn't know— We hadn't talked about it,' said Nate. 'So I just thought we were both doing our own thing.'

'Really?' she asked and Nate shrugged his shoulders. 'So meeting my friends, all those dinners and talks and everything else, that's what you call "doing our own thing"?'

'We've never had The Talk.'

His mentioning of The Talk made her even more frustrated. She'd never realised how someone so apparently carefree could be so hung up about The Talk, which brought every relationship crashing down to reality.

'I thought our feelings for each other were pretty clear, to be honest,' Tia sighed. 'But I guess not.'

Nate came towards her and placed his hands on her shoulders. He looked for her face until she finally lifted her head. His eyes pierced her icy facade.

'Look, I didn't expect a connection like this to happen, at all.'

'I didn't expect it either,' she said, staring back at him.

'But I'm glad that it did. So glad.'

'Me too.'

She couldn't help but reciprocate his tenderness. She missed him, and she was sick of telling herself to hate Nate and forget all about him. He meant too much for her to just shut him out like that. He slipped his fingers behind the nape of her neck and drew Tia's face close to his. She was entranced by the ticklish feeling of his pillowy lips grazing over hers. She took hold of his hands in a half-hearted attempt to stop him, but he enveloped her in a kiss before she could think any more. A rush of helplessness took over her body, and a soft moan escaped her as the butterflies in her stomach rendered her weak. Like the first bite of a ripened peach, the kiss was slow but fierce and sweet, as if he was trying to say he was sorry with every motion of his tongue. He tore himself away from her face, his hands still clasping her jaw.

'I don't want to stop this,' he said in a hushed tone. She smiled while being adorned by more of his kisses, letting him have his way with her lips. 'So let's just go with the flow.'

She had never wanted him to take something back so quickly. The muscles that formed her lips into a pout were completely flatlined by his vague statement. She opened her eyes and saw his still closed, unbothered and unfazed by the lack of assurance in his words. Tia pulled her face away from Nate's grip and he asked if she was okay.

'What does that even mean?'

She pushed her curls back and began to fan her face. Nate tried to hold on to her arms but she moved her body even further away from him.

'It means we keep spending time togeth—'

'Until?'

'Until . . . I dunno,' he half laughed. 'I'm not really thinking that far ahead.'

'But see, that's the problem. I do want someone who is thinking that far ahead,' Tia said, still trying to find the right words. 'I want someone who's scared to lose me.'

Nate huffed and looked down with widened eyes, rubbing the back of his head like he always did when he didn't know what to say.

'I just can't do this half-hearted shit, Nate. It's not me.'

She fidgeted with the hem of her shirt, unable to tell whether his silence was out of disappointment or disbelief, until he finally looked back at her.

'I'm just not in that headspace right now.'

Tia nodded.

'Fine. That's fine.'

It was far from fine, of course. Finally hearing where Nate was coming from, and not hearing him take everything he'd said back and that he wanted to start over, felt like a punch to the gut. Tia had so many questions. She wanted to understand why she wasn't enough, why what they'd shared wasn't worth trying for. But the sudden clarity also felt like someone had finally drawn the curtains and opened the windows to her mind which had been kept in the dark for so long.

'I don't know what else to say,' Nate said.

'I don't think there is anything left to say.'

Her fingers stroked the table beneath her and she

got to her feet and turned to pick up her bag, too despondent to even look in Nate's direction.

'So that's it?'

Tia looked at the wooden floorboards, then her eyes followed the mottled windows up towards the high ceilings. She peered over her shoulders at the rest of the studio space, as if she wanted to get one last look at the place. She turned around and forced a half-grin.

'That's it.'

29

A crumpled napkin flew onto Tia's lap, breaking the concentration she'd been holding while staring at the traffic outside the modest restaurant she, Hannah and Luca were sitting in. When she turned around, she looked at the other diners near them, chatting over stuffed aubergines and falafel. The older chefs joked around and shouted at the juvenile lanky waiters through the kitchen's pass-through window, over the sounds of Turkish music videos playing on the flatscreen television. It hung above the little wooden cubby where customers paid for their meals then left with a handful of boiled sweets from a large gaudy bowl.

Luca was yapping about something while waving his arms about and shaking his phone at the girls' faces. Hannah tried to calm him down but eventually joined in the hysteria too, powerless to his shrieks. He slammed his hand on the table.

'T, did you hear what I just said?'

Tia shook her head and smiled before jutting her mouth out towards the straw bobbing in her icy glass of Coke.

'I said Dawn Butler just tweeted about your story!'

'Oh, shit.' Tia looked at the screen of the phone he held out. 'Wow, that's mad.'

'Try to sound a bit excited, babe.'

'She's jaded,' joked Hannah. 'Her phone's been blowing up all weekend – it's not easy going viral, you know.'

'Oh, please!' said Tia, rolling her eyes.

'Well, as long as she's not thinking about that prick,' Luca said with a smize before taking a sip of his mojito.

'Really?' Hannah sighed.

'What?' said Luca, before turning to Tia. 'You're not actually thinking about that prick, right?'

'Well, of course she is! He took the photos, innit!'

'So? He and his film camera were full of shit. Like, we get it: you have a Contax! Now fuck off.'

'She can't just switch her feelings off.'

They carried on while Tia looked for the waiter who'd taken their order, figuring they'd be done by the time she had checked on their meze platters. A failed relationship always left an embarrassing stain Tia wished could be ignored and covered up. It felt like having 'This Person Sucks At Being Loved' tattooed on her forehead, but she knew her friends wouldn't rest until they had got some kind of statement from her.

'I just feel . . .'

'Pissed off? Because you have every right,' said Luca.

'Heartbroken?' Hannah interjected. 'Because it's okay, sis – he just wasn't the one. There's plent—'

'Dumb,' she sighed. 'I feel dumb.'

Tia shoved a chunk of warm bread into her mouth, as if that could stop the tears she could feel forming in her eyes.

'And sad. I don't even know why I'm so sad. We weren't even together like that.'

'Yeah, but that doesn't mean it wasn't real. You cared about him.'

Hannah put her arm around Tia, resting her braided head on her shoulder.

'I still don't get it. Like, he was doing all the right things—'

'Until he wasn't,' Luca said flatly.

'Why does this keep happening to me?' Tia sat up in her chair. 'First Aaron and now Nate. Like, is it me? Is there something wrong with me?'

'Ew, stop!' Luca hated anything remotely on the border of self-deprecation. 'There's nothing wrong with you, okay? You just haven't met the one who matches your energy.'

'Yeah. This keeps happening because you're not settling.'

'What do you mean?' asked Tia.

'Staying with either one of them would've been easier, right?' said Hannah. 'But you would've been ignoring what you really want. No dick is worth that kind of sacrifice.'

'Unless said dick is attached to a millionaire, then shut the fuck up and secure the Birkin bag.'

Tia cackled as Hannah threw a napkin at Luca's face. 'You're so dumb, you know that?' she hissed. 'But real talk, I think you did the right thing,' Hannah added, while dodging Luca's revenge shot. 'You know what you want and what he offered wasn't enough. And that's okay.'

'Just dust yourself off and try againnn,' Luca badly sang before finishing his drink.

'You guys are right.' Tia sighed and poked at the half-melted ice cubes in her glass with her straw. 'I just . . . For once, I just want to be soft with someone and not regret it.'

Luca stretched out his hand to Tia's then glared at Hannah to join them with her own.

'Well, you can be that with us,' he sighed. Being this sentimental was out of his comfort zone, but that only made the girls appreciate it even more. 'Until someone who's worthy enough comes along.'

Luca gave their hands another squeeze, but then his phone buzzed beside his cutlery and he immediately whipped his wrist up in the air and snatched it to see who had texted. He smiled as the screen glowed in his face and Hannah kissed her teeth.

'I swear, if you're lodging us for a dick appointment, you're paying for this dinner right now.'

'Have you got a date tonight?' asked Tia.

Luca remained quiet, his face concealed by his phone, as he frantically typed his reply. He tried to ignore them until he had sent his message but Hannah and Tia kept throwing torn pieces of pitta at him, nagging Luca to answer them.

'Will you guys fucking stop?' he shrieked while the girls laughed. 'It's Hassan.'

The girls grabbed hold of each other in shock, speechless at the name that had just left Luca's mouth, the very name he had declared dead in their group chat.

'We're just grabbing coffee.'

'At eight p.m.?' asked Hannah with a mischievous grin. 'Bitch, please.'

'Wait – so, what does this mean? Are you getting back together or . . . ?'

'I don't know about that' Luca shrugged his shoulders. 'He called by accident the other day and we ended up talking for over an hour, just catching up. It was nice. I guess we just miss each other?'

'So getting under someone isn't the best way to get over someone? Huh, who would've thought!' scoffed Tia.

The girls couldn't remember the last time they had seen Luca look so nervous. He fidgeted with the sleeve of his shirt and bit his lip as Hannah grilled him on the inevitable make-up sex that was bound to happen, though Luca was adamant that tonight was strictly on a wholesome vibe.

'You're gonna get in some holes alright,' said Hannah, dodging the olive Luca had flicked.

Tia couldn't remember the last time she had laughed so hard, quietly watching her two most favourite people in her life bicker, praying she'd never have to face anything without them.

'I love you guys,' she declared.

'Oh my days, is she drunk?' asked Hannah before throwing her arms over Tia. 'We love you more.'

'Now can we fucking celebrate, please?' asked Luca. 'Because Elaine Welteroth just retweeted you!'

'SHUT THE FUCK UP.'

'WAIT, WHAT?!' screamed Tia.

The three screamed and shrieked in their seats as nearby diners and waiters looked at their corner of the restaurant, some visibly annoyed but most of them laughing, though they couldn't tell what all the excitement was about.

Though parts of the weekend had disappointed Tia, she was glad to have the people who meant most to her right by her side to lift her up.

Still reeling from the feature's success, Tia was consumed by all the quote tweets and mentions in her notifications, trying to commit every positive comment to memory. She grinned from ear to ear throughout her entire commute, refreshing her screen to find even more likes and retweets the closer she got to the office. She breezed through the bustling reception and slapped her ID badge on the sensor at the glass doors with more force than usual, her newfound confidence secured by the thrill of a successful story.

Tia wished every colleague a good morning on her way to the Collaboration Zone, unable to remember the last time she had ever been this excited or on time for a meeting first thing in the morning. She pulled out a chair between two older colleagues and took part in some pleasant small talk about the weather, until Camilla sat down with a takeaway cup from Gail's and her leather journal tucked into her armpit. She looked around at all the faces surrounding the table with a grin, her way of telling everyone to wrap up their conversations and quieten down.

'Before we begin, I just want to say a massive well done to everyone we interviewed last week. To have made it that far is already a huge achievement you should all be proud of.'

Tia nodded with enthusiasm and looked at Camilla with earnest eyes, as if her manager were only addressing her. She knew damn well that the success of her feature had cemented her chances of securing the promotion.

'It was incredibly competitive and it's difficult to choose from so many brilliant candidates, but you'll all hear from us by the end of the week,' added Camilla.

Before she could move on to the next item on her agenda, Marc finally arrived. His eyes were locked on his iPhone as he plopped himself down into the chair beside Camilla and lifted one skinny-jean-covered leg over the other, revealing his worn-out Chelsea boots. Everyone sat up in their seats a little and adjusted themselves, though, as ever, Marc did not notice the way his presence had changed the atmosphere. Gbemi followed close behind, her arm supporting her opened laptop as she stroked the buttons of her keyboard with her other hand.

'Ah, Gbemi, perfect timing,' said Camilla. 'Would you mind giving us the stats for this weekend?'

'Sure thing,' she said, double-clicking something. 'I don't think I could start this without first mentioning Tia's hair feature.'

Tia's heart began to pound harder than ever before. While her friends and mutuals loved the story, everything was a numbers game these days. No matter how heartfelt or passionate you were about a story, if it didn't benefit LCN's interests then it didn't matter.

'Weekends are often a bit dead for us, since our readers are typically out and about, and though it got a fair bit of space on the homepage, the stories typically placed there get around fifteen to twenty thousand page views in twenty-four hours,' she explained.

Tia's leg began to bounce under the table, wishing Gbemi would get to the all-important figure.

'Tia's story, however, attracted over one hundred and fifty thousand views in a single day.'

'Bloody hell!' piped up Harrison. 'Not bad at all, Tia.'

Eloise quietly clapped, patting her fingertips together. Several others followed suit and joined in, congratulating Tia, as Gbemi continued to reel off the rest of her feature's impressive stats.

'By the end of the weekend, it grew to well over three hundred thousand views thanks to a few prominent figures sharing it onto their socials.'

Tia could hardly contain her grin and wrapped her arms around her stomach, attempting to subdue the intense flutters she could feel. *Is this what liking your job feels like?* she asked herself.

'Shannon's name was trending in London within a few hours of the feature going live, and the quality of the photos resonated with a lot of our under-served readers, particularly on Twitter. UK Moments even shared it,' Gbemi proudly added. She smiled at Tia who was still too stunned to speak. 'The socials team have estimated it'll reach a million views within a week or so.'

'Well, that's brilliant,' said Camilla, barely looking up from her journal. 'And yes, that makes sense, Nathaniel's photos were a lovely addition to Tia's work.'

I'm sorry but was that an actual compliment? From Camilla Hastings? This was all starting to feel too good to be true. Marc looked up from the phone in his palm and slid his thick black frames up his narrow nose bridge before looking at Tia.

'Very well done, Tia,' he said in a monotone. 'Do keep pitching us stuff like this.'

Now Marc wants more ideas? And knows my name! Tia thought, fighting every natural urge to squeal and buss a whine in her chair. She smiled and nodded instead.

The following days at work felt like something out of a fantasy for Tia, who was still revelling in the success of her feature. On Wednesday the website received a spike in engagement after the photos were reposted on The Shade Room and Essence, reaching a large number of LCN's American readers, who they could never usually attract even if Meghan Markle was in the headline. The day after that, Cheryl was contacted by a producer from LCN's children's department, saying they'd like to invite Shannon down to host a segment for its news programme after being blown away by her own writing for the feature, and on Friday morning, Gbemi begged Tia to reformat the content into a video for the organisation's TikTok and Instagram accounts, saying that LCN's social media editor loved the story.

Tia got to work on it straightaway, using audio files from her interviews with the likes of Shannon and Leanne, weaving them in with behind-the-scenes clips she'd filmed from her phone during the shoot as well as the main photos. She took hardly any bathroom breaks and only got up to get a limp, overpriced sandwich from LCN's canteen, scoffing it down at her desk while adding the final touches to the videos for Gbemi's approval. After emailing her a file named 'FINAL FINAL EDIT', Tia raised her sore neck up from the laptop screen she'd been glued to and got up to finally relieve her bladder, which had been paining her for at least an hour.

When she walked into the bathroom, she saw Camilla chatting by the sinks with Liz Baker, the sub-editor. It was the first time Tia had seen them together since the interview. She flashed a grin in their direction before teetering into the first free cubicle she could find, hoping they'd both be gone by the time she was done. The whirring of the hand dryers and the sounds of other women all giddy and restless for the weekend made it nearly impossible for Tia to eavesdrop on their conversation. She unlocked the cubicle door and found Camilla, alone this time, checking her reflection for any bits of food in her teeth. Tia walked to the only other free sink, right beside Camilla, and began washing her hands. She kept a smile on the entire time, out of fear her resting bitch face would start a conversation, but it was too late.

'Not feeling well, Tia? You look tired.'

'Oh, no, I'm fine. Just completed an edit for the Social team. They were keen to post a video about the hair feature.' She moved over to the hand dryer.

'That's marvellous,' said Camilla. 'Good to see you so productive despite the unfortunate news!'

'Huh?'

Tia whipped her hands from underneath the hand dryer and waited for the blast of hot air to stop so she could hear properly.

'What unfortunate news?'

Camilla stared blankly at her, then raised her eyebrows ever so slightly, realising Tia didn't know. Her stunned expression and the mirthless grin that followed began to make Tia feel uneasy.

'Oh, I thought you would've seen the email by now,' Camilla began. 'But, um . . . you didn't get the writer's position, I'm afraid.'

Tia's eyes widened in disbelief as Camilla began regurgitating the same corny lines everyone always heard when they were being rejected. Things like how it was really tough competition; it was between her and one other candidate, but how they'd been chosen because they had slightly more experience and were a better fit for the team – the team she had been working in for nearly three years. Her chest tightened and the blood in Tia's body rushed to her face so intensely she could hardly hear the spiel coming from Camilla's coffee-stained teeth. Though it didn't stop her from performing and playing along like she had always done in the office, keeping quiet, smiling sweetly, showing enthusiasm by nodding her head profusely. It wasn't safe to express discontentment or disappointment. You could only be happy and grateful to be there.

'However, we'd obviously love to extend your researcher contract, so do keep an eye out for that.'

'Sure.'

Camilla put her hand on Tia's shoulder for a brief moment before retracting it. She then picked her leather journal up from the sink's countertop and walked over to the bathroom door. She looked over her shoulder before reaching out for the handle.

'Better luck next time, eh? But definitely, definitely keep pitching, alright?'

'Of course.'

30

One Month Later

When she could no longer feel the breeze hitting the back of her neck, Tia pried open her sore eyes and quickly realised she was about to miss her stop. The early-stage panic attack pulled her up from leaning against the emergency door and she launched herself out of the carriage before the doors closed, much to the annoyance of the tourists who had already boarded the tube, their suitcases blocking the exit. *Dickheads,* Tia thought to herself. She kissed her teeth at their sweaty pink faces and passive-aggressive stares before her body was carried away in the sea of white button-downs and bulky backpacks. She yawned twice while ascending the escalators, blankly staring at digital posters of West End musicals she had never seen and MADE.com furniture she could only dream of filling her non-existent flat with. Tia stretched her arms while dragging herself up the stairs of the Underground, regretting every minute she had spent binging *Emily in*

Paris the night before, though the ditsy dilemmas and far-fetched faux pas had been a welcome distraction from the irremediable angst that weighed Tia's chest down whenever she thought about another day at the office.

Every day she tried to alleviate that heaviness with a cigarette before walking into LCN, as if the hit of nicotine were some kind of reward for managing to get to work on time. It kept her satisfied until she reached the fourth floor. She plastered on her best grin before the elevator doors opened on to the communal kitchen, filled with her zealous colleagues and their paper bags of artisan coffee beans, talking about the super-sick weekend one of them had had at Miffy's dad's place in Oxfordshire, or was it Muffy? Tia never really cared to remember.

Since finding out she hadn't got the job, the meetings at the Collaboration Zone had felt duller than usual, and Tia often spent them scrolling through her Twitter timeline or texting Gbemi about what they should have for lunch. Today was no different, until Camilla called her name out.

'Tia? Would it be okay to have a chat with Eloise after this? I think she'll need your help on this story.'

Tia scribbled gibberish into her notebook to look like she was actively listening.

'Uh, sure.'

When the meeting finally adjourned, she met Eloise

by her new desk near all the other writers and dutifully took notes as she explained her feature again, knowing Tia hadn't listened during her pitch at the Collaboration Zone. It was about Londoners staying childless to save the planet, which was, of course, right up Camilla's street. Eloise had finally started to relax into her new position and act normal around Tia, after weeks of keeping her head down or never knowing what to say every time they interacted with each other. It irked Tia initially, having to facilitate the apparent white guilt and reassure Eloise that she wasn't at all angry with her about how everything went down. Sure, Tia was disappointed. She thought the incontestable success of her hair feature would seal the deal. But what would being upset at Eloise achieve? She wasn't the problem. She was just a beneficiary of another problem much bigger than her and Tia. So Tia did as she had always done when faced with such issues at LCN: she got on with it. She just wasn't sure how much longer she could do it for.

After taking a bathroom break, which actually consisted of Tia sitting on the closed toilet seat while scrolling through TikTok for fifteen minutes, she finally got back to her makeshift workspace: a bit of free table space and a random chair she'd nicked from a meeting room, in a bid to be as far away from Camilla as possible, and got straight to work. She rang a few environmentalist groups, spoke to an influencer couple she'd found via Twitter, and posted dozens of call-outs across Facebook and Reddit, until she could no longer ignore the growls coming from her stomach and reached for phone. She had a text from Gbemi saying she'd completely forgotten about the lunch meeting she was having with some boring social media producers. Tia sighed, already anticipating the sad Tesco meal deal she was going to eat at her desk, since the nearby Pret and Abokado were almost always packed around this time of day.

She weaved through the bodies of staff members congregating by the microwave over plastic tubs of meat-free bolognese and leftover Thai green curry and threw the cold remnants of her morning brew into the sink of the communal kitchen before trying to shove her stained mug into the crowded dishwasher. After admitting defeat and washing it by hand, Tia dragged her feet over to the elevators, trying to figure out which one was approaching first.

When the doors slid open, her eyes met the same pair of Air Forces she herself was currently wearing. Brogues, TOMS or something a seasoned hiker would recommend were the usual vibe at LCN; actual trainers were few and far between.

'Nice kicks,' said a voice.

Tia cracked her first real smile of the day and was about to give a friendly laugh until she looked up and saw Nate. She froze and immediately noticed the absence of his curly high-top, instead his hair was shaven down to a low fade that only made you focus even more on his handsome, blemish-free face and gold hoop earring. Tia couldn't believe he had the audacity to look even sexier than the last time she had seen him.

'Hey, trouble,' he said through a grin that still somehow gave Tia goosebumps.

He stepped out of the lift, and she blinked several times, until she quickly realised that this was actually happening and she returned the smile. The pair of writers behind Nate soon realised the two were acquainted and made themselves scarce, telling Nate they were going to grab coffees in the kitchen. He nodded at them before turning his eyes back to Tia.

'What are you doing here?' she asked.

'I was hoping I'd bump into you.'

Tia jokingly rolled her eyes at him until he actually answered her question.

'Uh, LCN Longlist – you heard of it?'

It was the Music department's prestigious list of all the new artists set for global domination, hand-selected by the Editorial team and over a hundred experts, critics and just about anyone who was anyone in the industry. Almost every past nominee had gone on to win a Grammy, a BRIT, a Billboard or all three. Everyone with internet connection had heard of the Longlist.

'They want your boy to shoot the portraits, innit.'

'That's amazing!' said Tia. He laughed like he didn't believe her reaction. 'Nah, for real. That's huge.'

'Yeah, I'm hyped for it, still. I mean, I'm hoping they let me have fun with it, but it's the Longlist – I'll probably do whatever they say, to be honest.'

'Ah, there's that artistic integrity I've always admired.'

'Integrity don't always pay—'

'The bills. I know.'

'I've taught you well.'

'Oh, please!' laughed Tia, nudging Nate's shoulder. 'But if they chose you, that probably means they're looking for something different, so stand your ground, innit.'

'Thanks, T.'

'No problem.'

She knew later on she'd regret being this jovial with him considering how everything had gone down. Lord knows Luca would be furious, having declared Nate dead to him. But talking and joking around like this was effortless. Tia wasn't sure she'd ever find that again with someone else. When they looked into each other's eyes, it wasn't as awkward as Tia had assumed their first encounter would feel. Seeing his smile felt like putting on the freshly washed jumper you'd specially laid out on the radiator: warm, comforting, and something you wanted to nuzzle your face into. Her cheeks began to feel hot when he bit his bottom lip, his eyes still locked onto hers.

'This wouldn't have happened without you,' he said, slipping his hands into the pockets of his jeans. 'I owe you, for real.'

She laughed it off and quickly pressed the button for the lift, already anticipating where their conversation was heading.

'Let me take you out for a drink, have a catch-up and that,' he said with come-hither eyes. 'I've missed you.'

And there it was, Tia thought to herself. She hated herself for wanting to immediately say she'd missed him too, but her pride held it in for her. She sighed and laughed it off again, wondering what was taking the lift so damn long.

'Wow, we can't even have a drink together?' he joked. 'You're gonna do me like that?'

Before she could answer, her phone began to vibrate. Seeing Yvonne's name made Tia's stomach flip.

'Uh, I'm sorry but I really have to take this,' she said to Nate, stepping into the lift that had just arrived.

'Don't worry, I'll holla tonight, yeah?' he said with a self-assured grin.

She nodded before the doors closed and thanked God for the boon that was Yvonne's call.

31

Tia was surprised that Yvonne had instructed her to come to the ground-floor cafe of LCN's building, since she often complained that the fluorescent lighting was bothersome and unflattering, favouring the boulangeries and cafes nestled on the streets behind the office. Today it was crowded with tour groups of families and elderly folk, and fellow staff members who needed to stretch their legs but didn't want to venture out too far for food. Yvonne could be spotted from a mile away, with her signature model-esque glow and her eternally chic wardrobe. Today's look comprised a white cotton blouse with a ruffled broderie-anglaise yoke that Tia suspected was Chloé. The top was tucked into a pair of flared jeans that perfectly accentuated Yvonne's legs (which were rumoured to be insured for three million pounds, though Tia hadn't been brazen enough to ask about the truth in that . . . yet).

'Hello, my darling!' Yvonne moved her Birkin from

the table to the chair beside her and tried to get up but Tia bent down for a hug instead. Yvonne shoved her Amex into Tia's hand. 'Get whatever you want.'

Given that she'd been at the top her game for nearly twenty years, Yvonne possessed an astonishing ability to hold a lengthy conversation with someone without dropping in so much as a word about herself. She asked Tia question after question about work and what had happened after the interview and so on and so forth. This wasn't unusual for Yvonne. She was always so gracious and humble in the way she spoke to the younger journalists in the building, which was partly why everyone loved her so much (also the fact that she was a fucking icon and always looked runway ready).

But part of Tia couldn't help but wonder if Yvonne was doing this to avoid the elephant in the room. No one had seen her since the announcement of the Arts editor role, with some people wondering if her conveniently timed trip to Saint Barts was indefinite, and Tia hadn't been the only one aware of her absence, noticing how every passer-by in the cafe couldn't stop staring and whispering among themselves. A selfie request or a flock of admirers wasn't an unusual sight when in Yvonne's company – Tia had actually lost count of all the times she'd had to play photographer for fans – but today's attention felt especially intense.

'This is weird, right?' she joked. 'Has something happened?'

She glanced over at the monitor playing LCN's midday broadcast, when something in the moving banner caught her eye, though part of it was cut off. Her phone suddenly pinged with a news notification.

YVONNE ANDERSON INKS 8-FIGURE DEAL WITH IBN

'Is this for real?' asked Tia. 'IBN! As in, Independent British News IBN? LCN's biggest competitor IBN?'

Yvonne picked up her cup and took a sip of her coffee with a mischievous grin, as Tia skimmed Twitter until she found a press release, skimming all the fluff to get to the juicy part.

'"We have no doubt this partnership will result in various projects many viewers old and new will enjoy . . ." Blah, blah, blah . . . Wait, what's Role Model Media?'

'My brand-new production company. And my future.'

'Wow,' said Tia.

'It's something I've been mulling over for years, and that LCN Lead shite gave me the final push I needed.' Yvonne smiled. 'I'm not begging people to see my worth anymore.'

'This is huge!'

'And it can be your future too, Tia.'

'What do you mean?'

'I mean, I want you to join me.' She placed her cup

back in its saucer and leaned in. 'I was wrong when I told you to stick it out in this place. It's not worth the imposter syndrome, believe me.'

She couldn't believe the words coming out of Yvonne's mouth.

'I mean, you're not wrong there . . . but what would I even do?'

'I need an assistant. Someone who is capable, creative, and has their ear to the ground. Someone like you.'

Tia rarely felt capable, but who was she to argue with *the* Yvonne Anderson?

'And it won't be all coffee runs. If you're interested in sound mixing, graphics, or even bloody PR,' said Yvonne, waving her manicured hands in the air, 'I'll help you get there. I want you to grow.'

'I . . . I don't know what to say.'

'Don't say anything for now, but I'll need an answer soon. You'll need a visa for the doc we're about to start.'

'A visa?'

Yvonne nodded. 'We start filming in New York the week after next.'

'New York?!'

'Then Miami, Atlanta, New Orleans. We'll be gone for about three months or so? All summer, practically.'

Yvonne began to spill all the details of her

upcoming documentary, damn near frothing at the mouth she was so excited to explain. 'A deep dive into modern Black beauty from the streets that birthed today's biggest trends – it's going to be brilliant!' she said before listing the other rising talent she'd already recruited for the production, like the celebrated music video director who would be doing television for the first time, and the location scout whose clients were behind some of the scene's most decorated indie films. It sounded exciting, wonderfully creative, and all the other things that Tia had been craving for so long.

However, the thought of leaving behind the years she'd built at LCN held her off from jumping up and down at Yvonne's offer. She didn't have the status to protect her should this all go tits-up. Hell, she didn't even have a degree, whatever that was worth nowadays.

'I know it's a lot to consider. It's taken me a bloody decade to finally listen to my gut and say good riddance to this place,' Yvonne began. 'But if there's one thing I've learned, it's to go where you are loved and valued.'

She reached out for Tia's hands and gave them a squeeze.

'And I don't want you to waste as much time as I have trying to figure that out. Learn from my mistakes.'

Before Tia could say anything, Yvonne chuckled at Tia's doe-eyed expression and got to her Dior-covered feet, throwing her bag over her arm. She slid a pair of Linda Farrows onto her dark, chiselled face, and Tia followed her out to the main entrance. The bright flash of a camera startled Tia, though Yvonne seemed totally unfazed and barely flinched at the paparazzi stationed outside the building yelling her name. Calling Tia to meet her in the building within the hour of the press release being published suddenly made perfect sense.

'Let me know what you decide by tonight,' she said, pulling Tia in for a firm hug before sashaying out of the revolving doors.

Tia returned to her desk at a zombie-like pace and stared at her lifeless computer for what felt like ten minutes. She looked around at her colleagues, polishing off the last of their lunches or chatting on the phone. She was baffled at how they could all operate as normal, like they too were meant to be aware of the possibly life-changing lunch break she had just had. She tried her best to push on with her endless list of tasks, and put on her headphones, blasting her ears with Kaytranada's top hits, the cure for even the most jacked up of moods. But between seeing Nate (which she still hadn't even begun to process) and the job offer from Yvonne, her entire equilibrium had been disrupted. Tia zoned in and out of her tasks until 6 p.m., and when she left the office, she unwittingly walked past the Underground entrance and carried on marching down Regent Street all the way to Charing Cross station, her mind consumed by Yvonne's offer and Nate's proposition.

Tia made a list of pros and cons on the train

journey home; she flipped a coin several times; she picked the petals off a single gerbera she'd nicked from a Tesco bouquet; she therapised herself while taking a shower; and she talked her mum's ear off after dinner, until she was ready for bed.

Yvonne only worked with the best of the very best, so the fact that she had come to Tia with such an opportunity could only mean there were bigger and better things for her on the horizon. *But what if I fuck up? What if I'm not good enough?* Tia thought, then tried to battle her anxious disposition with some optimism for a change: *What if this is exactly what I need? Something exciting, something way out of my comfort zone.* She tried to clear her head, flicking through the songs in her latest playlist until it stopped on a track she'd once heard in Nate's room.

It had been good seeing him. Talking to him still felt so nice, as it had always done, as if nothing had happened, Tia thought, thinking of the way he'd looked at her earlier that day by the lifts. It was that same intense gaze he'd always give her right before he was about to kiss her. He probably would have if they hadn't been in the office. She smiled to herself. Tia hadn't told her friends about bumping into Nate, knowing they'd talk her out of making any further contact with Film Camera Fuckboy (as Luca now called him). And they'd be right to. But Tia couldn't help the way he made her feel like she was the most interesting thing in the room. She was addicted to the feeling of capturing his attention and the way he made her feel desired. But so many questions crossed her mind the longer she stared at his texts.

If we hadn't seen each other today would he have reached out? Why wait a month to tell someone you miss them? What does that even mean?

She hadn't felt this confused since Aaron, but at least Nate had reached out, Tia thought to herself. After their almost-hook-up, she hadn't heard a thing from Aaron. The radio silence would have stung her in the past, but according to Hannah's weekly status reports he seemed to be doing fine, solely focused on getting Motive off the ground, which comforted her.

Tia threw herself onto her bed and groaned into her satin pillowcase, until her phone pinged. When it pinged again several minutes later, she opened one eye and flipped her phone over to see who was disturbing her existential crisis. She sat up once she saw all the messages. Three from Nate:

It was good seeing you, trouble

So how about that drink . . .

Work is mad atm. Is the week after next good for you?

One from Yvonne:

So, are you in?

She reread the texts again before lying face-down again on her duvet, praying for some kind of clarity, a eureka moment, a strike of lightning – anything. And then it finally hit her. She unlocked her phone and began to frantically type out a message before deleting it and rewriting it over and over, repeating the frustrating cycle, until she finally gave up trying to write an epistle, settling on something simpler instead.

I'm down.

She shoved her phone under her pillow and stayed up with the third season of *Girlfriends*, anxiously waiting for a reply until her heavy eyes closed. Suddenly, the ping of her phone jolted her awake. Tia smiled at the screen.

Yvonne
Oh, this is going to be fun!

Acknowledgements

It's only by the grace of God that I'm here today, in the right frame of mind, doing what I love. I don't know a lot of scriptures off by heart, fasting is bloody hard and I struggle to drag myself out of bed to make it to service on time. But I can say with all my heart that God is real and every obstacle I've faced thus far hasn't been in vain. I couldn't have done this without the strength He supplied during some of my saddest, loneliest moments when no one else was around. Thank you, God! I don't know what'll happen in the next chapter of my journey but I know that I'm not scared any more. I trust Him because He is the author of my life.

Mum: I love you. I can't thank you enough for everything you've done for me and for supporting me in every way you could, especially when it came to writing this book during some of the toughest moments of our lives. Thank you for easing my anxieties and talking me out of my monthly existential crises; I couldn't have done this without you, your prayers and your belief in me. I'm so grateful to have a parent that has never once doubted my dreams. I thank both you and Dad for making me feel like I can do anything I put my mind to. Your love is my strength.

Aunty Yasmine, Israel, Ania and my baby sister, Miah: I love you guys so much! And I hope I've made you proud.

To my pastor, Mike White of Tab London: Thank you for your words of wisdom. I couldn't have fathomed some of my most trying times without the way you interpret the word.

To my real-life Luca, Michael: Thank you for the inspiration and for the gift of your friendship.

Rianna: I love you deep. You're the definition of a true sister. I'm so blessed to have someone so beautiful, inside and out, in my life.

To the rest of my day 1s and dear friends: Thank you for holding me down during some of the shittiest moments of my life, for the words of encouragement and for the laughter when I needed it the most. It doesn't go unnoticed.

To my family: Thank you for the prayers, love and support. I deeply appreciate every bit of it.

To my 'London 4' family – Maisie, Izin and Ameer: You were the most precious part of my time at the Beeb and I'm so happy I got to experience such a pivotal moment with you all. Mais, our red sofa kikis legit kept me from going mad. Thank you for bringing me so much relief and joy during those days, and for inspiring Tia and Gbemi's friendship.

To my mentor, Brenda Emmanus: I still get so giddy that I even get to call you that. I have idolised you ever since I was a little girl, watching you report on TV from the red carpet with so much effortless charisma and elegance. You know what they say about never meeting your heroes? Yeah, my experience with you was the complete opposite of that sentiment. I'm so grateful to you for all the ways you took me under your wing and I cherish every pearl of wisdom, cup of tea and evening out with you. Thank you for not only inspiring me and one of my favourite characters in this story but for all the hard work you've been doing in front of and behind the camera. You are a true trailblazer. You deserve all the flowers and more.

I also wanted to give a special mention to my personal heroes: Elaine Welteroth, Edward Enninful and Issa Rae, whose own journeys and contributions to the culture have deeply impacted this kid from Catford to dream big and work hard; who have made the impossible feel possible; and whose work has given me hope and joy during *so many* days when I felt lost and not good enough.

To my wonderful editor, Tallulah Lyons: Working with you has been an absolute dream come true! Thank you from the bottom of my heart for believing in this story, for loving these characters and for all your hard work. I'm so grateful for all the care you put into this and I'm so happy I got to be on this journey with you. I feel like I've made a friend for life.

Lemara, thank you for your words of encouragement right before my first ever meeting at Penguin. I was a nervous wreck and imposter syndrome was mashing me up differently that day, but you immediately put me at ease and made me feel like a real writer. It was the moment I was even more certain about wanting to go on this journey with Merky – I'm so glad I did.

To Laura O'Donnell, Hope Butler, Joanna Taylor, Becca Wright, Holly Ovenden and the rest of the team at Penguin: thank you so much for all your hard work, passion and support. This has been a total dream come true and I'm so grateful to each and every one of you.

And last but certainly not least! To the best agent in the world, Seren Adams: None of this would've been possible without you, S. You saw something in me that I definitely didn't know I had. You took a chance on me and believed in me when I didn't feel like you should have. I still remember airing your first ever email to me because I thought it was spam and there was no way someone would be interested in my writing! Your unwavering belief, patience and support has meant the world to me. I'm so blessed to have you.